EIGHT NIGHTS TO WIN HER HEART

EIGHT NIGHTS TO WIN HER HEART

A Novel

MIRI WHITE

alcove
press

Published in the United States by Alcove Press, an imprint of The Quick Brown Fox & Company LLC.

Alcove Press and its logo are trademarks of The Quick Brown Fox & Company LLC.

Library of Congress Catalog-in-Publication data available upon request.

ISBN (hardcover): 978-1-63910-892-3
ISBN (ebook): 978-1-63910-893-0

Cover design by Stephanie Singleton

Printed in the United States.

www.alcovepress.com

Alcove Press
34 West 27th St., 10th Floor
New York, NY 10001

First Edition: October 2024

10 9 8 7 6 5 4 3 2 1

To every child who needed
more Chanukah in their world.

CHAPTER ONE

"What do you want?" Leo Dentz called out to the distraction in his workshop, the one currently banging around, potentially toppling over one of the antiques.

As suspected, his sister's voice responded, not that he could understand her with all the clattering. He tossed down his rag, no way would he be able to finish cleaning up this English boot scraper now. It didn't need a lot of work, mostly a good shine, and he had banked on having it finished ten minutes from now. Another bang, this one metallic, which didn't mesh well with his hearing aids or bode well for damage control. Damage he'd be blamed for even if he resided on the moon when it happened. Still no sign of his sister, with any luck her destruction to the shop would be minimal. He couldn't afford any more setbacks.

"Stop destroying the goods and come where I can see you."

It took a moment, and another loud noise, but his sister appeared. Jodie's brown hair piled on top of her head in her signature messy bun. She still wore her thick winter coat and held a large box that dwarfed her frame. Her purse had slid down to the crook of her arm and bumped into her leg with every step she took.

At the sight of what she carried and what it might contain, he instantly forgave her for the chaos, assuming nothing had been broken. He wasn't that magnanimous.

"I said I had something for you, not that you deserve it." Jodie's deadpan delivery was accompanied by her signature smirk. As the oldest sibling she used the phrase often, typically accompanied by some sweet treat. She hefted the package onto his table, the contents jostling around.

"You want Dad to sell the shop or do you want me to save it?" He asked. Dentz Antiques, started by their grandfather, had been in the family for its entire seventy-year operation. Only now, five years after his grandfather's death, his father and current owner wanted to sell. "I don't trust you kids," he'd claimed, referring to Leo and his younger brother, Dean. Two misdeeds, admittedly big ones, hung like an ecological dome, trapping everyone inside and threatening to destroy a lineage no matter if he managed to start shitting gold.

"Of course I want to save Dentz Antiques! But I'm not about to help the ungrateful." Jodie crossed her arms, her stance turning into the familiar defiance he'd grown up with.

"I'm grateful." Okay, so he said it through clenched teeth, but he still said it.

"Younger brothers are a pain in my ass. You're lucky I love you."

He gave her a grin. He couldn't charm others with a look like his siblings could, but he knew how to get his older sister to steal him a cookie.

"Mom, you knocked over stuff!" His niece, Millie, bounded into the area, her long brown hair braided and draped over one shoulder, coat unzipped and flapping behind her.

"You pick them up for me, squirt?" he asked.

Millie nodded. "Yup. No casualties . . . this time."

"Hush." Jodie removed her coat and hung it over an old rocking chair in need of repair. The chair wobbled, but thankfully didn't topple. "I come bearing goods, you want me to take them to Dad instead?"

Leo forgot about the wobbling chair and grabbed the box, a worn one with the logo of a popular store. The items inside clattered together in the high pitches his hearing aids loved to amplify. "Don't even think about it."

He rummaged through, not waiting for her to speak. Antiques were his thing, in his blood. He didn't do this because the family needed him to follow a path. He did this because he loved it. The items represented comfort and home. Each one held a story, one he could either piece together or theorize. The quality and styles, representations from days gone by, were unique compared to the current trends.

So what if sixteen-year-old Leo thought otherwise? He'd grown since then, a hell of a lot and fast.

"From a member of my shul, the Wisenbergs. Mister passed at ninety-eight and the grandkids are more into modern than sentimental, and thus I was handed this potential treasure."

Leo pulled out a candelabra. A little beat up and worn down, but he could probably fix it up to be worth something. "They want us to buy them?"

"Nope. Just wanted it to go somewhere."

This could be the good score he needed. Something rare, something valuable that would bring attention and money to the shop. Something he could repair with his own two hands. His father saw him as the breaker of things. But his hands fixed, brought new life to possessions old and forgotten. He needed one good find to finally prove his worth in the only way his father could accept. Then maybe, just maybe, he'd earn his birthright back.

He reached to the bottom of the box and pulled out an old and well-loved menorah. The gold tarnished in areas, but the exquisite detailing had him entranced. It had a tree-like feel, with vines along each of the nine candle stems, all coming together at the base. A tree of life, as though the item was more powerful than a simple menorah.

He flipped it over, discovering Hebrew written on the bottom, not something he usually found:

נִיסִים הָיוּ בְּכָל מָקוֹם

"Hey, kid, can you read this?" he asked of his ten-year-old niece.

She scrunched her nose and came forward, looking at the bottom. "There's no vowels."

Jodie nudged her daughter. "Go ahead, try anyways."

"You two can't read it, that's why."

He chuckled and raised his hands. "Guilty. I'm rusty." Truth be told, he hadn't been good at reading it when he'd been Bar Mitzvah'ed. And since then, there hadn't been many opportunities to keep up his limited skills.

She studied it for a bit before speaking, "Ni..ssim hai..yu b'khol ma . . . kom. I think."

"Sounds right to me," Jodie said.

"And what does that mean?" He asked.

Millie threw up her hands. "You think I know?! I'm not taught to understand, only to read. Seriously, you adults are all the . . ." she turned and stomped off into the shop.

Jodie chuckled. "I don't think there's anything in there that is going to fit your restoration goals, but you always got this stuff better than the rest of us."

"Which is exactly why Dad should sell the business to me," Leo grumbled, placing the menorah aside and checking out the other contents.

"He'll come around," Jodie said.

Leo scoffed. "Before or after he signs it over to someone who isn't a Dentz?" He'd seen his father attend mysterious meetings, the business suits walking around the shop; he needed a miracle, and he needed one now.

"Hopefully before, but the stubborn streak does run dominant in our family."

4

Leo's own brand of stubborn had gotten him into this mess in the first place. The rest of the box held some potential for the sales floor, but nothing that called out for his specific skill set. He moved the items to a different bench when Millie picked up the menorah, her cell phone in hand.

"What'cha doing?" he asked.

"You wanted to know what it meant." Millie studied her screen, then the menorah, then her screen again. "I think it means 'miracles happen everywhere.' Oh! Like the dreidels!"

She ran off and came back moments later with one of the antique dreidels in the shop. "Nun, gimel, hey, shin," Millie pointed to the different letters on each side of the dreidel. "It stands for nes gadol hayay sham, which means a great miracle happened here, or there, really, since we're not in Jerusalem. The dreidels tell the story of the miracle of the oil lasting eight nights, but this menorah claims that miracles happen everywhere, almost like it's magic."

Millie placed the menorah down and looked up at the adults with shining eyes. "I bet it's magic. You should light it and make a wish!"

He blinked at his niece. "Is this a Jewish/Chanukah/Birthday cake thing?"

Millie laughed. "No, silly. But Chanukah is about magic and miracles and getting what you need." She suddenly frowned. "Although our near constant persecution is often because of others thinking our artifacts are magic. So maybe this is haunted instead."

Jodie crossed her arms. "We just went from making a wish on a menorah to it bringing back the dead?"

Millie shrugged.

"Am I Scrooge? Are ghosts going to visit me?"

Jodie placed a hand on his shoulder. "Or we give it to Dad and the ghosts will visit him." She faced Millie. "Does Chanukah not have enough magic for you?"

"I didn't put the Hebrew on the menorah." Millie walked off, disappearing into the shop.

Jodie picked up her jacket. "Kid does have a point, maybe you could use some hope this holiday season."

He raised his eyebrows. "Hope as in . . . You really don't think Dad is going to sell the business to me? Cause I'm not saving this business with a wish."

"I'm not talking about the business for a moment here. You only ever talk about the business. I want you to act on something else. Like that cute neighbor you've got a crush on."

Andie.

He shook those thoughts aside. No. Business first. Once he owned the place outright and had it steady, then he could consider his love life, or lack thereof.

"Am I that hopeless if I need a magic menorah?"

"No, but I'd like to see you do something other than stare longingly at your shared wall."

"Jodie," he groaned. Couldn't his sister leave him alone already? Just because his bedroom wall butted up against his neighbor's didn't mean he spent time staring at it.

"Look, you have your plans to try and convince Dad to sell to you. But maybe this holiday season you need something outside of business and family."

He thought about it. He thought about it often. He didn't need magic or a push to do something different, he needed the right timing. But Jodie didn't need to know that.

Millie skipped into the area. "Are you coming for the Chanukah party?" Her big brown eyes pleaded with his.

He'd been roped in months ago, first by Jodie, then, when he claimed he had too much work, she sent Millie and her big eyes after him. In other words, she sent his kryptonite. The same reason she knew any time Uncle Leo kid-sat, said kid got whatever she asked for.

"I'm going to do my best to make it." Leo said.

Millie flung her arms around him, a surefire tactic to up the guilt if he missed it. "You'll be there, I know you will."

6

"Okay, squirt, laying it on a bit thick." Jodie waved to Leo, heading for the exit.

Millie let go. "Bye, Uncle Leo. And if the menorah is magic maybe it'll help with that cute neighbor!" She scampered off after her mother before he could respond.

His sister had a skill for being the puppet master of the family, but he suspected her daughter would soon outshine her. Millie had ears on everything and was often listening when she appeared not to be. So her little parting gesture was not a complete surprise.

Leo picked up the menorah again. A magic menorah, that would be something. But he much preferred the magic of the story, the oil lasting for eight nights. While he could use a little magic in his life, he'd settle for the magic from his holidays. Still—he set the menorah in his bag—it might be nice to light something new tonight when the sun sets.

* * *

Andie Williams juggled a paper bag in one arm and a cardboard box under the other arm and tried to remember which pocket she stuffed her keys into. The elevator doors closed behind her and she prayed she hadn't dropped anything.

"Maybe I should have gotten the box another time," she mumbled to herself as she realized the keys definitely were not in her right pocket.

That's what she got for being excited about something, rational thought always took a back seat to whatever whim she hyperfocused on. Truly, the opportunity was right there, waiting for her, it had to be done. After months of searching for a job, thanks to her current preschool program closing at the end of the school year, she finally had an offer! Sure, it involved a big move, on a preschool teacher's salary, but better to move than be unemployed.

At least that's what she told herself.

So, the move didn't come without some drawbacks, but determination had her looking forward, figuratively and literally as she tripped over the carpet bump in her apartment complex hallway—the one she should have remembered was there and avoided at all costs. Nope, not her luck of the day. No, her luck involved her jerky movements causing the paper bag to rip, spewing all her belongings out onto the worn gray rug.

Andie sighed at the mess puddled at her feet and dropped the useless ripped bag. "Karma, if this is a sign, I'm not liking it." She placed her box against her apartment door and prepared to see how many of her belongings she could cradle in her hands, when the door to unit 42 swung open.

Squatting in the midst of her bag contents was not the time for her hot neighbor to open his door. But, alas, there she squatted and there Leo stood, looking even more handsome from her angle. She often thought of him as a younger Ryan Reynolds, with darker hair and a more curved nose. So naturally she'd been flirting with him for over a year, but the man had yet to take the bait. Only now, there he stood, handsome as ever, while her tampons, tissues, and cheap pharmacy Chanukah candles were strewn across the hallway floor. He took in the mess, all tall and strong, making her want to find her phone and take a picture. The man made her drool, and to momentarily forget the embarrassing clutter between them.

"Trouble?" A man of few words and oh, how she liked that trait.

She rose, even on tiptoes she'd have to look up to see him. Her angle had been nice, but nothing beat being closer. He always smelled like old wood and polish, a combination she somehow found alluring and a perfect match for the man. She gestured to the torn bag by her scuffed-up shoe. "Just another moment that I kick myself for forgetting my reusable shopping bag when these paper ones love to break on me."

He chuckled and, dear no, bent. "I've got two hands. It's a long walk to your unit, but I can handle it."

She cringed as he picked up her tampons and the candles. He didn't have any decorations on his door, but neither did most of their neighbors. They'd never discussed anything related to religion, and she really did not want to find out if her hot neighbor was an anti-Semite. She needed her nighttime fantasies for those cold winter nights.

"Cutting it close to sunset, aren't you?" He tossed the candles before catching them.

Andie pressed her lips together, debating how to answer. Her people had been attacked, or simply made fun of, for less and she wasn't in the mood for either. Tonight would be a cold winter night, bye-bye fantasy.

Something on her face must have telecast her feelings, because his expression softened. "Hey, I'm teasing. I barely found my own candles in time."

She breathed in relief. Fantasy back on board! He could still be a candle snob, but she'd take that over certain danger. She quickly gathered up the rest of her belongings. "I thought I had some, turned out I had two left, and one had broken."

She turned to her door, juggling everything in one arm and managing to get the door unlocked before things tumbled, again. When she faced Leo, he stared at her box.

"Donating things?" he asked.

What did it say about him that his first thought was donation? "Moving, actually." It felt strange to say it out loud, another step toward making this her new reality.

The box slipped, but he caught it before it fell. "Moving?"

She entered her unit. The entry area opened up in between her small U-shaped kitchen and dining area before leading to the rest of the living space. She headed for her table, unloading her items in a heap. He followed, placing his items down to join hers. "Yeah. My program is being cut and there are not a lot of job options. I finally found something, but it's far away."

"How far?"

"I haven't done the math yet, but . . . Ohio."

"Ohio's a long way from Massachusetts."

She nodded. "I know. It's a great opportunity, but it's a lot. So I thought a box and packing would make it real and help me settle."

"You're really moving."

His dark eyebrows hung low, making him look so sad. Maybe he regretted the missed chances like she did. Why did that spark hope deep inside of her?

"Probably." She sighed. "Anyways, thanks for the help. I appreciate it."

Someone knocked in the hall, but Leo didn't seem to notice. She took in that he wore a snug-fitting gray Henley, worn jeans that lovingly hugged his legs, and white socks, no shoes. Not exactly head-out-into-the-hall attire. "Why'd you leave your unit?"

He looked down at his feet. "I forgot shoes again, didn't I? I always forget shoes. I had a delivery coming up, which should be here by now."

"Someone knocked."

His eyes widened and he stepped out of her unit. Andie watched him head to his door, where a very confused delivery driver stood. "I had the wrong number, I'm sorry."

"No, I was helping a neighbor."

Leo paid the guy and turned back to Andie.

"Since you've got a new box of candles for the first night of Chanukah, and you're moving, and I've got enough Chinese here for several people, might I make a proposition?"

The smells of Chinese wafted through the hall, making her stomach grumble. Of course she forgot about dinner in her haste to get candles. "What's the proposition?"

"I'd like to light the candles with you and share my meal. What do you say?"

CHAPTER TWO

Andie's heart picked up a few notches as she stared at Leo, his proposition a swirl of glitter hanging in the air between them. Light the candles with Leo? She had no one to celebrate with this year, not since her father passed away. Dinner with her hot neighbor fell firmly under the perk heading. The timing stunk, since she'd be moving soon, but it couldn't hurt to have a little fun this Chanukah, right?

Her father would want her to celebrate with someone. And he'd know she'd jump in with both feet. The only person to trust her instincts more than her.

"Sure, come on in."

He stepped into her unit, bringing the delicious scents of food right under her nose. She closed the door behind him, shedding her coat and purse by the hook. Leo placed the food on her well-loved square dining table that had seen better days. Unfortunately, her other belongings had been placed there, and tampons did not inspire her to eat good food with a good-looking man, so she scooped up everything but the candles, walked down the short hall to her bedroom, deposited them on her unmade bed, and closed the door.

There, better.

She returned to her dining room, pushing up the leather cuff bracelet on her wrist as she walked.

"That's an interesting cuff," Leo said.

She lifted her sweater higher to show off the band. "I had it made recently, the thicker leather is from a belt of my father's, the thinner is from one my mother had." The thinner leather crossed over the thicker, a perfect match for her style.

"It's nice."

"Thanks." She came to the table and rested on the back of a chair. "No plans yourself for the first night of Chanukah?"

"I've been too busy with work. I'll see family toward the end for the big get-together."

Big get-together. The words said so casually, and they resonated deep within her. It hinted at a close-knit extended family where laughter reined. The type of gathering she longed for even though she never had the experience.

The type of gathering she wouldn't want to wait for night eight to enjoy.

"But nothing before then?" The concept felt strange to her. When her father was alive she spent at least a few sunsets with him, and often lit candles with friends as well. This year she had no concrete plans, and it made her feel her loss all the more.

A big, loving family had always been her dream. All she had left were a few distant relatives who were so drama-filled that her father cut ties when she was small. As a result, she didn't know them. The only numbers she had were found in her father's handwritten contact list, and a great number of those proved outdated when she tried them after he died.

"Just volunteering for the Hebrew school Chanukah party that my conniving niece roped me into." His voice held an amused tone and the glint in his eyes said his niece held a soft spot in his heart.

It nearly made her purr. *Large family with cherished children.* She pushed it aside. "Is it still volunteering if you were roped in?"

"As I said, I've been busy."

A Leo-shaped puzzle piece began sliding into place: works long hours, doting uncle. She focused on the former because she liked the doting uncle side far too much. "Workaholic then. You know, they have programs for that."

Leo chuckled; eyebrows raised. "They do?"

Andie nodded. "They do. It starts with helping a neighbor with a ripped bag and lighting candles together."

His grin grew large, crinkling the corner of his eyes, and she felt the flames of the candles they hadn't yet lit, warming up the space between them.

"What about you?"

She pulled down two plates and two cups and brought them over to the table. "I don't think I'd consider myself a workaholic, but I do enjoy my job."

"No family to celebrate with?"

She sighed and brought over silverware as Leo unpacked his bag. "My father passed eight months ago. Before that it had been just the two of us for as long as I can remember. Now it's just me." She tried to smile, to put on her brave orphan face, but this was her first Chanukah without him and it hurt. Probably why she only managed to uncover her menorah this morning.

"I'm sorry," Leo said. "Explains the bracelet."

She fingered the leather around her wrist, working to contain the ache in her chest. "That it does. And the rest is not your fault. We should light the menorah before we eat." She collected the candles and moved away from the table, doing her best to leave her sad memories behind. She could be sad later.

She had her menorah set up on a small table in front of her window. A simple but old one. It had been her father's. A strange mix of hurt and family warmth filled her, and she was glad Leo had helped her, because she really did not want to be alone the first night.

"That's a nice menorah," he said.

"Thanks. I think my grandmother gave it to my father as a gift, something she had when she was young."

He brushed a hand along the tarnished base. "Antiques are my thing. I figured it was old."

"Antiques, huh? Don't find that much in people our age."

"Family business. I grew up with it and wouldn't want to do anything else." His words felt heavy, some other meaning stirring underneath.

She shook out two candles from the box, one blue, one yellow. "There's something there, in the way you said it. Is that the truth or is it one of those 'you'll follow the family business or else' things?"

He blinked at her, a note of surprise in his brown eyes. "You caught that, huh?"

"I'm good at reading people."

"Not wanting to do anything else is true. However, my father wants to sell the family business, and his sons are not his first choice."

"Ouch. That sucks. I'm sorry." Andie set the two candles in the menorah. She didn't get family conflicts. Life was too short. She wanted a warm, loving family to walk in to. Sure, perhaps she was swayed by life with her dad and holiday movies, but her gut said it existed, and she wouldn't settle for less.

She grabbed her matches, facing her companion. "How long has it been since you've celebrated?"

Leo raised a single eyebrow. How did he do that? She'd tried practicing as a kid and eventually gave up. On him it looked sexy as hell and she nearly leaned in. "Are you asking if I forgo my own candles when alone?"

"I'm asking if you can read the Hebrew or need the phonetics?"

"I've got it memorized, does that help?"

"Very much so, since I didn't find my paper with the prayers written on it."

He grinned at her, smooth cheeks rising, and a part of her grew sad that they'd only tried this now.

She lit the match, and they said the three prayers together as she lit the shamash, then used the shamash to light the sole candle on the right. His tenor voice blended in with her higher one, taking this moment and adding a bit of something new and special to it. Three prayers with only one candle to light meant the shamash was safely back in its raised center position as the last words rang in the air.

"Happy Chanukah, Andie," Leo said. His face held something in the glow of the candles, a warmth she wouldn't expect from someone she only sorta knew. Yet it felt good, tempting her to bottle up this moment for later.

"Happy Chanukah."

Her stomach chose that moment to grumble. Her hands sailed to the noisy fiend. "I guess it's a good thing I'm not rummaging through my freezer for sustenance now."

Leo chuckled. "Then let's eat."

They settled in at her table, passing food back and forth until both their plates were piled high. Seasoned aromas wafted to Andie's nose, creating an eager grumble deep in her empty stomach. The moment her plate landed before her she picked up her fork and dove in, too hungry to be polite.

"So what is this job that's taking you all the way to Ohio?"

She had to quickly chew the lo mein in her mouth. "Lead teacher in a preschool that specializes in underprivileged kids."

"You can't do that here?"

She smiled at him, but it grew tight at the clueless expression on his face. This felt like any other conversation she'd had where the person knowingly, or unknowingly, put down her profession, or equated it to glorified babysitting. "The program I work at is being hit by budget cuts, many are. We're closing down and all of my coworkers are looking for work. A few found positions, most of us have not, and I'd love to give something back to a community that truly needs it."

He took a bite of chicken, talking as he chewed. "I get budget cuts and limited options, times are rough, but moving that far for a teaching position? I don't get it."

She stabbed at something on her plate, not even registering what. "You wouldn't move if there were no job options in this area for you? If your father sells the business to someone else and the next best match isn't local?"

"I'm getting the business. If I don't, well, I'll figure something out. But wouldn't working for a Walmart or Amazon or something make more money? Then you wouldn't have the burden of moving and could wait for something better to come along?"

She dropped her smile completely. The evening had started off great and now this. "So you'll figure something out that doesn't involve Walmart or Amazon? If you're so comfortable, why are you living here with the rest of us low-income workers?"

"I . . ." Leo rubbed the back of his neck. "I didn't mean . . . I guess with the right support systems it could work."

Andie scoffed; she couldn't help it. Support systems. Sure, the current setup of the economy meant she'd continue to struggle on her own. "I've got no one." A notion she felt even more strongly— so much for company for Chanukah. "But there are kids struggling everywhere, and I have an opportunity to help. This school needs me." One of the many things that had drawn her to this job.

"But what about the kids struggling here?"

She resisted rolling her eyes. "The ones in programs that have no teacher openings? Or that are being shoved into overcrowded class-rooms due to budget cuts? Or not able to get a spot in the wait-listed programs? There's nothing I can personally do to change that."

Would Daddy Warbucks over there suggest she open her own center, right after thinking she'd be better off driving around in an Amazon truck? How out of touch with reality was this guy? Apparently, hot neighbor was the look at, don't talk to, type. Shame. She'd heard all this before. The few extended family members that came to sit shiva after her father died were full of condescending state-ments about her job, and hints that now she should get a real one. As though caring for children and shaping their future held no value.

Leo looked up, alarmed. "Shit, I'm sorry. This isn't going well."

"Should young children not need preschool because they stay home with their mothers while the fathers work?"

"What? No, Andie, I'm not like that."

Caution warned her to calm down, but anger fueled her on. She couldn't talk back to so many who questioned her work, but she could to this man across her table. "Could have fooled me right now. I know people look down on teaching, especially when it comes to the younger kids. But not everyone comes from a two-parent, picket fence life. Some kids need the socialization, and not because their parents are bad par-ents. Some parents have work, some kids have a lot of needs that the parents struggle to meet. So maybe moving is going to take up all my savings and then some, but it will be worth it to do what I love."

Leo had stopped eating. "Andie, I really am sorry, I didn't mean it that way."

"Then what did you mean?"

"I uh . . ." He rubbed the back of his neck, clearly whatever he did mean he didn't have words for.

Why was she getting into this with this oblivious man? So much for getting to know her neighbor better. He didn't deserve to know that she'd been feeling a bit lost since her father died. She raised a hand. "Look. The candles are burning, the food is good and I'm much too hungry to send you home without finishing. Why don't we eat in silence?"

He looked like he wanted to speak again, and she was tempted to raise her knife to warn him off, but figured that would only add another log to the uncomfortable fire at the table. Eventually he faced his food, as did she.

Five minutes later, he took the remnants of their dinner and left without another word.

"Good riddance."

Only now Andie felt well and truly alone. She walked over to the remaining embers of her candles, and the yellow wax dried in a dripping pattern down the base.

"Always the yellow."

No matter the box or the brand, for some cosmic reason, yellow never burned cleanly, always leaving a trail of wax behind.

She sighed and settled in on her couch, touching her cuff. "Happy Chanukah, Dad. Miss you, wish you were here." One day, she'd have a family to light the candles with. Maybe she'd find that family in Ohio.

* * *

Leo closed the refrigerator door, after tossing the leftover Chinese food in there. Then, he rammed his forehead against the freezer door. The narrow, neutral-toned U-shaped kitchen spread out to his left, the same as Andie's except in reverse, even if his had more than one antique salvage on the counters.

"Can you mess things up any harder if you tried?" he mumbled to himself. His "open mouth, insert foot" bad habit had reared its ugly head, timing, as always, impeccable. Now, his one shot with Andie was gone in a violent flash of smoke.

Maybe it was better that way, for her. His track record with women sucked to high heaven, the curse of being the uncharismatic one in the family.

He left the kitchen, heading for the dining room, where he'd set up the new menorah. Everything he touched seemed to turn to coal, and he didn't even celebrate Christmas.

"Dentz, you are a putz. A no-good, messes everything up, putz."

He didn't mean to put down her career. He was just shocked, since most teachers he knew wouldn't relocate for a job. Instead of thinking his words over, he let them out in the worst possible way. One of the many reasons for his painfully single status.

"I need a do-over." One that involved duct tape over his mouth.

He studied the new menorah, his favorite type of new, since the item in front of him was in fact very old. The night would have gone differently if he had lit it and studied its charm, rather than how the glow of candles danced in Andie's eyes.

"That's it. I'm lighting them again."

Not exactly protocol, but he didn't care. He pulled out his candles, and his matches, and lit the candles a second time. Soon the dual flames flickered in his apartment and he could almost forget the night had turned sour.

Almost.

"And this pity party is officially over."

He took a picture of his menorah, sent it to Millie. Five minutes later, he got an image of her smaller menorah next to his sister's bigger one, both with candles burning.

Millie: Happy Chanukah! Is that the new menorah Mom
brought you?

Leo: Happy Chanukah! And yes, it is.

Millie: It looks like it really is magic, not haunted. Bet
you could make a wish and it would come true.

Leo: A wish? On a menorah?

Millie: Why not?

Leo: Because it's a menorah. Go beat
your father at dreidels for me.

Millie: Already on it!

Another picture loaded, of Millie's large pile of gelt in front of a dreidel, with his brother-in-law's much smaller pile across the way.

Leo: Good job!

Sure, he worked long hours to make up for his misdeeds, but he had Millie, and a drive to succeed. That would have to be enough.

CHAPTER THREE

Leo tapped his fingers on the antique desk in the back of his workshop, the one that had charm and character but was better suited for ambience than selling. It had two large gashes on top and a replacement leg of different style and quality. He had worked with his grandfather back in the day on the gashes, but even their combined skill couldn't make the desk suitable for selling. Especially as it was part of a set that matched the grandfather clock that stood in a corner. A constant reminder to all that Leonard Dentz had the middle name of *Trouble*.

The clock had busted glass, bent hands, and a crack in the wood. It had at one point been a beauty, almost a decade ago, when teen Leo had a chip on his shoulder about being stuck watching the store. Leo's kid brother, Dean, and that chip resulted in a tug of war over a football in a place where "you break it you bought it" could cost thousands. The football had taken the grandfather clock from glory to ruins and demolished an entire row of antique plates. Leo had been grounded for so long he wasn't entirely sure it had ended.

So now, Leo did year-end work while facing the clock. He'd built himself back up to be trusted with managing the numbers, and nearly had his foot planted into the business door to open it wide. But then incident number two occurred, and the door slammed shut with bolts and plywood.

Footsteps echoed into the area, before his younger brother appeared. Dean had all the Dentz charm and could sell an item with a flash of a smile. Leo sold it with his brains and knowledge, and, yeah, a bit of that charm as well. Together, they made an unbeatable team, but tell that to their father. Leo's misdeeds affected them all, and while Dean could sell antiques, managing a shop was not his thing.

"Millie says you've got a magic menorah. What's she snorting at Hebrew school?" Dean propped on the edge of the desk, running his fingers through his hair while studying his reflection in the nearby glass cabinet.

"You think she's snorting something and not a child who still has some youthful magic in her life? Why'd she tell you about it, anyways?"

Dean picked up a paper weight and tossed it in the air before catching it. "Said I should take a stab at it if you didn't." Dean put the weighted cube back down. "So tell me, brother, did you make a wish as this very tall tale instructs?"

Leo moved the paperweight back to its previous position. "No. I lit it, it's a nice piece."

"Too bad it wasn't a fixer you could use to woo Dad over. However, will you find a way to show off your talents. A shame there isn't something tall and broken for you to save . . ." Dean nodded his head in the direction of the clock.

"Give it up. I need to find something I didn't damage. Dad will have my hide if I touch that thing again."

"So don't get caught while you fix it." Dean pulled out his phone, thumbed through. Leo knew from experience it wasn't work on his phone.

"You can swipe right after hours."

Dean shoved his phone into his pocket. "You want to continue having this conversation?"

Leo leaned back and sighed. No, he didn't. He hadn't wanted to have this conversation back when the clock first broke, and the years that followed didn't help.

"That's what I thought."

Leo groaned and pulled the paperwork toward him. "Get back to work, maybe your pretty face will sell something today."

Dean flashed a smile. "You admit I'm pretty."

"Do I need to plan another tea party for you and Millie?"

Dean rubbed his chin. "Pencil me in for after the New Year." He pushed away from the table and walked back through the shop toward the showroom.

Leo pulled out his phone and marked it into his calendar app. He then scrolled back and stared at the week ahead. Chanukah. A week before Christmas. And all he had to show for himself was an empty calendar.

He'd had a glimmer of hope that he'd have someone to spend the week with. Not a random someone either. Andie. He'd extinguished that hope. He thought back to her scowl the previous night, the one that had darkened her face, highlighting the hurt in her brown eyes. It cut into him. It had the night before, but he couldn't think fast enough on his feet to rectify the situation. Why didn't life come with reverse buttons? She had haunted his dreams, all the potential they had dying before it had a chance. It demanded fixing, though Leo could admit his desire to fix things was stronger than his ability. At the very least, Andie deserved a peace offering before moving far away. Her store-bought candles had lingered in his mind, and the excessive dripping he caught before leaving. She deserved a nice set and he knew where to get one.

After inserting his foot so far in his mouth he kicked his own ass that way, it really was the least he could do.

He checked his work schedule. If he did a bit of juggling, he could pull this off in between appointments. He'd get Andie some candles, wish her luck, and then leave her alone.

It stung. He'd wanted the chance for something more with her. But karma had spoken, and really, it was his own damn fault for waiting so long. He'd fix the bad vibes, not that he had the best track record with that either.

"Dentz, you need a New Year's Resolution not to be a dick."

One step at a time. For now, work awaited.

* * *

The last of Andie's sugared-up students bounced next to her in the cold midday air, waiting for one of her fathers to show up. No gloves, no hat, and only a light sweatshirt for protection against the day that had turned cold, despite the sun shining high overhead. Andie squatted down, rubbing the little girl's hands in between her mitten-covered ones, debating loaning them, even if she knew that loan meant losing yet another pair.

"Did you enjoy the gingerbread people?" Andie asked, as much to entertain herself as her student.

Emma nodded, pigtails swaying with the motion. "Uh-huh. I made a green one!"

Andie smiled. Some of the green food coloring had lingered on Emma's hands, announcing to all her color of choice without words. Andie's own hands had a little of each color lingering on her skin.

She rose as footsteps bounded toward them to see Patrick had finally arrived. He skidded to a stop and scooped Emma up. Patrick, Andie noted, did have gloves on. She got gloves on twenty kids multiple times a day and some parents couldn't even find shoes.

"Sorry, the baby was crying all night and Samuel brought her to the doctors. Ear infection. I hope Emma didn't catch it."

"I don't catch baby cooties." Emma crossed her arms. She was not taking the new addition well.

Andie softened. Overtired parents with a sick baby made perfect sense for being late and missing a few layers of warmth for their oldest. She knew better than to make assumptions, at least until a pattern emerged. Then she had to investigate, not assume.

"Nothing this petri dish of a school hasn't already seen."

Patrick held Emma close as he hurried off to his car. Andie chided herself, again, for jumping to conclusions. How easy it was to think something quick and not consider all the facts. A lot like her conversation with Leo the previous night.

It had lingered in her mind, haunting her as she tried to sleep. Did she overreact? Because if she had mentioned the lack of gloves or her thoughts to Patrick, she'd expect him to come back at her with a dose of his own justification.

Lesson learned. Good thing she was a lifelong learner.

A gust of cold air broke her from her thoughts and slipped up through her jacket. Best to get inside. Andie rubbed her aching lower back and hurried inside for warmth. The quiet halls of the old school welcomed her in. Student artwork lined the walls, and a variety of decorations for multiple holidays added to the ambience. The building may be old, but it was well loved.

Andie already missed it.

She didn't know what would happen to the place after the program closed. The chipping paint and cracks in the walls suggested it needed more than a little work, but whether the town would or would not do that remained to be seen. Either it would be torn down and rebuilt or sold or refurbished for older students. The end result she'd never know unless any of her friends updated her.

The room blurred before her and she had to stop moving. An image of older kids running through these halls, tearing down the preschoolers' pictures. A wrecking ball shattering the stairs. A bunch of suits reorganizing the layout to some office park. She pushed it aside. Not her problem, even as it chipped away at the memories she'd made. She loved it here. Loved her students and her coworkers. This had been her first post-college job, and while she knew she'd leave it behind eventually, she hadn't anticipated it being so soon.

"Let it go, Andie, you can wallow later."

She took the stairs two at a time until she could collapse into a blue child-sized chair in her friend's room.

"Four more days," Sarah said while wiping down a table. "I hate looking forward to break so much when we won't be here next year, but I need a breather."

Andie nodded, resisting the ache in her chest. "I know exactly what you mean."

"Of course you do, Miss I'm-Moving-Far-Away-For-An-Amazing-Opportunity."

She grinned. Like it or not the "amazing opportunity" lessened the ache. "You'll find something." Sarah was one of the many teachers still looking.

"I know I will, and I've got time." Sarah tossed her paper towel in the trash. "Still stinks. All these kids will be split. Some won't find a new preschool; others will end up in overcrowded classrooms or without the support systems we've been creating for them."

Andie said nothing, she knew Sarah spoke the truth. She also knew they needed a conversation change. Discussions like this dominated all their minds.

"I had dinner with my hot neighbor last night."

Sarah's eyes grew wide and she lowered herself to the chair next to Andie. "And?"

Andie sighed. "And it didn't go well. He questioned me moving for my job and it got worse from there." Perhaps part of her reaction had to do with pent-up aggression on a mostly innocent bystander.

Sarah's dark hair slid over her shoulder as she leaned in close. "You went off on him, didn't you?"

Andie held up two fingers very close together. "Little bit."

Sarah laughed. "Oh, that poor man."

"That was wrong of me, wasn't it?"

Sarah rubbed her neck. "Wrong? Never. Reactive? High possibility."

"I'm moving though, it shouldn't matter."

"You're moving. Why not have some fun before you do? Then it doesn't matter whether he understands your job or not."

Andie tried to find fault with that but couldn't. "I could apologize."

"Ooh, now we're talking! Apologize while wearing clothing unacceptable for the classroom, please! Oh! Strip dreidels!"

Andie blinked at Sarah as the words registered. "Did you really just say 'strip dreidels' in a preschool classroom?"

Sarah threw her head back, laughing. "I did, and there are no students in the building, so I'll do it again. STRIP DREIDELS!"

Andie glanced at the door, expecting someone to rush in and shush them, but no one came. "How would that even work?"

Sarah's lips curved in a Cheshire cat grin. "Why don't you find out?"

Leo, landing on a shin, unbuttoning his shirt . . . Andie's cheeks burned. "I think you're the one who needs a date."

"On that we agree. What do you have to lose?"

The shirt slipping off his shoulders and landing on the floor. "A lot of clothes if we're playing strip dreidels."

"And that's the point!"

Andie shook the image of Leo reaching for his belt buckle aside and stood, stretching as she did so. "I'll consider the dreidels, not so much the stripping." Those thoughts were for fantasies, not reality.

Sarah stuck out her lower lip in a pout. "Don't force my hand and have me send my afternoon kids pouting to your room."

"I think we need a foam snowball war."

Sarah stood, stretching as well. "Oh, definitely. I'm thinking Thursday, closer to the break."

"Deal."

They shook on it, and Andie headed back to her classroom. Giving Leo a second chance felt right. Better than being alone for Chanukah. Maybe like her thoughts with Emma's parents, Leo had a change of heart about her job. What did it matter what he thought about her job anyways? In a few months she'd be gone.

That sent a fresh wave of sadness over her. She'd grown up in this area. She had memories with her father here. Sure, she kept to herself enough that the few friends she had would stay in touch, but a big move didn't come without some drawbacks.

What would her father say? Something along the lines of, life hands us opportunities and takes others away. When we're handed something, we're smart to listen. So she'd listen to this one, on the job and the neighbor.

* * *

The midday sun sent a ray of bright light over the city street. A few slender trees dotted the walkways around the urban buildings. Brookline, Massachusetts, was one of the few local places to get truly authentic Jewish artifacts. Leo hadn't been here in years but luck had given him an appointment nearby, and if he had any chance of finding quality candles after the start of Chanukah, this was the place to be.

The bell above the door chimed as he entered the shop, leaving the cool December air behind. Leo breathed in the scents of things both old and new, a feeling of home and tradition. The store was jam-packed with books, food, tchotchkes, and other items. He could get yarmulkas or yahrzeit candles, fancy menorahs that cost more than the last antique he sold, or the one item he was here for.

If he had any luck.

He weaved around the aisles until he came to the candle section. Picked through, of course, Chanukah had already begun, but he skipped over the three short boxes that were no better than the one Andie already had, checking for the beeswax and premium handcrafted options, finding one sole box remaining. In white. Broken.

Of course. He put the box back hard enough that the wire shelf wobbled, taking out his frustration on an inanimate object. Finding the right candles had been a needle in the haystack hope. He turned away from the display. He'd find another way to make it up to Andie, some other peace offering. As soon as he figured out what.

The shop was relatively quiet, but a voice rose above the rest, and he wiggled his hearing aid, not connecting the sound to speech until it got closer and louder.

"Can I help you?"

Leo turned to an older gentleman who stood nearby. With one last hope for a miracle—Chanukah was the holiday of miracles after all—Leo pointed toward the candles. "Any chance you have a few more boxes out back?"

The guy shook his head. "Maybe yesterday but not today."

There went Leo's last hope for the candle option. "Thanks."

He exited the shop, sun blinding him for a moment, and headed to his car. Once there, he reached for the GPS, setting it up for his next appointment. It took twenty minutes until the familiar streets came into view, and he found himself idling in front of his client's house. A nice older lady, like the quirky family aunt, with a bit of a hoarding tendency. Which worked for Leo, since Rose kept items from multiple generations, slowly reducing her inventory as she felt able.

She wouldn't have the candles for Andie, but maybe he'd acquire the score to save the business.

Leo got out of his car and ambled up the four steps to the front door. He pressed the doorbell then shoved his hands in his pockets. Rose moved slower than she used to and needed a bit of time to get down the stairs of the split-level. A leaf blew across the yard. It had snowed a few weeks ago, only a couple inches, not enough to stay with the rising temperatures.

The door creaked open. "Oh, Leo, you made it!"

Rose stood before him, barely five feet if she stood up straight. Her hair dyed black, matching the large cat eye glasses he suspected had been her style since they were popular the first time.

"Of course I made it! Anything for you, Rose."

She gestured him in and headed down the stairs, to where chaos lived. The top level of the home didn't display clutter or anything overflowing. She saved it all for the bottom level.

The lower level had a living area that he only got glimpses of. He followed Rose down the hall, to the massive storage area set up like a maze with all her supplies. A place like this should be a dust trap, but it wasn't. The setup would put any stock person to shame.

He let his gaze wander as he followed her, spotting at least five different menorahs two rows over, and what looked like more candles than she'd be able to use in her lifetime. Rose had never let him touch an item off of her designated shelf, and yet he'd be a fool not to take advantage of the opportunity.

Later. He made it to where she waited and poked around while she stood there, explaining what she knew of the different items. He had to keep looking back at her to hear, asking for repetition when he missed something. A stack of newspapers from the 1800s, two complete silverware sets, a variety of different glasses—first glance suggested Depression era—and a very old clock that, while it might be valuable, had seen much better days.

Unsalvageable clocks had become his thing. He knew not to touch this particular artifact.

"What do you think?" she asked.

He rummaged around a bit more, calculating and contemplating. "If those glasses are Depression era they may be worth something."

Rose stood taller. "They are."

Leo grinned. "Then you'll want to let me investigate them further. The silverware is good, as are the newspapers. The clock, however, might be too beat up."

"A few falls will do that for anyone. Shame, it was once a beauty." She picked it up with gentle, shaking hands, holding it up to the light, a forlorn smile on her face. Whatever she saw wasn't the beat-up item she held.

His father did the same thing with the damaged clock, no forlorn smile to be had. The two clocks held a note of resemblance—parts might be compatible, but not enough to save both.

"I know, it's worthless now, but it comes with such fond memories." Rose sighed. "It might not make sense to you youngsters, but I want it to continue to be involved in those good times."

"Would I be here if I didn't get it?"

Rose smiled up at him and patted his cheek. "Such a good boy. You'll take it then?"

He wanted to back up, but if he did, he ran the risk of knocking over a shelf, or twelve. "I don't know if I can save it."

"Then you weren't listening. I'm not asking for it to be saved."

"What would you want for it?"

Rose used the same hand that patted his cheek to pat the clock. "A chance for it to be a part of more good memories." She leveled him with a sharp glare over the rim of her glasses, and he doubted she saw anything more than a blurry blob. "I think you can give me this favor."

Laughter bubbled up in his chest; but he swallowed it in place of a professional smile. "Of course." Two words and he'd cracked open a door to a creative bargain. "Though I decide the proper match for this favor."

Rose pushed her glasses up. "What do you want?"

He nodded in the direction of the menorahs. "I'm in need of some good quality Chanukah candles, and you know the stores won't have anything left."

Rose crossed her arms. "Why?"

He opened his mouth. Closed it. How could he even begin to explain Andie, to a client, no less?

Rose pressed her hands together in a single clap. "I knew it, it is a girl, isn't it? Mr. Workaholic finally found someone."

Now his mouth hung open.

Rose laughed and turned, heading toward the menorahs. "I talk. As does your family. Is it serious?" She glanced over her shoulder, shrewd gaze locking on him.

"Uh." He scratched the back of his neck. "It's to make amends for a bad start."

Rose nodded and arrived at the shelf, studying her collection. Up close, he realized it was even larger than he thought, and some were quite old by the looks of it. "Sounds like a story. The best starts are a story. Much like that clock. What colors does she like?"

Shit, what color would Andie like? He thought of her apartment, of the neutral tones with pops of bright color. Some blueish-greenish shade. At the very least, it would match her décor.

"Teal."

"Ahh, a hard one to find. But don't worry. I think I have something." She pulled out a bunch, handing them to him, and then piling more and more on top until his chin held them steady. She rose to her tiptoes, one arm stretching to snag a box from near the back. The lighting in this part of the room was dim, and she angled it to catch the light.

"Will this do? I think that's the best I've got."

He studied the color, it felt close to the shades in Andie's apartment. At the very least, it was a damn good option. "That's perfect."

She placed it on a higher shelf, then took the items in his arms and lined them back up to their former state of perfection.

Satisfied with her layout, she turned to him. "Do we have a deal?"

Leo nodded. "We do."

"And pay for it?"

He held up the candles. "These are my commission, yes?"

Rose smiled.

Leo took a second look at his items, figured out the rates. Everything came with a bit of risk in this business, but he knew Rose and she knew her items. With the exception of the clock, he rarely had a bust with her.

He also didn't have a huge win like he needed, but the glasses might be hiding something they both overlooked. If so, he'd make it up to her.

He turned his phone around, with the calculator app on screen. "This work for you?"

Rose lowered her glasses to get a better look. "Yes. It'll do. Keep me updated on the clock. And the candles."

Leo chuckled. "Will do."

CHAPTER FOUR

Andie struggled to fold down the box lid, crisscrossing the flaps to be secured without being taped up. Box one was packed. It was kitchen items mostly, the rarely used ones with a thick coating of dust she doubted she'd use before she moved. But it was a step forward, an attempt at making this all real.

She stretched, hand to her lower back. There was a lot of bending in her world working with three and four-year-olds. The box sat at her feet, her kitchen showing no signs of change. And yet she knew her cabinets held fewer items; it would be one step closer to easier packing.

With a huff, she prodded the box with her foot, sliding it to an empty corner in her living room, next to the desk she inherited from her mother. Broken and worthless, but also priceless. Now she had a reminder of her job offer and move, as if she'd presented the idea to the mother she didn't remember for approval. She'd made a decision.

Sort of.

She hadn't accepted it yet, still wanted to give herself the entire week. Too often, Andie made decisions on the fly, jumped into something new without thinking it through. Those decisions hadn't come back to bite her in the ass, but none involved as much change as this one did.

One box packed. No regrets. Though granted, some of those items might be better off in a storage unit.

Andie clapped her hands and faced the direction of her neighbor. Leo. He'd hit a soft spot and she'd gone off on him. Not his fault. She'd go over there and make amends. Her gaze tracked to her menorah, still with dried yellow wax clinging to it. The darkening sky displayed behind it through her windows. A barricade-like sensation sprouted and grew roots between her and the candles. If she tried to light them, she'd have to climb a mountain first. How odd, she could pack a box, but she couldn't light those candles alone. At least not without giving Leo a second chance.

She stuffed her phone in her pocket and grabbed her keys, walking the few feet down the hall to Leo's unit. This walk felt as smooth as butter. It was the right decision for tonight, the only explanation she had. That gave her a little kick to her step, a drop of adrenaline coursing through her system. With any luck, the conflict from the previous night had been a fluke. Either way, she'd come prepared to find out.

Leo's blank door stood in front of her, the gold forty-two under the peephole. The same setup as all the units, with mirroring layouts. She knocked, a light rasp of her knuckles against the dark wood. And waited.

And waited.

Her foot tapped the carpet. Perhaps she knocked too lightly? She knocked again, louder this time, bringing a sting to her knuckles, and waited.

Nothing.

She sighed. He might be out. Or perhaps he didn't want round two with his bitchy neighbor. Couldn't blame him for that. With any luck, this attempt at talking to him would allow her to light her menorah, even if the thought of being alone felt just plain wrong.

Her keys were in hand and her back to his door, when it clicked open. "Andie?"

She turned, catching Leo standing there, hair all mussed up, a dress shirt open at the collar and stretched across broad shoulders, dark jeans hugging his legs, and white socks on his feet.

Damn, she'd forgotten how gorgeous he was.

"Hi," she waved. "Look, I wanted to apologize."

"Apologize?" His eyebrows attempted to reach the wayward lock of hair on his forehead. "I thought I needed to apologize."

She warmed at his words but held to her reason for being there. "I might have been a bit harsh last night and reactive. I get like that. One can only take so much of their career being put down before being a tad oversensitive. Anyway . . . I didn't know if you had plans for the second night or if you would be up for company?"

She bit her lip, wondering when she'd turned into a rambling fool. She talked students and parents out of meltdowns, flirted her way to free drinks, and yet fumbled with her words in front of her neighbor.

He looks like Ryan Reynolds, you'd fumble in front of Ryan Reynolds, too.

A smile grew over Leo's face, strong and sure. And suddenly she wasn't thinking of the celebrity he resembled; she was thinking of him and his smile. One she wanted to taste.

"I'd very much like to spend the second night with you." He stepped back, welcoming her into his apartment.

Andie took in the unit. The same layout as hers reversed, though that was where the similarities stopped. Her unit was filled, albeit sparsely, with modern and secondhand items. Leo's reminded her of her grandparents' place, but in a good way. No question about him being an antique dealer, or at least an antique lover. Dark furniture with gold accents covered the place, probably worth more than her Ikea couch. And yet, the place felt light and comfortable.

"You really do deal with antiques," she said as she continued to examine his place. "I think this makes your unit more valuable than mine."

Leo chuckled. "That's only if I'm having an estate sale."

"I don't think there's anything here that isn't old."

"I have modern technology, I'll have you know. And while I enjoy antiques, I'm not a fan of secondhand mattresses. The bed set is old, however."

She faced him, forgetting about his living area. Now, she wanted to see his bedroom. What kind of set did he have? A soft, plush one in dark, masculine tones? Perhaps one she could sink into, or be tied up to, or . . . Andie really needed to stop her thoughts from traveling any further down that particular path. Leo's cheeks pinked, clearly catching the same drift. At least some of it. Adorable. And sexy. Was it warm in here?

He tugged at his collar. "Uh, a lot of the other furniture has been reupholstered, so a bit of new mixed in with old."

She nodded. "That's nice. There are stories here that don't involve a crowded Ikea trip. Though I will have you know I have some epic Ikea stories."

"Oh really?"

Andie did her best to smother her grin. "Indeed. Besides catching some amazing finds and grabbing a cinnamon roll on the way out, have you ever had a scavenger hunt there?

Confusion crossed Leo's face. "A scavenger hunt?"

Andie laughed, lost in the memory. "Yes. Two preschool teachers on a shopping trip with a bit too much caffeine energy. Some of the most fun I've ever had while shopping." Sarah and she had raced through the place, trying to find all the odd items, laughing so hard they got not-so-friendly looks from strangers.

She'd do it again in a heartbeat.

"That does sound like fun. I might like to do that someday."

"And perhaps someday I'll bring you on one." Where did that come from? One minute she thought of fun with Sarah, the next she invited Leo somewhere as if they were dating or at least good friends, not neighbors with an end date all but stamped on.

"I, uh, got you something."

She refocused on his face and the hand scratching the back of his neck. She bet his hair was smooth and silky. "You did?"

"Yeah, I felt bad about yesterday and your candle situation. I was planning on dropping it off soon, hang on." He turned and rummaged through a workbag. The whole apartment had a gold tone to it that had nothing to do with the setting sun. The shade looked good on Leo, somehow luring her toward him.

He turned and held up a box. "For your menorah. I hope you like the color."

She collected the box of beeswax candles with teal and white accents, her heart warming. "Teal's my favorite color, I don't think I've ever seen candles this color. How did you know?"

He rubbed that neck of his again, a nervous gesture she realized, and darn cute. "I, uh, remembered you had a lot of teal items in your place."

Many men didn't recognize a drastic haircut and this man caught the color of the accents in her apartment. He paid attention, a rare trait to find. "And you just happened to have a box on hand?"

"I had a visit to one of my collector clients. She had more candle boxes than she knew what to do with, so I offered it a good home."

She turned the box over in her hands, touched that he went through the trouble for her. "Well, thank you for this."

He gestured to the dining room table where his menorah sat. An old one, for sure, gold—naturally—with a tree-like look. "Would you do me the honor of lighting them with me?"

The vines on the menorah held so much detail, exquisitely depicted and carried out. Someone took a lot of time in designing this, and the years that had since passed only enhanced the mystique. "That's beautiful." Andie walked over, brushing a finger down one side. It brought to mind a different menorah, also with a tree-like feel, and all the warmth that other menorah held. "It reminds me of one my grandparents had. I don't know what happened to it after they passed, but I'd secretly wanted it for myself."

"I'm sorry you lost track of it. This one came into my workshop. I want to clean it up a bit, but couldn't resist using it."

"I can see that. Sure, let's light it."

"Really?" He looked so surprised, like she'd came over just to scurry back to her apartment.

"Yes. Fresh start, right here."

"No pressure or anything, I have a bad habit of putting my foot in the mouth."

Andie grinned, he really was cute with those two spots of pink on his cheeks above the hint of a five-o'clock shadow. "Well, you try and keep that foot out and I'll try and let you have a mishap or two."

"Only two?" The color faded and knowingly or not, he leaned into her, heating up the space between them.

"I need to have my standards, don't I?"

"Well then, let's light the candles and see if I can behave."

Maybe you can not behave in other areas. Down girl, there was plenty of time left to have some fun. Whatever had turned her off the previous night didn't seem to be a problem anymore, making this moment all the more special.

Leo gestured to the box of candles she still held. "Would you like to use your candles? Your candles, my menorah, and this fresh start?"

He might put his foot in his mouth, but the man was considerate, thinking of others in ways she wasn't used to. It touched her, proved there was more to Leo than what met the eye.

"I would, thank you." Andie tapped out three candles and set them up in Leo's menorah. He lit a match, lighting the shamash. "Words are on the paper over there, but we proved yesterday we don't need it." A folded yellow paper with the words lay to the side.

"That we have, and yet, we're both going to read it anyways, aren't we?"

"Or pretend to."

He reached for the shamash, then stopped. "Did you want to light them?"

She intended to reach out, but standing back, enjoying the view of his menorah, her candles, and the man himself, she wanted to keep this visual and savor it. "No, you go ahead."

He nodded and plucked the center candle from its holder. Their voices rang out together again, saying the prayers. "Baruch atah, Adonai Eloheinu, Melech haolam, asher kid'shanu b'mitzvotav v'tsivanu l'hadlik ner shel Chanukah. Baruch atah, Adonai Eloheinu, Melech haolam, she-asah nisim laavoteinu v'imoteinu bayamim hahaeim baz'man hazeh."

Andie stepped back, watching the three flames flickering back at them. She wanted to make this night a better one, wanted this magical moment to continue. With any luck, Leo and she wouldn't clash, and they'd be able to enjoy their time together. In more ways than one.

* * *

Leo watched the flames lick high into the air, teal candles bright against his menorah. Andie stood beside him, also watching. He couldn't believe his good fortune that she'd had a change of heart. Instead of the awkward uncomfortable moments of the previous night, here felt comfort. The flames cast a flickering glow on her face, bringing out her beauty, and he wanted to see her lit by all nine candles.

Maybe if he played his cards right—and managed to keep his foot out of his mouth—he'd have a shot at it. Until then, he'd make the best of this moment here and now and see where the night brought them.

"How are you at dreidel?" Andie asked, pulling him from his runaway thoughts.

The words took a moment to register. "Dreidels?" *Goodness, Dentz, enough with being a shmuck!*

"Yes, you know the spinning tops with Hebrew on the side, the ones that indicate the words to 'a great miracle happened there.'" Her lips tilted with a tease that looked as sweet as honey and nearly made him forget how to speak.

"Uh. Yes. I know what they are. I just wasn't expecting it." *Or hearing it right.*

"We could make it interesting?" In addition to her tempting grin, her eyes shone with a glow not from the candles.

He didn't know if she meant it to be seductive, but he wanted a taste, a big one.

"How do you make dreidels interesting besides winning the most gelt or candy?"

"My friend and coworker suggested strip dreidels, but I don't think we're up to that, are we?" She batted her eyelashes at him, a tilt to her head, exposing a strip of her smooth neck.

All his blood ran south at airplane speed. He had to swallow to ensure he didn't squeak. "No. But I'm always game for that."

Andie laughed, head tilting to the other side, showing off more of her neck. "Of course you are. What I'm thinking is this: we play now and winner decides what we do tomorrow night."

"There's going to be a tomorrow night?" One would think he had cobwebs on his dating skills. In fact, he probably did, more so than some of the antiques he worked with.

"If you spin your dreidels right there could be." A flash of vulnerability crossed over her face. "Unless you have plans?"

He shook his head. "No plans."

"What do you say? You have supplies or do I need to go rummaging around in a box at home?"

"I've got some supplies. No gelt, though. My niece won most of mine the last time we played."

"How old is she?"

"She's ten. A sweet exterior with a calculating soul."

"The type that cries to get what she wants?"

"Not since she was four."

He loved his niece, but she was a handful. Jodie claims it to be the reason she only had one, but he knew infertility played a heavy hand.

"I do have some M&Ms we can use, if you don't mind Christmas colors."

"Tis the season and all that. A full bag should make for an interesting game. All right, Leo, you're on."

A full bag? He didn't think his hearing aids were giving him issues, but tell that to everything he stumbled over. "You want to use an entire bag of candy?" He posed the question carefully; aware he risked inserting his foot back in his mouth.

Humor danced in Andie's eyes. "Why not? This game is a bit like war and can go on for a while. Leo, would you like to go on for a while with me?"

His brain turned to mush, complete and utter mush. Half of him wanted to take up flirting like a second job, continue down the tease Andie dropped before him. The other half still appalled at wasting that much precious candy.

"And what happens to the M&Ms?"

Andie threw her head back, laughing. "Winner takes all? Or, if it matters to you, the candy can stay here."

"But if you win . . ." He really knew how to dig himself a hole. Any hole. Anywhere. But he didn't buy candy to be used only as gelt.

"Then I'll have tomorrow night's plans as my winnings, won't I?" Her brown hair hung in its typical waves around her face.

Focus, Dentz, she's here and wants more. "Works for me." He held out a hand. "May the odds be ever in your favor."

Andie laughed and shook his hand, her skin silky smooth against his roughened palm. "A *Hunger Games* fan, I take it?"

He shrugged as he shuffled through a drawer until he found his dreidels. The candles sparked and wavered, the dance of ancient times, as he shifted the menorah to the side so they had room to play.

"I wouldn't call myself a fan. More like I saw it and enjoyed it."

"You didn't read the book."

He grabbed the M&M bag and brought it over to the table. "I did not read the book. That doesn't mean I don't enjoy reading, just further proof that the movie wasn't a strong interest. I probably saw it because everyone was talking about it."

"I get that."

He grasped two sides of the candy bag, prepared to yank it open. He pulled, hands straining, bag not even attempting to tear. He altered his grip and tried again, the material threatening to slip through his fingers. Not even a slight rip.

Leo put the bag down and hung his head. So much for creating a good second impression. "That did not go well."

Andie chuckled, the glow of the candles on her raised cheeks, bringing out gold specks in her brown eyes. "Go ahead, try again."

She made him feel like a kid given an extra dollar to give the strong man game another try, one he had no plans to waste. He grabbed the bag, getting a different grip, and wrenching with all his might. His male ego wanted to puff his chest and turn all Hulk super strength to impress her. Instead, his fingers slipped as he tugged and his ego slinked off to a corner to pout. "We're going to pretend I didn't do that."

Andie dropped her head, laughing. He liked the sound, just not at his expense. He went into his junk drawer and grabbed a pair of scissors, snipping the bag open. "On the topic of movies, what does everyone love and you dislike?"

"You said you liked *Hunger Games*."

"I did. It was okay, but it made me think of this question." He dumped the contents of the bag into the center of the table, stealing a few to pop in his mouth. "Humor me."

"You think you can handle this?"

A smile spread across her face. Damn, she was beautiful. One day, if he was lucky, he'd get the chance to tell her so.

"Try me." He opened the cloth bag that held his dreidels, spreading them out to be chosen.

"This will probably have you packing up and taking the dreidels away, but I'm so not a *Star Wars* fan." Andie folded her hands in front of her and settled her chin on them. The expression on her face could only be described as "deal with it." A multicolored beaded bracelet slid down her wrist.

"While I have seen the movies and enjoyed them, they were just okay. I'm not camping out to watch them or fretting over any story-line changes."

"Ahh, but you know about them."

He grinned. "It's a lot like *Hunger Games*. Family, friends, social media, they all know and talk about it so it's in all of our faces. The bigger question, why don't you like it?"

She picked up a wooden dreidel, twirled it between two fingers. "Because it's so overdone. The hype alone is everywhere, and the attitude people have about it is blown out of proportion."

"So, because it's overly hyped, you won't give it a chance?"

She sighed, laying the dreidel on its side. "That's the thing. I did give it a chance, and it left me bored after the first twenty minutes. I don't get the appeal."

Leo began sorting out the candy. "I can accept that."

"What about you?" Her gaze studied him with an intensity he wasn't used to and be damned if he didn't like it.

"*Terminator*."

"Well, the fifth one was pretty bad. I'll give you that."

He shook his head. "Never saw the fifth. I'm talking about the first."

A hand went to her heart. "Not *Terminator*!"

"'Fraid so."

Andie leaned forward, angling the table toward her. A few candies skittered closer. "Come on. Sarah and Kyle are adorable together."

You're adorable. "They know each other a week. We're supposed to buy everlasting love in a week?"

"Wow, you're a cynic."

Was he? "No. I like my fair share of romance movies that my buddies tease me about. I just don't buy this whirlwind romance. A week and sex? Sure. But not love. Then, the whole concept falls apart. If robots were going to take over, we'd all be gone by now."

"Ahh, but it's a parable, a warning for what might come."

"Bodybuilder robots who have a change of heart? No. You don't believe in the dark side, and I don't believe in the robot revolt."

Andie's eyes slid to his iPhone resting on the table. "And your phone isn't listening to you? You never mentioned a product and then saw an ad for it on social media an hour later?"

"Oh, my phone one hundred percent is listening to me. I play it Mozart at night to fall asleep."

She threw her head back and laughed. Her cheeks rose with the humor and had the strongest urge to kiss each one. *Hold it together, man, you're on your second chance. There won't be a third one.*

"Okay, so no *Star Wars*, no *Terminator*, and *Hunger Games* only if the mood strikes, am I following our movie options correctly?"

Andie collected the pile of M&Ms he pushed toward her. "I never said what I thought of *Hunger Games*."

He settled into his seat. "And . . .?"

"I suspect we both are not huge fans of the hype. I probably enjoyed it more than you, but have no burning desire to see it again. And yes, I did read the books."

"Which was better?"

"I think, at the end of the day, I enjoyed the book better. But they both bring a lot to the table."

"Speaking of tables, who goes first?"

Andie grinned. "Spin for it? I'm surprised your dreidels aren't older."

He held up a finger, scrapped his chair back and went into his living room. The glass door on the old cabinet squeaked uncomfortably as he opened it. He returned to Andie, setting a very old and very fragile silver dreidel in her hands.

"Oh, that's beautiful." She turned it around, examining the sides. It was rounded instead of squared, with ornate detailing.

"Not one to spin and play with, and I doubt it ever was. But I couldn't let this leave my hands. I don't get many through my shop that are good for playing, so newer is better, though a lot of these dreidels I've had since I was a kid."

"Fair enough." Andie handed him back the dreidel. He returned it to its home, Andie's voice hitting his ears from across the room. With her distance, and not being able to see her, he couldn't make out a word.

"What was that?" He asked when he got back to the table.

"Oh, I was just saying that the dreidels from my youth are sometimes better than the cheap plastic ones made now."

He rejoined her at the table. "Ah, perhaps there is an antique appreciator in you after all, or at least a retro/vintage one." And where did that come from? He really did excel at sticking his foot in his mouth.

Andie didn't seem phased. "I do appreciate an occasional older relic. But my taste is more modern and my budget is mass-marketed cheap crap."

"It's not always accessible, I'll give you that. But if you ever have your eye on an item let me know, I can usually work out something."

She studied him for a moment. He knew the offer was bigger than whatever got them to this table, and she'd be moving soon, but he couldn't not drop that into the conversation. He couldn't sway her future, but he also wouldn't hold himself back.

"Thank you." She spun a dreidel and they watched it sail into a smooth twirl, then sputter, then stumble and land on the letter hay.

"Beat that."

He grabbed his own dreidel and spun it. It sputtered more than hers did, but landed on a gimel. He grinned. "My win."

Andie dropped a green candy into the center pot. "Your win indeed. Let's see what you've got."

CHAPTER FIVE

An hour later, the candles were burned down, and Andie had one red candy left in front of her. Even with Leo munching on his winnings she didn't have a chance at catching up. She'd never had much of a competitive streak, and times like this proved it. The fun existed more in playing the game than in the winning or losing. Despite the previous night's sour note, she did enjoy this time with Leo. "Either this game ends here, or we'll be going at it for another hour."

Leo raised an eyebrow, lips curving. "Going at it?" He leaned forward and she swore his eyes darkened, as though an invitation not related to dreidels had landed on the table.

Her entire body grew warm and tingly. Who knew not-strip dreidel still came with flirting? "You know what I mean."

He added two candies to the center—and one to his mouth—body still angled toward her. "Maybe I like the idea."

If there hadn't been an additional invitation on the table, there certainly was one now. He only needed to add one candy, but she accepted the encouragement and spun her dreidel. Gimel, she'd accept the unspoken invitation. Nun, she'd pass. It twirled in wobbly loops, her thoughts pinging back and forth between the two options, unsure which she wanted for tonight. The dreidel's loops grew haphazard before skidding to a halt near the center pile, landing on a shin.

She didn't know whether to sigh in relief or be bummed.

"Welp, I'm out. Can't put two in the pot when I have nothing left." She leaned back, marveling over how two evenings could be so different. The previous night must have been an off one for him. She'd take it. "The win is yours."

Leo fiddled with a few of his candies. "I guess it is. The question being, you still on for something tomorrow night of my choosing?"

She studied his face, and the caution suddenly lurking on his cheeks. Adorable, absolutely adorable. Did she want another night in his company? She looked inward: a content and happy feeling filled her, and it had nothing to do with avoiding being alone for the holiday. She wanted more of his pink cheeks and sexy smile. "Yes. I am."

"Then I'd like to take you out for dinner. Not takeout that I hadn't intended to share. Andie, will you have dinner with me tomorrow?" He leaned his elbows on the table. He'd rolled his sleeves up, and sturdy forearms dusted with hair shifted the table toward him, biceps struggling against the bunched-up fabric. The kind of arms she wanted banded around her or propping him up next to her.

She pressed her lips together. This had changed from two neighbors hanging out during Chanukah to something that most definitely spelled out d-a-t-e. She wanted to enjoy herself this Chanukah, didn't she? She deserved the potential of nice forearms in her immediate future.

"Okay, you're on. A date it is." No use not labeling it appropriately.

He grinned, those smooth cheeks rising, and she nearly swooned. "Excellent. And thank you."

His face had sobered, the grin slipping, and she found herself reaching a hand across the table, covering one of his. The contact created a jolt, but she didn't pull back, she welcomed it. "Hey, what's wrong?"

He shook his head. "Nothing. I'm just grateful you gave me this second night. I'm enjoying spending time with you."

"I'm enjoying spending time with you, too." Much more than she would have expected.

"Even after last night?"

She let him go, though her cheeks were definitely smiling. "How do you feel about me being a preschool teacher?"

"I think it's wonderful and you should move wherever you need to."

Andie laughed.

"Never say I'm a man who doesn't learn."

"And that is why I'll see you again tomorrow. Goodnight, Leo."

She rose, gathered up her new candles, and headed for the door before she investigated those sexy arms prematurely. Hand on the knob she turned, catching him standing but not going after her. A light stubble covered his jaw, accentuated his lips, calling her to him. She could walk back and kiss him, see where else this night could go.

No. She might be on borrowed time, but no need to rush. She had tomorrow and most of the nights of Chanukah. Perhaps one of those nights she'd manage to scratch this itch.

She made the short trek back to her apartment and let herself in. Darkness greeted her, and before her eyes could adjust she flipped on the lights. Her place didn't have the charm that Leo's did, but it was home. Her belongings. Her memories.

For a little while longer, at least.

She placed the candles on her desk, next to the two pictures she kept on display. One of her entire family from when she was baby. Her mother cradling her, looking down at her daughter in such a way that Andie had never needed to doubt her mother loved her. Her father with his arm around her mother, smiling at the wife he didn't know he'd lose so soon. The second photo was of her and her father at her college graduation. Her smile filled her face, and her father's eyes shone with pride.

Life would have been different if her mother had lived, but her father did his best to make her life a good one.

Now it was up to her to make the rest good.

She ran her fingers over the chipped varnish on the desk, over the drawer that had been stuck in a closed position so long she wondered if it ever was supposed to move. Like the pictures above, this desk represented love. Oh, she wished it wasn't falling apart, but this desk helped her mother with homework, and her with homework, and she'd carry the broken fragments of it wherever life took her to continue the tradition.

Moving. Her parents would want her to reach for the stars and accomplish all her dreams. Those dream directed her to Ohio, where a new job offer awaited her acceptance. They'd want her to accept and not hang back for memories, as precious as they were.

"I wish you were here to guide me."

The figures in her photos didn't answer her. Grief wrapped around her, the loss of her father still fresh and would be for years to come. How she wanted a family to support her again. Someone to go to and cry on their shoulders, to steal a meal from the freezer, or ask for outlandish Chanukah gifts. Someone to confide in and provide that unconditional support her father had doled out in waves.

"I'll find it again."

She had time. It just wouldn't be in the same place of her youth.

Her gaze flitted to her wall shared with Leo's apartment. She'd miss him, miss the potential of where this fun night went. Who knew, maybe she'd find someone intriguing in her next apartment building.

That made her sad and she welcomed it. Moving would be sad. On so many levels. But life had handed her an opportunity for a rewarding new start and she'd be a fool to pass it up.

"I guess I'm going to need more boxes."

* * *

Leo finished loading his dishwasher after dinner when his phone vibrated with a message from Millie.

Millie: Did you light the magic menorah again?

He laughed and snapped a photo. The flames had burned out a long time ago, but the few wax drippings served as proof.

Millie: Yay! And did you make a wish?
    Come on Uncle Leo, tell me you made a wish!
                            Leo: No, I did not make a wish.
Millie: Awwww! Come on, give it a try. Or I can try.
    Can I come over and make a wish?
                            Leo: And what would you wish for?
Millie: I already gave you my Chanukah list.

Leo chuckled and propped a hip against his counter, firing off a response. Millie had sent a group text on November first with all of her top wish list items, first come, first served. He wished he had half her confidence.

                  Leo: I know you did. I already bought your present.
                          What would you wish for?
Millie: Nope. Wishes are meant to be secret,
    that's how they come true.
Millie: You should at least try. Light them tomorrow.
    Make a wish.
                  Leo: I don't think that's necessary.
Millie: ☹ Think of it as a science experiment.
                  Leo: With an antique menorah.
Millie: Fine. Do it for your niece!

She sent a picture of her looking up at the camera with doe eyes and a stuck-out lip.

Leo's heart rolled over in his chest. "Damn, she's good." Not wanting to suck out the magic left in her life, especially as a child for whom Santa was never a real entity, Leo opted to not point out that menorahs really weren't magic.

Leo: Okay. For you. What should I wish for?
Millie: Nope, that will ensure it doesn't work.
But if I were to lend some suggestions, I might
mention that neighbor you are too chicken to ask out.

Leo nearly dropped his phone. Good thing they weren't on video, if they were she'd be dancing around and twirling and thinking the menorah really had magic and it had worked. Because apparently he'd never make a move any other way.

Leo: Chicken?

Millie sent a gif of a chicken being choked.
Leo nearly doubled over with laughter.

Leo: Don't use that gif.
Millie: Why not?
Leo: Ask your mother.

No way was he getting into that.

Millie: Fine. Don't ask out your neighbor.

Leo grinned. Maybe his own initiative would give Millie a little holiday magic, no menorah required.

Leo: I can't tell you my wish anyways, according
to your rules it won't come true.

Millie: Good point! Tomorrow night, make a wish!

Leo: For you, tomorrow, I will.

Millie: Yay!!!

He put his phone away, chuckling at his niece. He'd light the candles tomorrow and then the next day tell her that he had a date planned with Andie. And if it all felt a little magical to him, that was simply the power of the holiday season.

CHAPTER SIX

Andie was used to crying children. Their hugs and teary grins often made a difficult day completely worth it. She wasn't used to inconsolable children that flung themselves around her legs and wouldn't let go.

There were days she wished for an assistant teacher. Today, for instance. An extra set of hands, and arms, would always be welcomed in her world. The rest of her students played contently, so Andie slid to the floor to address her clinger.

"Hey, Emma, what's wrong?" Andie hoped the baby wasn't sick again.

Emma sniffled and rubbed her nose into Andie's shoulder.

Andie shifted until her back was supported by a wall and rubbed a hand up and down the little girl's back. At least she could see most of her room. It took a few minutes, and more calming words, but Emma's sniffles slowed. She spoke, the words muffled by Andie's now wet shirt.

"Sweetheart, it's going to be okay."

Emma pulled back, wiping her nose with her sleeve. "I don't want you to go."

Andie knew from experience there were multiple possible meanings behind that sentence. "What do you mean, sweetie?"

"I don't want the school to close. I want you to stay!" Emma burst into tears again and sagged into Andie's arms.

Gut punch delivered, preschooler style. Andie took a deep breath. A few kids glanced her way and she worried she'd have more crying students on her hands. She tapped a finger to Emma's nose and looked into those watery blue eyes. "Now, where did you hear that?"

"Dad and Papa were talking about how they need to find a new school for me next year. But I don't want a new school. I want to stay here. With you!"

Andie's heart tore a bit. Change was hard. Especially at four years old. "You'd have a new teacher next year anyways." And soon, kindergarten.

"No. I don't want a new teacher. I want you here." Emma stomped.

Andie needed a redirection, and fast. "I know. I understand you. But I have a question for you. What did you get your fathers for Christmas?"

"They buy me gifts. I don't have money to buy for them."

"What if we made them something?"

Emma sniffed and ran a sleeve under her nose. "Okay."

Andie brought Emma over to the crafts table to get her started on a handmade gift. She knew the less she said the better. Small ears picked up things and she didn't know what any of the other students had overheard or been told.

She wanted to tell Emma that an appeal had been filed, and they could save the school. But that would give Emma hope that Andie struggled to hold onto. They'd filed appeal after appeal already, and all had been denied. All the love that everyone had for the school had yet to be enough to save it. Because in the end, it came down to the dollars and cents, and the town simply didn't have enough.

With Emma refocused, Andie stood and checked on each of her students. No more tears, no one else seemed affected by Emma's outburst. So far. It had taken Emma nearly halfway through the day to crumble.

"Miss Andie, I made a tower!"

Andie smiled at Kayden, beaming up at her with the biggest smile. "I see. That is a big tower."

"I made it myself!"

"Nuh-uh, I helped!" Xavier said.

"Did not." Kayden pushed Xavier.

"Did too!" Xavier pushed Kayden back.

Andie sprung into action as the tower fell, separating the two amid the fallen blocks. Never a dull moment in her job. She wouldn't change a thing.

Except for the appeal to go through with budget for an assistant. That she would change.

* * *

The scents of wood and dust filled the air as Leo investigated the midcentury modern dining set Dean had brought in from an estate sale. Dentz Antiques tended to have older styles, but Leo couldn't deny this beauty had potential, and it belonged in a shop like theirs.

After he got a chance to play up that potential for all to see.

The sleek lines exuded grace. A warm cherry wood lurked under years of neglect. One corner had water damage stripping away at the finish. Cup rings existed in other parts, but only this area had the extensive damage. He touched the wood, seeking its story. Household leak? Kids' corner where things spilled on the regular? Had it been left outside and this corner got uncovered? So many options. He'd never quite know the answer, but one thing held true: This table had been well loved.

He'd make sure it would be loved again. It had the character someone would spend good money for.

Family dinners could happen here again, children working on homework. All that the table had already experienced would happen again—as soon as Leo finished shining it up and showing others what he saw.

The fourth chair wobbled more than he liked, and he had it upside down, studying how it originally went together, when heavy footsteps alerted him to company.

"You're still here?" Dean asked, sliding up next to him, hands in his pockets.

"Yeah, I'm still here. Where do you expect me to be after you dump a truckload of furniture?"

Dean looked around at the items Leo had spread out, each with papers attached to them chronicling what they needed and their potential worth. "You've got to save something for tomorrow."

Leo fiddled with the leg some more. "Why put off to tomorrow what you can get done today?"

Dean laughed. "That one only works if you took a day off every now and then. Did you even eat lunch?"

Leo flipped the chair upright and rubbed his forehead. Then did so again with his other arm to remove the dust. "Is it noon?"

"Oh man," Dean snorted.

"One?"

"Try three forty-five."

Leo faced his brother, sure he had misheard. Dean repeated the same scary chronological number sequence.

Leo scrubbed a hand down his face. It was nearly four. He'd planned to leave by four to get ready for his date. He even arrived at the shop early to make up for it, too. None of that mattered when he'd been in the zone. Didn't matter how many times he'd been teased for it, he never quite managed to not get lost in a work-related time warp.

If Dean hadn't interrupted him, he would have kept going until he finished the job.

And then he would have been late for his date with Andie.

"Aren't you hungry? If I miss a meal my stomach yells at me. You just go into a work-mode coma."

Coma. Time warp. He'd heard it all. "Yeah, yeah, yeah." His stomach took that moment to grumble, not in the past three hours. At least, he didn't think his stomach had grumbled.

Dean walked around the dining room set. "I knew this one would be a good one for us. Hoped it would be a really outstanding one." Dean gave Leo puppy dog eyes.

Leo shook his head. "It's good, but not that good. I need to fix at least one of the chairs."

"And the armoire?"

They both turned to the item in question.

"A bit more worn than the rest. It'll make someone happy."

"But no dollar signs in our eyes. Got it." The words may have been casual, but they held the heavy weight of their reality.

"We'll keep this place."

Dean flashed a smile, a fake one, that Leo could see through because he knew his brother well. "Of course. We break it, we bought it, right?"

Leo groaned and began putting items away to close up for the day. "If that were true, we'd be the owners by now."

Dean helped, and they worked together side by side like they'd done for years.

"Got any other estate sales booked?" Leo asked.

"Just one, I'm not expecting much. Might be a few good odds and ends but that's it."

They needed more than that. Time was running out, and their options dwindled by the day. Leo wouldn't give up. He'd find a way, even if it took him until the very last second.

The large white envelope that arrived for his father suggested the last second could be as early as tomorrow. In truth, he didn't know what information was in the letter, only that it was from the business lawyer, and he doubted it was paperwork to pass Dentz Antiques onto the next blood generation.

His stomach grumbled again.

"Feed that thing already. I'll finish up here."

Leo paused. He took in all the items out of place and had flashbacks to a younger Dean assisting in putting away Legos. Leo had organized the blocks, he just needed a few pieces put back. Dean had created a tornado that never got back together again. "I'll be fine." He had an order and a way of organization for new items coming into the shop. There were systems to uphold. If Dean put something away wrong, he'd be lost trying to get back on track.

Dean opened his mouth, ready to protest, as usual.

"I've got this."

Dean snapped his mouth closed and turned, but not before Leo caught the hurt on his face. His voice bounced into the shop, echoing and losing clarity.

"What was that?" Leo spoke loud, a force of habit when he couldn't hear.

Dean angled his head back, not stopping. "I said, suit yourself," He yelled.

Leo watched him walk away, wondering what he missed.

* * *

Andie stood in her closet, in her bathrobe, staring at her clothes. Her hands still sported a light red and green tint from the art project of the day, and no amount of exfoliating brought her back to normal.

"I guess I'm going be festive tonight," she grumbled to herself. "What goes with red and green?"

Her phone rang from the pocket of her robe and she pulled it out to find an incoming call from Sarah. She clicked answer. "Exactly the person I needed; help dress me for this date."

"Well hello to you, too," Sarah said, voice lifting at the end in amusement.

Andie switched ears. "Hi. Thanks for calling. Can you help me?"

Sarah's chirpy laughter echoed through the line. "Not much better, but considering I called to check in on your upcoming date, I'll give it a pass. What are you currently wearing?"

Andie tightened the sash, swallowing a laugh. How kind of Sarah to think she'd gotten farther than this. "A bathrobe."

"Oh, so you don't need my help."

Andie sighed and rummaged through the colorful array of her tops. "I'm getting dressed for dinner, with no immediate plans for after."

"I'm pouting at you."

Andie chuckled and pulled out a black top. "What goes with the lingering dye of red and green?"

"Ouch. Wrong holiday colors."

"No kidding."

"What are your options?"

Andie studied the silky material in her hand. "Black?"

"I know it's slimming and all, but don't you want something cheery?"

She hung the shirt back on the rack. "And we're back to the red and green."

Andie ruffled through her clothes to the sounds of Sarah's laughter.

"If this guy really likes you, he's going to like you in whatever you wear. Be you. Be comfortable."

Andie considered that, and it gave her zip ideas on direction. "You know that doesn't help the indecisive!"

"Has it really been that long since you went on a date that this is such an issue?"

Andie slumped to the floor in front of her clothes. "Perhaps." She'd been focused on her father as his health declined, and between his care and her students, there hadn't been much time for anything else. That didn't change when he passed and with the school closing and her job search there were days Andie simply collapsed into her bed at the end with no desire for socialization.

Sarah sighed. "Switch to video."

Andie pulled her phone away from her ear and did as she was told.

"Good, now slowly scroll your closet."

"Must you use your teacher voice for this?"

"If you don't slow down I'm going to have to!"

Andie's arm started to hurt as she held her phone, slowly shifting through her closet until an "ooohhhh" came through the line.

She faced the camera. "What?"

"My two o'clock, teal and sparkly. Red and green won't clash but it's a more blueish tone so doesn't scream 'jingle my bell.'"

"'Jingle my bell?' Really?"

"Well, I'm all for some jingling, but this is your life not mine. Yesssss! That could work."

Andie held the dress out and had to admit, it was nice. A clearance find from last year, never worn, as the tag clearly informed her. The silky feeling material had a fun shimmer to it, the sleeves poofing just enough to add more flair.

"Thoughts?"

Andie bit her lip. She'd bought it because it was cute and looked good on her. But clearly with the tags still on, she hadn't found a chance to wear it.

Maybe that had changed. And if it hadn't, maybe she needed to make it change.

"I think a date is a perfect excuse to cut off the tags."

Sarah squealed. "Yes! Try it on and show me!"

Andie put the phone down and changed into the dress. It slipped on, silky against her skin, hugging her curves. She felt good in it, and it looked just as good as she remembered.

She collected her phone.

"Ooh, yes! Hot! Leo's going to swallow his tongue!"

Andie slid a hand down her side. "It's good, isn't it?" She displayed her more colorful hand. "Huh, it kinda blends."

"Multicolor works for art-day mishaps. Why has it taken us so long to learn?"

"Because we both need to get out more." Andie caught a glimpse of the time and swallowed. "He'll be here in ten."

"Then what are you doing talking to me! Go get finished! And have fun!"

The call disconnected and Andie hurried into the bathroom to fix her curls. At least its normal state was messy; she'd given up on smooth years ago. A fresh coat of makeup and she managed to exit her bedroom the same time as the knock at her door.

"Showtime."

Her heels clicked against her hardwood floor as she walked across the room, opening the door to Leo. He stood there, haloed by the poor hall lighting, hair slicked back, blue shirt, collar open at the neck, and a black jacket. It looked as though he hadn't shaved since the morning, the five-o'clock shadow darkening his jaw.

Andie nearly swooned.

His dark eyes raked her in from head to toe, before settling on her face. "You look beautiful."

Her cheeks lifted, part in thanks and part in embarrassment. Compliments always gave her a little kick, albeit an awkward one. "Thanks. You look nice yourself."

He cleared his throat. "Shall we? I know we're going to the same place but if you prefer to take separate cars, I understand."

She swooned in a completely different manner. "My friend knows where I am and who I'm with, but the fact you acknowledge it means a lot." She grabbed her jacket and purse.

"I have an older sister. She made sure to tell both me and my brother her reality."

"Smart woman."

They exited to the hall and she locked her door.

"And she has a daughter, so if we even dared to try and forget and get comfortable with our privilege, my niece would remind us."

"Your niece and not your sister?"

They hadn't moved beyond her door, standing there in the dimmed lighting of the hall.

"Yes, my niece. A firecracker from day one."

"You've mentioned this niece before. I suspect she's a handful."

"Not one you'd want in your class?"

"Depends on if she's a helpful firecracker or pot-stirring one."

Leo faced down the hall to the elevators and began walking. Andie fell into step beside him. "A bit of both. Depends on her mood."

Andie chuckled. "Then I'm sure she would have been a blast, and part of the reason why I am extra colorful for this date." She held out her hands, and even in the dim lighting her chosen career showed loud and clear.

"Oh, wow." Leo reached out, gently cupping his hands under hers. The contact barely there and still able to send a spark right up her arm. "If that was your day, Millie would have arrived home looking like a Christmas tree stand-in."

Andie laughed and lowered her hands. The loss of contact didn't diminish the lingering spark—the kind that made her want more. She hoped the quick rub of his hand on the back of his neck meant Leo felt it, too. "I did have a handful of students who will need a good bubble bath tonight."

"Not staying festive?"

Andie held up her hands again as Leo pressed the button to call the elevator. "Considering this is after exfoliating, I suspect we all will be a little extra festive for a few days. If only I got some blue in there." Andie tried to pout, but she ended up laughing at herself instead.

The elevator arrived and they stepped in. "Well, I think you look lovely, and that includes the festive coloring."

"You really are being careful not to put down my job," Andie smirked.

"I learn from my mistakes when I can."

His words held a weight she suspected didn't tie into their conversation. The elevator doors closed and the metal box lurched into action. Curiosity welled up inside, but she suppressed it. Leo would be a person to enjoy in the moment. Whatever troubles he had going on in his life would still be there after she left.

* * *

Leo didn't choose the fanciest restaurant in the area. Truth be told, he wouldn't even begin to know where they were and if the food was any good. He worked too much, sacrificing his personal life to try and repair his professional one. If he didn't sway his father soon, he would have failed in every direction.

He pushed those thoughts aside. He could worry about it after Chanukah. Certainly not when he had Andie sitting across the booth from him. The midweek crowd meant the tables on either side of them were empty, creating an intimate experience. It also created a quieter one, which gave him a better chance at hearing. He'd been here a few times before, found the food to be good, the staff friendly, and the atmosphere comforting. Maybe not on a wine-and-dine level, but he never claimed to be a wine-and-dine guy.

"You've mentioned your niece a few times, who else will be at your family Chanukah celebration?"

Leo reached forward to grab a roll from the basket. "You're curious about that?"

Andie waved a hand in the air. "Humor me, what does Leo's family tree look like?" In contrast to her hand, her aura felt heavy, like this simple conversation held more weight than he could imagine. Her leather cuff caught his vision and something clicked. His

64

family was alive and well and often giving him grief. Andie's was gone.

He leaned back, taking a bite of the still-warm sourdough roll. He took on a light tone, wanting to lift the mood. "So you want to know about my family now?"

Andie smiled, but he noted not as wide as usual. "Families fascinate me. Especially as I no longer have much of one of my own."

He studied her face, the way the lighting smoothed over her cheeks, the leather cuff she wore even with her dress. "And this helps you?"

"For some reason, yes. Even if I'm missing the small one I used to have, I can still be interested in others." She wiped a line of condensation off her water glass. "Besides, I hope to have a big family one day, or at least, a bigger one."

Leo didn't understand it. The beauty across from him had a mesmerizing aura. Who wouldn't want Andie to brighten up their family? "I hope you do as well."

She smiled at him, this one full. It lit him up, a warmth tumbling out from deep within. An urge for more than this night and this week welled, but he quashed the notion as fast as it began.

"I'm one of three kids. The middle child."

"Is it as bad as they say to be the middle child?"

He glanced down at the crumbs on his plate. He wasn't your typical middle child, not since his hearing changed. But that wasn't what she asked for. "Well, I'm the oldest boy, so take middle with a grain of salt. My sister is the oldest, she's the mother of my niece. My younger brother is single and works with me. Mom and Dad are still alive. Sometimes my uncles will join us, but the extended family doesn't do much outside of the big events."

"That reads like a generic family tree. What does it feel like?"

He'd never been asked, but Andie leaned forward, elbows on table, as if Leo prepared to share the secret of the universe. "We're . . . complicated." He took a sip of his drink. Andie didn't move, not allowing him off the hook but also not pushing him. "Mostly we're a family that gets along, enjoys each other's company. My brother and I work for my dad."

"That's nice."

He couldn't stop the harsh, quick laugh. "No, it's not. I was an asshole of a teenager, roped Dean into my antics, and that's why Dad won't sell the business to us."

"Ouch."

"He has other reasons besides that, but I'm trying to win him over."

"Well, I hope you succeed."

A silence encompassed them, accentuating the lively chatter at other tables. "What was it like, before your father passed?"

Andie sighed and fiddled one red-and-green hand on her cuff. "It was nice. Quiet. Just the two of us, since the rest of my family is not worth the drama. We spent a lot of time together in general, but he always made the holidays special. Maybe it was just the way he was or to make up for missing my mother and not having a large supportive family. But it shaped me."

Lights practically danced in her eyes as she talked about her upbringing. "It suits you."

She grinned. "Thanks."

Cheering erupted from a large group in the corner. A woman held up something she pulled out of a bag. Andie turned, watching the commotion with him. When she faced him again her eyebrows were raised, a question on her face, and he hadn't a glimmer of an idea why.

"Did you hear me?"

An uncomfortable vibe settled over him. In his experience, people looked at him different after knowing he had a disability. Especially his father.

"No, I did not. I'm hard of hearing." He pointed to one of his hearing aids. He didn't have long enough hair to cover them, but the neutral tones of the aids and the thin tubing, along with the general low observance level of the population, meant he'd only had one person who had spotted them on their own, and that person happened to wear hearing aids as well.

"Oh, I'm sorry. I asked what was going on over there." Her voice came louder than it had before.

"Don't be sorry. I hadn't told you."

She studied his face, what she looked for he couldn't begin to guess. "Fair enough. Have you always worn hearing aids?"

"No."

She waited but he didn't want to get into it, not here, not now. Didn't want to give her a reason to look at him differently.

He nodded to the noisy table. "Whatever is going on over there seems to involve the bags they have on the table."

Andie nodded and checked on the table. She made sure to face him before speaking. Or she faced him after he didn't respond—either option held possibility. "Family gathering or business Yankee swap?"

He studied the group. Most appeared around the same age, and not all the same race. Another person opened a bag, pulled out what appeared to be a stuffed chicken toy. "If it's family then it's a chosen-family situation."

This person pointed across the table, where a man held up his hands in surrender and the crowd laughed some more.

"Oh, perhaps a secret Santa?" Andie scooted her chair so she could see the crowd and him. "And I think 'chosen family' works for them."

"Where's your chosen family, Andie?"

She fixed her chair, her brown eyes landing on his. "I have a few good friends, but I mostly haven't found them yet." She shrugged. "Maybe they are in Ohio, waiting for me."

His smile slipped but he forced it back in place, though he didn't like her answer. He wanted her family to be here, with him.

Not chosen but family family. It filled him up, a missing part now found. The feelings crawled out of all the locked boxes he held deep inside, from the two years he wanted to be right here, with Andie, and hadn't. Bigger than their short time together allowed for. He'd thought his feelings were a crush, a desire for her when life didn't allow for it. He'd underestimated his own emotions. Their meal arrived with such perfect timing he could have kissed their waiter. A distraction was exactly what he needed. Andie wouldn't be his family. She'd be merely a beautiful *CliffsNotes*, a holiday tale.

"I know there is a family out there waiting for you, because any family would be lucky to have you as part of them."

Andie paused with a fork in her hands. "That's really sweet. Thank you."

He focused on his food. Kicking himself for waiting too long to make his move. If he hadn't . . . well, no use in wondering, he couldn't change the past any more than he could prevent damaging the grandfather clock in the first place.

CHAPTER SEVEN

At the end of the night, Andie stood in front of her door with her keys in hand. The night had been wonderful, a bit magical even, and she could admit to herself she didn't want it to end.

Leo stood in front of her, bypassing his own unit to wish her good night. Or maybe his thoughts aligned with hers, that a wonderful night like this shouldn't be wasted?

"Thank you for dinner. I had a good time," Andie said.

"Thanks for allowing me to treat you." He seemed to shift closer, though neither of them moved. Something about the long hall, the dim lighting, and the holiday season. It made the dull area come to life, filled it with a cheer it normally didn't have—as though they were inside a snow globe, fake snow floating down around them.

A smile stretched her lips. "You won that dreidel game fair and square."

Leo laughed, the soft sound tickling her ears, a sweet melody to their night. "You still could have said no."

She shook her head, not breaking eye contact. "A deal is a deal." She took a chance, inched closer to him. "Besides, I wanted to come."

A connection solidified between them. They breathed as one, the location fading away, creating a special orb around them. The thing of movies and books, not a common experience for Andie. As though something much bigger than a holiday fling started here, in this building. She wanted to reach up, grab the lapels of his open jacket, and yank him in. Or, no, better yet, let the night continue to shift them closer, a slow uniting heightened by the moment.

Leo swallowed and Andie tracked the movement in his Adam's apple. "I have to repeat myself and tell you how beautiful you are."

The man knew how to talk or, at least, did so tonight. "You're not so bad yourself."

Leo chuckled.

"I might have described you as a darker-haired Ryan Reynolds."

Leo's eyebrows lowered. "Ryan Reynolds? *Deadpool?*"

Andie shrugged. "You going to tell me he's not good-looking?"

Leo's head gave a slight shake. "I can honestly tell you I've never heard that one before. And no, that's not a joke on my ears."

Andie laughed. Curiosity swirled. She wanted to know more about his hearing loss, what had happened to turn him into the man who stood before her. But she knew now wasn't the time. "Then take it as a compliment."

Two spots of color appeared on his cheeks. "Thank you, Andie. Though I'll never watch *Deadpool* the same way again."

"He wears a mask and scar makeup, you'll survive."

Leo reached up, brushing a lock of her hair behind her ear. "I guess I will." His head angled downward, and he held that position, a silent invitation extended, waiting on her response. Oh, how this man drew her to him. And how she wanted a taste. She stretched up, eager for the moment when they would touch. Would it continue the vibe, or be a call back to the first night of Chanukah?

A loud creak echoed from down the hall, followed by a door slam.

They jumped apart, like teenagers caught doing much more than an almost kiss. Their eyes held for another second, a shared look of remorse for the moment now lost. Then they turned to their interrupter.

"Hey, Leo, Andie, nice night, huh?" Thomas Landry waved, pocketing his keys in his pocket. He was around seventy, with white, thinning hair and a slight stoop. On a normal day Andie wouldn't mind chatting with him. Tonight wasn't normal.

"Hi, Tom," Leo said, sending a wave down the hall. Andie prayed Tom would continue on to whatever adventure had him leaving his unit.

Her prayer was not answered. Tom headed in their direction, away from the elevator and stairs. "What are you two up to tonight?"

Andie and Leo shared a look. There wasn't much to share, especially not to a random nosey neighbor.

"Oh, just got to talking in the elevator," Andie said, catching Leo's eyes to see if he agreed with her swerve tactic.

"The timing worked out, usually I have to ride the elevator alone." Leo sent her a wink and she relaxed.

"I try to use the stairs, but my knees don't like them like they used to." Tom rubbed his lower back, and Andie didn't know if that somehow related to his knees or not.

"I just get lazy and will take company any day of the week," Leo said.

"I keep telling you to get out more." Tom shook his head. "You work too much. You'll never have a family."

Andie swallowed her laughter.

"Noted. Thank you, Tom."

"Well, you kids have a good night then." He waved and walked off, taking his blunt conversation with him.

"That family topic is such a big concern for people our age," Andie whispered, laughter in her voice. "Even after they call us 'kids.'" Sure, she wanted a family, craved it, but her situation was a bit different than most people her age.

"Was he a Jewish mother in a past life?"

Tom waited at the closed elevator doors, foot tapping.

"Perhaps. Or maybe he had a good bubbe to show him what really matters in life."

"More children and less business?"

Leo's eyes watered with humor and Andie struggled to keep her laughter down.

"I think both are needed, after the marriage."

"Arranged marriages made this so much simpler."

She covered her mouth, laughter threatening to overflow. Tom still waited for the elevator and glanced back at them.

Leo cleared his throat and Andie turned to him. "I guess we'll need a rain check here," Leo spoke softly, and then, in a louder voice "Good night, Andie. Thank you for a wonderful elevator ride."

Andie opened her mouth to say something, but Leo walked off, back to his apartment. She wanted to reach out and continue their conversation long enough for Tom to disappear. To keep the sizzling chemistry or the joyful laughter flowing, but the mood had been broken, and Leo slipped inside just as the elevator dinged. Andie had a moment, thinking she could go after Leo after Tom left, but Tom waved and Andie slinked into her apartment.

Alone.

She switched on the lights, the loneliness making the space seem empty and sparse. Not the nightcap she wanted. There hadn't been any plans for after, no concrete thoughts or wants in her head. But standing there, alone, torn between prepped for a kiss and more laughter, had her all sorts of off kilter.

"Damn you, Leo, why do you have to be so darn adorable?"

Andie deposited her purse and jacket on their hooks, then unzipped her boots and stepped out of them. Her feet stretched without the confinement, and even that good feeling did not make up for the loss.

"Let it go, Andie." With a shake of her head, she made her way to her kitchen, grabbing items and prepping her lunch for the following day. Normal evening rituals, even if this particular evening did not feel normal.

On her counter, her bag of potatoes called to her. She'd hoped to bake latkes this Chanukah but hadn't known if she'd have the energy and desire. Next to them were two packages of latke mix, the instant potatoes of the latke options. She planned to make them with her students tomorrow, and she would, but nothing beat the real potato version. Thanks to Leo, she wanted to bake the real ones. A bit of the night's magic came back as an idea formed, so strong and sure she had her phone in her hands before she could finish thinking it through.

> Andie: I'm thinking of making latkes tomorrow night, want to join me?

Andie bit her lip, staring at the message she had typed. One click and it would be waiting for Leo. One click and she'd find out if the interruption had changed things on his end.

Andie clicked send.

> Leo: What kind of latkes are you thinking of?

She took a picture of the box waiting for her students.

> Andie: Not this one. These will be made with my students tomorrow.
> Leo: LOL. Good start. I'm going to need more.
> Andie: Oh, are you a latke snob now?
> Leo: Maybe a little bit.

She leaned against her counter, grinning at her phone wider than she'd grinned at her dinner date minutes earlier.

Andie: Your recipe can't top mine.

Leo: Oh really?

Andie: Really.

It was one of the few things she got from her mother. She might never have witnessed her mother make it, but thanks to her dad she at least got to enjoy it.

Leo: Then how do we settle this?

Andie: You get your ingredients. I'll get mine. Bring them over. We'll have a cook-off.

Leo: A cook-off? With one stove?

Andie: You could cook at home, but then how will I know if it's not store-bought?

Leo: I'm laughing, just so you know. I'd rather spend more time with you anyways.

Warmth filled Andie as though the latkes already sizzled in front of her. She nearly suggested they get back to where they were before Tom's untimely hall meeting.

No. Let the anticipation build. She only had one week with this man, one last Chanukah before her move.

Andie: Then I'll see you tomorrow night. Don't light your candles, we'll light mine.

Leo: Wouldn't miss it for the world.

* * *

When Leo pulled into the parking lot behind Dentz Antiques the next morning, he nearly hit the curb at the sight before him: Dean Dentz, never early for anything in his life, including his own birth, sat on the back of the company pickup, feet swinging like he'd done since childhood.

Leo very carefully parked a few empty spaces over. By the time he exited his car, Dean had already crossed half the distance, hands in his back pockets, with a casual stroll that meant the man felt far from casual.

Leo's pulse spiked. He stopped walking. Dean raised his hands in a peace gesture.

"Yeah, I'm not buying that," Leo said.

Dean stopped a few feet in front of him, hands back in his pockets. "I found something."

"I gathered. But I think you mean 'I bought something.'"

Dean cringed, no doubt because the last time he bought something it had been at a huge loss. Both in the financial sense and in their relationship with their father, as all steps toward peace had been eliminated. "Curbside freebie."

Leo groaned. Better than another financial blow, but the last "curbside freebie" came with roaches, and that unpleasant discovery didn't occur until after it had been brought into the shop.

"I inspected it, but thanks for your vote of confidence. I don't have your skills; I'm not made to take over this business without you. Partner? Sure. Sole owner? I'd tank the place."

"Now who's downvoting his own confidence?"

"Bite me. You want my help or not? Because it took both of us to create this mess in the first place."

Leo sighed. He took the burden of the blame because he'd been the oldest, and in charge, and he damn well knew better than to wrestle his twelve-year-old brother for a football while in the shop. But he'd been sixteen and missing the biggest party of the season. The chip on his shoulder had been too large for rational thought to exist.

It was still his fault and his problem, but Dean had stepped up to take his share of the blame even then. He didn't deserve to be stuck in that shadow any more than Leo did.

"All right. Show me what you got."

Dean's eyes lit up with excitement, sparking memories of him as a little kid, even if the stubble proved he hadn't been a kid for a while. No other displays of excitement filtered out, Dean resumed his casual walk over to the truck and hopped up.

Leo joined.

On the truck, a hall bench was still strapped in. Leo circled it, trying to remain neutral, studying the item from different angles.

"What do you think?" Dean asked, bouncing on his feet.

"It's worn, there are tears in the wood, scratches, a few filaments missing . . ."

"I can see that. I think it has potential, but I'm not the one fixing it."

Leo rubbed his jaw, contemplating the condition and the work needed to restore it. Some of the wood might need to be reinforced, but nothing outside of his abilities. "It has potential."

Dean stood taller.

"I'll have to examine it more, but I get why you picked it up." He didn't know if he would have stopped to get it like Dean had, but he didn't mind having it to work with now.

Dean grinned.

"Come on, let's get this into the shop."

They undid the hold-downs and maneuvered it to the edge and onto the ground. Not too difficult with the two of them, but it had surely given Dean a sweat to get it in.

"Millie wants to know why you aren't answering her texts. Not a good uncle move, dear brother."

"I meant to text her back after my date last night. I guess I forgot." He'd been too preoccupied with the almost kiss, and the promise of another night with Andie. The hallway distraction was enough to mess with more than one brain cell. He had nearly waited for the elevator to leave and go back to Andie's unit but had talked himself out of it.

Dean dropped his end and Leo plowed into it, the wood digging into his stomach. "Date?"

"Yes. A date. Pick up your end and I'll explain."

Dean did as he was told and got the bench away from trying to dig a hole in Leo's jacket.

"I had a date with Andie. Millie thinks the menorah is magic. I'm going to tell her I wished for a date, as she suggested, and am going out with Andie tonight."

"But your date was last night."

Dean propped open the door and they got the new item inside. Leo picked up his end but Dean crossed his arms.

"I'm seeing Andie again tonight. We're baking latkes."

"Nice Jewish girl. Millie won't be the only one excited."

"We can make latkes if she isn't Jewish."

Dean raised his eyebrows.

"But, yes, she is."

Dean laughed. "Oh man, don't tell mom, you know she's got wooden menorahs just waiting to add a family member name to them." Their mother had made and engraved one for each of them and threatened she could create another at a moment's notice. Leo wasn't the only family member with a thing for woodwork.

He groaned. "You going to be a pest and make me leave this here or are you going to be a nice guy who doesn't leave large items to block traffic?"

"Can't I be both?"

They worked together, getting the bench to the back of the workroom, over to the side where other repair items were kept. Some were for customers, while others were items Leo had purchased to be resold. All had potential beyond keeping him busy.

"She's moving soon. So it's just a short-term thing. No engraved menorahs necessary."

"You sure about that?"

"She's moving to Ohio, not south of Boston. I think that's too far for both of us."

Dean dusted off his hands. "Well, that sucks. Don't tell Millie."

Leo wasn't born yesterday. He ignored his brother and pulled out his phone.

> Leo: Sorry, bad uncle. I made a wish. Guess who has a date planned for tonight?

He went to put his phone away and it dinged.

Millie: I KNEW IT! IT IS MAGIC!

"Why is Millie responding? It's schooltime."
Dean chuckled. "You underestimate our niece."

> Leo: Aren't you supposed to be in school?

Millie: I am.

> Leo: Then put your phone away!

Millie: I'm doing research, give me a break.

> Leo: I'm not research.

Millie: No, but the minerals page
you keep pulling me away from is.

She sent an emoji sticking its tongue out.
"See. Smart kid," Dean said from over Leo's shoulder.
Leo laughed and put his phone away. He didn't know if Millie truly was allowed to have her phone with her, but he figured he'd let his sister worry about that one.

CHAPTER EIGHT

Andie cleaned up a table after her morning students had left for the day. The latke mix had been a success, as the mess left behind surely indicated. She even inducted the students into the age-old "applesauce versus sour cream" debate. The morning class had applesauce winning by a single point, although Andie did need to add two new categories: plain and ketchup. She still couldn't figure out where the student had found a packet of ketchup to begin with.

Sarah knocked once at the door and entered. "Did you hear?"

Andie tossed some towels in the trash. "Hear what?"

"About the appeal."

Andie paused, chemical spray in hand, ready to give the table another rinse. Andie's gaze slid up to Sarah. "No."

Sarah pulled out a chair and slumped down to the child-sized height. "Another bust. And our last chance." She glanced around, a somber note on her face. "Say goodbye."

Andie dropped her items and joined Sarah. "At this point there wasn't much hope. That's why we're all job searching."

"I know. I know that. I just . . . had hope, you know? A holiday season miracle to keep my bestie nearby." She reached out and squeezed Andie's hand.

Andie squeezed back. A holiday miracle would be lovely right about now, but if those existed, she'd still have her father this Chanukah. "Want me to see if my new job is hiring?"

Sarah sat up straight, eyes wide. "You accepted it."

"Not yet."

"But you will."

With no other strong prospects, she'd be a fool to pass on such a good match for her goals. "More than likely."

Sarah slumped back down. "I can barely handle the winters here. If I move anywhere, it's going to be for warmer pastures."

"Don't discount global warming, you might get your wish wherever you land."

"Wow, you went dark there."

Andie stretched out her legs. "Sorry."

Sarah took two deep breaths, her mini-meditations method. "So tell me something good, like more about that date from last night that did not end in a kiss."

Andie scraped her chair back and returned to wiping down her table. "I've told you everything. Nice meal, good conversation, a moment in the hall, then the neighbor interruption."

"Way to make a date sound clinical." Sarah stood and stretched. "You going to get a kiss tonight? It is the fourth night, just about halfway through."

Andie thought of Leo, of him being in her apartment. No distractions. Tingles broke out on her arms and slid down lower. The two of them cooking side by side in her narrow kitchen, making it easy to brush up against each other. Was he thinking about her as she thought about him? "Why do you think I invited him over to bake in my tiny kitchen?"

Sarah laughed. "There. That is so much better than school closings or global warming."

Andie finished cleaning the table and put her supplies down. "You'll find something. Maybe even something better than this place."

"I know. I know. There will be more options in the spring, too. I just liked it here."

Andie glanced around at the many student drawings on her wall. "Me, too. But nothing in life stays the same."

"Wow, you are gloomy today."

Was she? The tingles faded to the heaviness of the brokenhearted. Leo gave her the holiday distraction she needed. It was hard to feel alone with him around. And yet, the memories pushed forward, her father's smiling face over a game of dreidels. Oh, how she missed him. "First holiday without Dad. I was experiencing a lot of change before the school closing news hit."

Sarah crossed the room and wrapped Andie up into a hug. "And because of that you get to spend Chanukah with your hot neighbor."

"Are you saying hot neighbor makes up for being an orphan?" Andie spoke with alarm and pulled out of Sarah's grasp.

"No. I mean you might not have taken Leo up on his offer if you already had plans with your father."

Andie mulled that one over and couldn't deny it held weight. For starters, she wouldn't have been scrambling to find candles before sunset, she'd have been with her father. "Take some of that weirdly backward logic and apply it to your own job hunt."

Sarah scrunched her nose, thinking. "I'll pay off my student loans faster if I move back in with my parents?"

Andie shook her head. "What am I going to do with you?"

Sarah blew Andie a kiss as she headed for the classroom door. "Stay in touch, because if you don't, I will."

Alone in her room, Andie straightened a few chairs. Her heart felt heavy with everything and everyone she would soon leave behind. She took faith in Sarah being a forever friend. A year into the future would be so different from now—new people, new school, new relationships. There would be a lot of unknowns. Andie hadn't always been a fan of the unknown. It led to holiday seasons like this, alone without her family. Sure, life could be better in a new location, but nothing in life came with guarantees. On the other hand, life really could be better. Maybe she'd find something, or someone, now missing in her life. Either way, Future Andie would have a story to tell.

"I'll make it work. Just like Dad always did." She'd carry on his legacy, especially during this transitional point in her life. Her father had the drive, and the heart, to make beanstalks grow from beans. He'd been a human service worker before he got sick. He'd made an impact on many lives, more than hers alone. She strived to do the same in her own way. Helping preschoolers develop a love of school allowed her to carry on some of his ambition.

Andie scrubbed a hand down her face. She had more boxed latkes to fry. And later, real latkes.

* * *

Leo shifted the paper bag in his arms in order to knock on Andie's door. He'd spent several hours with Dean working on his curbside find, only to discover the item had more damage than originally anticipated. Not to the point of belonging on the curb, Leo could fix it up to something tangible, but it wasn't the grand find they had both hoped for.

He still had some time. He hoped. Not a lot, but it would be enough. He'd make it so.

The door swung open and Andie stood before him. She wore a casual sweatshirt with the sleeves rolled up, revealing her cuff and three beaded bracelets tied together with thick orange string. Her cheeks were flushed and she blew some hair off of her face. "Hi, sorry, I'm not much of a baker normally, so I'm on the hunt for my grater. Come in."

She turned and headed into her unit and he followed, depositing his bag on her kitchen table. He found Andie in the corner of her living room, on her hands and knees, rummaging in a box. Her jeans-covered rear up in the air, calling him to the soft curves on display.

Leo swallowed and forced his gaze away, realizing the box had been stored under a desk. A very old desk. One that had seen better days, but no doubt was worth something.

Andie leaned back on her heels. "Aha! I found it!" She held up a red grater, smiling wide.

He was too caught up in the desk. A spinet, in what appeared to be solid mahogany. He'd guess from around the early twentieth century, based on other items he'd worked with. "That's a nice desk." His manners forgotten, he walked over, brushing a hand along the ornate detailing. If this had been Dean's curbside find, they'd be guaranteed their win.

"Oh, yeah. That belonged to my mom."

Leo faced her and saw the sentimental look on her face. "Then it's more valuable than whatever I could get it appraised for."

Andie smiled. "Not with all the nicks in the wood. Or the leg being propped up with a book and duct tape. Or the drawer that has been fused shut for so long I keep forgetting it's supposed to open."

Leo studied the item, and all of Andie's complaints. Sure, the wood had yellowed with age and had the markings of many mugs and cups. He'd bet his salary that it had been cleaned with chemicals that caused more damage than good, but he knew better than to get into that argument now. Still, the piece looked solid and he knew a few things about restoration. Perhaps a concern for a regular person, but he wasn't regular, not when antiques were involved. "I could fix it."

Andie laughed and headed to her kitchen. "That's sweet, but I'm okay."

He followed her. "I mean it. This is what I do. I can fix it for you."

She faced him, brown eyes large and wide. "I'm sure I can't afford you."

"I'm not asking you to pay me. Let me do this for you, as a parting gift." He wanted it to be a gift to bring them closer together, to show her how he cared, not to send her off into her next adventure.

But he could do this one thing, for this moment in time. He needed to leave her with some piece of him, as foolish as that felt.

She didn't have a family anymore and she was more than worthy of one. He wanted to fix that. Restoring her desk, bringing back this part of her mother, that he could do. He'd used that excuse to cover up this foreign feeling of wanting someone so deeply, like he felt for Andie. It was just the years of longing, that's all it could be.

"I don't part with valuable items lightly."

He placed a hand on his heart. "I won't let anything happen to it. Except for bringing it back to its former glory. Stronger, so it can withstand the trip and won't need a book to stand upright. Only if you promise me to stop using whatever you've been using to clean it."

Andie bit her lip, eyes on her desk. "It would be nice to have it look as good as it means to me." She turned to him. "Are you blaming my cleaner?"

"I'm . . ." Crap, there was no way around this. "Yes. In part. Not fully. I'll get you something that won't damage it."

"Are you sure?"

He smiled. "It would be an honor to work on an item like that."

She gave a quick nod. "Well, okay then." She held out a finger. "If anything happens to it—"

He took a step closer and wrapped his hand around her finger. "I will guard this with my life." He wanted to kiss her finger, even with the slight red dye lingering under her pink nail. Instead, he let her go.

"Thank you."

"I believe I have a cook-off to win."

Andie laughed, the heavy moment lightening. "Oh, I don't think so, Mister." She gestured to the outside windows where the sky had begun to darken. "But aren't you forgetting something?"

"Latke cook-off by candlelight?"

"The best kind of cook-off."

They lit the candles and said the prayers, and soon four teal candles and the shamash cast half the menorah in the glow of the flames.

Leo watched the lights flicker across Andie's face, bringing out the pink in her cheeks, and in that moment, nothing else mattered.

"It never gets old. I don't think I'll ever tire of watching the candles burn."

I don't think I'll ever tire of watching you in the glow of candlelight. "It does hold a special kind of magic." His phone chimed. "Speaking of magic, that is probably my niece, who thinks my new menorah is magic."

Andie looked away from the candles. "Really?"

"There's some Hebrew writing on it, we think the translation is 'miracles happen everywhere.' And she's a precocious ten-year-old."

Andie moved toward the kitchen and Leo followed. "What kind of magic?" Andie reached for a bag of potatoes.

"Light the candles and make a wish type of magic."

Leo's phone chimed again.

"Is she asking what you wished for?"

Leo debated his answer, but decided on honesty being the best policy, nieces excluded. "She's checking on my previous wish and wants to know how my date with my neighbor is going."

Andie paused with a potato in her hands and Leo realized he took honesty one step too far.

He scratched his neck, trying to get his foot out of his mouth. "I, uh, might have talked about you often."

"So what does your niece think?"

His phone chimed again, and he held up a finger to check on it.

Millie: Happy 4th Night!
Millie: Did you make another wish?
Millie: How's your date going?!?!

Leo held up his phone for Andie to see.

Andie's laughter filled the air. "Oh, she really is a handful."

"That she is." His phone chimed again.

Millie: Is she coming to the Chanukah party? She should come!

"More of your niece?" Andie asked.
Leo nodded and quickly fired back a response.

Leo: Happy Chanukah. No. Good. I don't think so.

"She wants you to join me in volunteering for the Hebrew School Chanukah party tomorrow night."
"I see. And what do you want?"
He put his phone on the table. "I want this holiday with you. And if you would enjoy Millie's Chanukah party, then I'd be honored for you to join me."
"I guess we better get cooking latkes so I can judge your skills."
"So you'll only go if I win?"
Andie turned on the water to rinse a potato. He stepped closer to hear her over the faucet sounds. "Or if I win. You'll have to take the gamble."
Leo laughed and began emptying his bag. "Just so you know, in case you do meet Millie, she thinks I made the wish last night and this is our first date."
Andie turned off the water and patted the potato dry. "She wastes no time, does she?"
"No, she does not."
Andie took in his supplies, a note of surprise on her face. "Sweet potato latkes?"
Leo nodded. "Are you up for a challenge, Andie?"
"On that, you are on."

* * *

"I can't believe we have dueling burners going on!"
Andie laughed as two very different batches of latkes sizzled, spurts of oil jumping out and attacking any arm within reaching distance.

"You did say this was a cook-off, didn't you?"

Leo grinned at her. His shirt had been rolled up to his elbows, even with the threat of oil stings. His sturdy arms were dusted with hair, and Andie hadn't realized how one could drool over a forearm before.

The kitchen had two areas prepped with paper towels and were nearly filled with warm oily potato pancakes. The smells filled the air, of oil and potatoes, onions, and the sweet cinnamon Leo used on his.

"I never expected this to be a savory-versus-sweet competition as well." Andie flipped her last latke, golden side up, sizzling side down.

Leo turned off his burner. "Now is probably not the time to mention where this recipe came from."

"Oh?" Andie shifted her attention from her latkes to Leo.

His cheeks sported a blush that had nothing to do with the heat in the kitchen. "High school girlfriend. I think she's a chef in a five-star restaurant now."

Andie moved a latke to the paper towel. "Oh, so now you tell me your recipe has won awards or something?"

He smiled, bringing his skillet over to settle his last few pancakes to cool. "I can safely say this will be the first thing I'll win with the recipe." His eyes found hers. "If I win."

Andie turned off her burner and got the last of her batch cooling. "And the high school girlfriend?"

"I'm not sure how far her latkes took her, but I never made it quite as good."

Andie laughed and tore off a piece of one of the first ones Leo cooked. She blew on the still warm latke, then popped it in her mouth. Sweet potatoes, cinnamon, and that classic latke feel exploded on her tongue. "Oh my." She closed her eyes, savoring the rest as she chewed.

"I don't need to win, watching you is my reward."

Her eyes popped open, finding him standing there, attention full on her, and suddenly she wanted to taste a different type of sweet. "It's good," she managed to whisper.

He stepped closer to her and reached past to grab a piece of one of her latkes. He didn't close his eyes as he chewed like she did, but a smile lit his face.

"This is delicious."

Somehow, she wondered if he had other things than the latkes in mind. She certainly did.

"I'm not sure how we choose a winner here."

He held out a hand. "A tie. Or yours is the best savory, mine is the best sweet."

She chuckled, placing her hand in his. "I guess those work."

He shook her hand once, then tugged, sending her stumbling into him. "I bet you taste delicious as well." Her pulse kicked and he loosened his grip. "Sorry, that was probably—"

She placed a finger on his mouth, cutting him off. They stared at each other and she cataloged his face, the hint of stubble, the way it gathered a little thicker under his bottom lip. Then she pushed up on her toes and meshed her mouth to his.

He kissed her back, slick and sweet, a shared breath. His arm snaked around her waist, holding her closer but not trapping her, his lips pressing firmer. He tasted like Chanukah, and like something much more potent, better than the best latkes she'd ever tasted.

Andie wrapped her arms around his neck, pressed in close, and opened just enough to take the kiss from sweet to smoking. His hand bunched in the fabric of her shirt, and her internal burner came to life.

Leo lightened the kiss, then put some air between them. He smoothed back a lock of her hair. "Forget the tie, your lips win."

Andie laughed and pulled away, grabbing two plates. "I'll take the win." She handed him a plate.

"So does that mean you'll join me tomorrow for the school Chanukah party?"

They grabbed a few of each latke and settled at her table. "Depends." She sat down and grabbed a fork.

Leo joined her. "On?"

"Whether or not there will be more kisses."

"Andie, for you, take all the kisses you want."

She leaned forward and did just that.

CHAPTER NINE

"So let me get this straight, you dragged me out of bed early to pick up an item that will not be sold, nor will you be paid for it?" Dean asked as they exited the truck.

"Like you haven't given away jewelry to dates?" The December air nipped around them as they headed to the building. Leo pulled out his keys to get through the outside door.

"And you're going to spend how much time and resources on this thing?"

Leo headed for the stairs. "It shouldn't take too much; I want to get it back to her by the end of Chanukah." He started up, taking them two at a time, only stopping when laughter echoed up from below.

He sucked in a breath, then faced the thorn in his side ten steps below.

"You really like her, huh?"

Leo glared.

Dean held up his hands. "I know, you've talked about her for years. But from what you said, this isn't a simple replacing the batteries or fixing a wobbly leg."

"It does have a wobbly leg."

Dean crossed his arms and waited.

"Your point?"

"This isn't something you do for a neighbor you have the hots for who will be moving away in a few months."

The words connected with the emotions swirling around inside Leo. "Think of it as a parting gift." Leo climbed the stairs again.

The soft sounds of mumbling hit his ears. He turned and Dean nearly plowed into him.

"What was that?"

Dean straightened. "I said, one hell of a parting gift. Maybe don't storm off if you want to hear what I'm saying."

"Maybe don't mumble things you know I can't hear."

They stared at each other for a moment before Dean sighed and moved ahead. Leo shook it off.

On his floor they bypassed his unit, going straight to Andie's. He'd had to get up earlier than usual to get the desk before she left for work. Today, he'd be surviving on caffeine and adrenaline alone.

Leo knocked, and shoved his hands in his pockets, waiting.

"So what do we have to look forward to? Next year we'll lose the business and you'll lose her—so much for a happy new year."

"We're not losing the business," Leo ground out.

"And Andie?"

He sighed. "She's got a good job offer. Fixing a desk doesn't make up for that."

The conversation stopped there when the door swung open and a bright-faced Andie stood in front of them. Her hair hung in damp waves around her face. "You made it."

She wore jeans and a red sweater, a beaded necklace around her neck he bet came from a student.

"Andie, this is my brother, Dean."

Dean waved and Andie stood back, letting them in.

"I see the resemblance."

Dean nudged Leo. "That means she realizes I'm the pretty one."

Leo shook his head and stopped in front of the desk. A new box sat nearby, holding all the items the desk used to store. "You got everything you need?" he asked Andie.

"Yup." She nodded and bit her lip nervously.

Leo stopped investigating the desk, even though Dean didn't. "What's wrong?"

Andie stepped over, placing a hand on the desk. "This hasn't been away from me for as long as I can remember."

"I'm going to make it better, nothing bad will happen to it."

A hesitant smile graced her lips. "I know. I trust you." She stepped back and the weight of her words carried through. He was just her neighbor, a momentary companion in her life. And yet she trusted him with something she wanted as a permanent fixture.

In some strange way, a small part of Leo would stay with Andie wherever she went. He'd make an impact on her life. Not the one he would have preferred, but knowing she trusted him warmed him deep inside.

"This is a real beauty," Dean said. "Who gave it to your mom?"

"Dad thinks it came from her grandparents, but unfortunately, we don't know the full story, just that she loved it dearly."

"Leo's the best at what he does. Don't you worry about a thing. It will look brand new when he's done with it."

Leo stood a little taller at his brother's praise, and Andie's smile widened. "I don't know if an antique needs to look brand new, but I'll settle for in better shape."

Dean patted Leo on the shoulder. "Your expectations are too low for his skills."

"Better than latkes?"

Leo laughed and shifted the desk out from the wall. "Decidedly so."

The brothers worked together and moved the desk to the door. It wasn't so heavy that one person couldn't maneuver it, but he wanted the extra person to be sure he didn't have any issues.

"Need a final goodbye? Picture for insurance purposes?" Dean joked.

"No, that's okay. I know where your brother lives."

They got the item into the hall, Andie lingering at her open door. "I promise you; you won't regret this."

The caution had vanished from her face, her eyes now sparkling in a hall that often didn't allow for such. "I don't think I will."

He nodded. "Good." And then, because she lingered, because he wanted to, he kissed her. Short and sweet, a hallway kiss. But a kiss nonetheless. "See you tonight, Andie."

She licked her lips. "Tonight."

Leo gave his brother credit, he waited until the door closed and they were by the elevator to talk. "Dang, that was hot."

"Shut up."

"Shame she's moving, you two seem good together."

The elevator dinged and they carried the desk inside. "Yeah. We are. But life doesn't care about that."

"Well maybe next time you won't take so long."

The doors closed. "Lesson learned."

*   *   *

Dean took off after the desk had been brought to the workroom, but Leo stayed back to investigate. He had the desk propped up on a workbench, checking it out on all sides. The wobbly leg wiggled too much for his liking, but he knew the type of construction and would be able to figure out the fix. It needed a good cleaning, if he was lucky, one good cleaning would be all it needed, but he wouldn't know for sure until he got to work. The drawer would need to be taken apart, but he'd get it working again.

Underneath all the years of harmful chemical cleaners—he really needed to educate Andie—it was still a beauty. A good, strong heirloom piece, one that easily fit in with multiple styles and decades.

He'd return this to Andie, and if she ever had kids, maybe one day they'd cherish it like she did.

The little things in life were the ones that truly mattered. A sentimental piece of furniture, a date with a neighbor. One of the things that made him proud to do his job, because he sold and repaired items that had meaning and history to them.

Leo got to work, starting with the drawer so he knew exactly what he was dealing with. He tested it, pushing and pulling, noting the thing was solid. Too solid. On his hands and knees, he checked the underside, flashlight in hand, blinking at what he found. A screw. He didn't know if this was a botched attempt at fixing it, or if it had ever had a purpose. Over time the screw had loosened and wedged the drawer shut.

"Who did this to you?"

He got up and grabbed some tools, wondering who in Andie's family thought this was a good idea. And why. But like most of the items he got in his shop, no one was alive to tell him the answer.

He settled back down, flashlight in his mouth, so he could cut the head off the stripped screw. Finally, the drawer came free and Leo stumbled over what he held in his hands.

Not an empty drawer.

In fact, the opposite of empty. The drawer was stuffed with items, mostly papers. A page on top had the word "Andie" written in large, loopy cursive. Cautious of snooping, but needing to know what he'd found, Leo lightly shuffled through, noting what looked like a great deal of notes and old photos along with other random mementos inside.

He didn't know what it all meant, for all he knew these would be not so welcome memories. Curiosity stirred, but it wasn't his desk or his belongings. He settled the findings back in the way he'd found them, careful to keep whatever organization they had, as much as he possibly could.

He cleaned the wood with alcohol and steel wool, scrubbing extra at anything that didn't bring character to the mahogany. He thought of Andie as he worked, paying close attention to all the rings and any scuffs, demanding a level of perfection higher than his usual perfectionist self adhered to. This was Andie—she deserved his best. When finished, he set it to dry.

Footsteps echoed in the shop, and before he had a chance to properly prepare himself, his father appeared. Glen Dentz stood tall and thin, with white hair and more forehead than he used to have. Wrinkles lined his eyes, and his trademark beard had been in place for longer than Leo could remember.

As usual, Glen spoke before getting close enough for Leo to hear. Twelve years with a hearing loss and his father still couldn't remember to speak up.

"I can't hear you."

Glen's eyes rolled as he came closer, a frown now accentuating his beard. "You can never hear. How can you run a business when you mishear?"

Leo clenched his jaw. If he could never hear then how did he hear that? The world had plenty of people with a variety of disabilities with successful jobs and careers. His ears didn't create the barrier, people like his father did.

"How can you run a business when you don't listen?" Sure, Leo missed a thing or twenty, but his father had stopped listening a long time ago.

"We need to talk about selling," Glen said, proving Leo's point.

"Gladly. How much do I owe you?" Leo crossed his arms, widened his stance, prepared for a fight that wouldn't turn physical.

Glen sighed as though he were the only one tired of this game. "You two have yet to prove you have what it takes to carry on this business."

"Why not? We haven't been running the shop mostly on our own for the past two years? Dentz Antiques was only supposed to be two generations? I'm here, I've got my blood, sweat, and tears in this shop. Both your sons are working here and ready to carry the mantle, but you don't want us to."

"Because our two biggest losses are due to both my sons."

Leo ground his back teeth together. "So let me fix the clock." It stood in the corner, in his peripheral vision, eavesdropping on nearly every fight about it and silently mocking him. Sure, it was only one of the issues, but it was the one he could make shine.

"And the money lost from the last brother purchase?"

"We're working on a solid find to cover that mishap. It won't happen again."

"Fool me once, shame on you, fool me twice, shame on me."

Leo glanced up at the heavens, wondering if his grandfather wanted to punch Glen or had brought out the popcorn. "You never made a mistake as a kid? Because if you never wanted me to take over, then maybe you shouldn't have stuck me on store duty when I was sixteen."

"You couldn't handle the store then and you can't manage it now."

Fire burned deep in Leo's gut. Back then he'd been a bratty teenager, now he had a disability.

"I have buyers interested, they're willing to pay what this business is worth. We're meeting the first week of January to sign papers."

Giving Leo or Dean a chance was never going to be an option. He pushed past his father, in desperate need of fresh air that had nothing to do with the chemicals he'd been using. It didn't matter what he did, all his father saw was the sick kid with too high fevers and too many ear infections. Or the spindly pimple-faced kid who had to make a few mistakes to figure himself out.

The memory held as clear as if it had just happened, the years slipping away and placing him back in his sixteen-year-old shoes. It had been the day of THE party, the biggest one of the season, hosted by the most popular kids at school and he had scored an invite. The ragged piece of paper had burned a hole in his back pocket. He'd been two feet out the door before his dad dragged him in, forcing him to not only look after the store, but also his brother.

Leo decided then and there that his life sucked.

He kicked at the leg of the old, worn table, the one his father had been working on for weeks to restore. On a normal day Leo would enjoy the time to inspect the progress, perhaps even do a little work on it himself.

Not today.

He kicked the table again, though he'd have to take something a lot harder than his sneaker to it to make any damage in the century old wood. His crush was going to be at the party. He'd be able to grab a drink, make a move. By next week she'd have been his girlfriend.

Instead, she started dating Rick Leibowitz and Leo got stuck in this old, stuffy store, with its old products and its old customers where nothing exciting would ever happen to him again.

He'd groaned and tugged at his too long hair. His mother would make him get a haircut soon, whether he wanted one or not. Story of his life, doing things he didn't want to do because he wasn't old enough to move out of the house or go to college like his sister.

"What's crawled up your shorts?"

Dean. His "little" brother. Though the twelve-year-old had already passed five feet.

"I'm here. And I'm not wearing shorts."

Dean snickered and tossed a football from one hand to the other. "Ever hear of an expression?"

"Ever hear that I can kick your ass?"

"Dude, you sure are sour." Dean tossed the ball and caught it again. "Go to the stupid party. I'll watch the store."

"You're twelve."

Dean stood taller, the thin line of hair on his upper lip becoming more pronounced. "I'm almost thirteen. My bar mitzvah's in two weeks."

"An almost adult of the temple does not mean you can handle customer questions and credit cards."

Dean tossed the ball again. Shrugged. "Your social funeral." He walked away, ball shooting above his head, then slapping into his hands. Above. Slap. Above. Slap.

Leo's last thread threatened to snap.

"Give that to me," he ground out between his teeth.

Above. Slap. Above. Slap.

"I said, 'give that to me!'"

Slap.

Dean turned. "What?"

"Give me the ball."

"What? No. What did I do?"

"Annoyed me." Leo stomped over to his brother and grasped at the football.

"Hey, wait, that's mine!"

Dean tugged back, but Leo refused to loosen his grip.

"This ball is annoying me. Let go."

"It's not your ball!"

They began shoving at each other, neither letting go, haphazardly moving around the shop.

"Do you really want to do this with me?"

"It's my ball, let go and I'll leave."

Leo groaned. "Fine."

He let go with a shove, his lanky brother thrown off balance. The next few moments played out in slow motion. Dean losing his balance. Dean stumbling backward. Dean colliding with the old grandfather clock that had been a staple of Dentz Antiques for longer than either of them had been alive combined.

Both Dean and the clock came crashing to the floor, taking a shelf of expensive plates with them. A chorus of crashes filled the air as one after the other shattered to the ground. Plates on display for a special sale that weekend.

Dust filled the air, or so it seemed, slowly dispersing to reveal the rubble of destruction left behind. One fight over a silly football and the damage had to be in the tens of thousands of dollars.

Leo knew how superheroes felt at the damage they left behind.

Dean groaned and Leo stepped over a pile of broken ceramic and wood to give his brother a hand. "You okay?"

Dean stood and brushed off the dust. "I . . . think so." He turned, surveying the damage. "You might as well kill me, I'm dead after this."

Leo swallowed some dust and managed not to choke. "No. I'm the one who's dead."

Dean looked up. "We both are."

In the end, Leo took the brunt of the blame, even if Dean never believed himself to be innocent. Dad blamed the oldest. Leo had been in charge, and even at sixteen, he knew better.

Two months later he'd gotten sick and nothing was ever the same again.

The cold air welcomed Leo as he stepped outside and brought him back to the present, helped by the wind rustling against his hearing aid microphones. Yeah, he had known better. But growing up meant making mistakes and learning from them. He learned from this one, as did Dean. The only person in the world who didn't see it was Glen. And now he'd take this grudge and not only destroy a family business, but also take away Leo and Dean's legacy.

Leo still believed he could prove his worth to his father. He knew he could take over the business and do it right. But unless his father learned the meaning of forgiveness, all would be lost.

If only Millie was right, and that menorah was magic. Because Leo knew exactly what he'd wish for.

CHAPTER TEN

Andie had driven by this temple many times but had never had the opportunity to stop. Out front, a large brass menorah stood year-round, only now it had the first four candles lit. Andie didn't know what, if any, traditions would take place at sunset to light the fifth but had to admit it made the night a bit extra special. In a land where large Christmas trees were the norm, it was nice to have this one portion of her religion celebrated on an equally large scale.

Leo parked in back of the building and turned off the engine. "You ready to be accosted by about two dozen tweens?"

Andie leaned over the center console. The late afternoon lighting made everything feel more intimate, wrapping them up and cocooning them inside the car without a care for the outside world. "Did you forget my job again?"

Leo shifted close, past casual conversation, a light tilt to his lips that she wanted to taste. "No, I did not. But these kids aren't preschool-aged."

"And I'm only good for preschoolers then?"

Leo shifted back, alarmed. "No, I didn't mean—"

Andie's laughter cut him off. He might have made her mad a few nights ago, but now she enjoyed his fumbling far too much. "I know. But I also know most people don't realize that I have experience working with multiple age groups and there are some basic commonalities among them."

"Such as?"

Andie reached for her door handle. "Every child wants and deserves respect."

The sky held dark purple tones mixed in with the blues. The area behind the temple consisted mostly of trees, creating a secluded atmosphere, and a playground that didn't seem to match the school-aged kids.

Leo appeared beside her, extending an elbow for her to hook her hand on. She didn't need to be asked twice, not when it allowed her to be close to his side, his broad shoulders protecting her from some of the cold winter air. "Do you belong to this temple?"

"Nah. I'll join Jodie here or Mom and Dad at my childhood one."

"I get that. I haven't found my place since Dad stopped attending."

They headed up the stone steps, parting as they entered the main doors to where a small group of adults bustled about, setting up. One young kid weaved in between the adults. All heads swiveled their way.

"Oh, Leo, thank goodness you're here." A short woman wandered over to them. "We need another table for all the food. Would you be a dear and go grab one?"

"I'm on it." Leo placed both hands on Andie's shoulders. "Whitney, this is Andie, she's here to help."

Whitney had short dark hair and wore a sweater rolled up at the elbows that had a large dreidel on the front. "Help is always appreciated. Come with me. You can help with the decorations."

Andie followed. The room felt like a large function hall, and Andie had no doubt that many an event had taken place here over the years, Chanukah parties were the tip of the iceberg.

"Are you a good friend of Leo's?" Whitney's voice held a curious note, one that wanted to deduce the true reason why this random person had joined a school celebration.

"You could say that. We're celebrating Chanukah together."

"I see." Whitney held out a streamer and Andie took her end. "Leo is quite the catch. We've got a few single mothers who would be upset if he was taken. And a few not looking for partners who would be as well." Whitney laughed.

Andie smiled and hung the end of her side around a tac in the wall. "He is a catch, no argument from me on that." A punch of jealousy hit her, but she ignored it. Leo wouldn't be hers for more than a blink of an eye, she could put in a good word for him.

"You two aren't a thing?" Whitney had finished with her side and stood in front of Andie. "I'm sorry, I'm too blunt for my own good."

"No, it's all right. And we might be a bit of one, but I'll be moving for a new job soon, so . . ." Andie flailed her hands, unsure of how to finish.

"I see. Shame, he seems to like your company. I mean, you're here."

"I think that's due to a precocious niece."

"Oh, yes, Millie. She makes my bluntness seem mild."

They hung up another streamer before Leo returned, carrying a banquet table as though it weighed nothing. He set it down not too far from Andie.

"How is it you needed your brother for my desk, but not that?" Andie asked.

When Leo didn't answer, keeping his focus on fixing the table legs, Andie figured he must have not heard her. There was chatter from those who were helping to set up. Andie realized the noise bounced off the walls, so she moved until he looked up and repeated herself.

"This is worth a whole lot less and will continue to get beaten up. If I drop it, no big deal."

Leo got pulled away again, and Andie found herself without a task to do. The multiple groups were all hard at work, and none appeared to need a new pair of hands. She wandered over to a table where plastic dreidels and candy gelt had been scattered. The layout suggested that the items had been dumped more than set up, and, being no stranger to organizing crafts and activities for kids, Andie set to work separating the dreidels from the gelt.

A boy was running around—about five, Andie guessed—wearing running shoes that lit up and a dinosaur shirt. His gaze locked on what she was setting up. He ran over to her table, bouncing on his feet when he arrived.

"Are you playing dreidels?" Hope shimmered in his blue eyes.

"I'm setting them up for the party."

"Oh." His head angled down, feet no longer bouncing, lights going dark on his shoes.

Andie pushed a blue dreidel his way. "Why don't you give it a spin, help me make sure it works."

He glanced up. "I like green."

Andie chuckled and swapped out the blue dreidel for a green one.

The boy happily twirled it, squealing when the dreidel spun right off the table to land on the floor.

"No, Evan, those aren't for you."

Evan picked up the dreidel and placed it on the table, head angled down.

Andie looked over at the woman with blond hair pulled back into a high ponytail, hoping she was Evan's mother. "That's my fault. I needed someone to test the dreidels and make sure they work."

Evan smiled brightly up at her.

The woman studied Andie, probably torn between keeping her son with people she knew and getting a small break. "He's not bothering you?"

Evan resumed twirling.

Andie gave the mother her best teacher smile. "Absolutely not."

She gave her son one final look before pushing up the sleeves to her pink sweater, returning to the food table.

"Does that dreidel pass the test?" Andie asked.

Evan pushed it toward the center. "Uh-huh."

Andie found another green dreidel. "Let me know how this one goes."

Evan began spinning it, not even letting it come to a complete stop before he spun it again.

A warm hand landed on Andie's back. She didn't need to look to know who it belonged to, not with the slight scent of wood that engulfed her. "You okay?" Leo asked.

She glanced up at him. "I'm good. I've acquired a helper." She nodded to Evan.

"This one works, too!" Evan bounced, pushing the dreidel to Andie.

"I've got a challenge. This pink one needs a test; think you can do it?"

"I like pink!" Evan grabbed it and began twirling.

Leo chuckled low, and somehow it vibrated through her, even in this environment. "I see you don't need my help then."

"I suspect they have other tasks for you."

Just then, Whitney waved for Leo.

Leo groaned. "I'm the resident handyman when I'm here."

He walked off, and Andie suspected some of the women liked to see him work, more than needed it. She didn't blame them.

With her pile nearly sorted, Andie handed Evan another pink dreidel. Across the room something fell, clattering and echoing through the space.

Evan dropped the dreidel and covered his ears, body hunching over. "It's loud in here." He didn't straighten, remained curled up into himself.

Andie went into caretaker mode. She had students who struggled in different environments, and while she'd just met Evan, she understood that the noise had created a shift in his environment. She glanced around, checking to see what options the open space had. Not much, and the openness meant the current noise level would only get worse. "I think it will be louder when the other kids arrive."

"I don't like that. I like it quiet."

He tugged at her heart. "I like the quiet, too. Are you staying for the party?"

He nodded. "Mom's helping and Dad had to work, so I'm stuck here." Evan threw his palm down, bouncing the dreidels. He picked one up, yellow, and gave it a spin.

Andie knew when reinforcements would be needed. She didn't know this place, but she suspected Evan needed a quiet break. "I'll be right back."

She got up and hurried to his mother, finding her standing with Whitney. "That's the longest he's been still all day," the mother said.

"He told me it's loud in here. I don't seem to have anything to do at the moment. If it's okay with you I can take some dreidels and Evan and I can play in the corner."

The mother looked at Whitney.

"This is Andie, she's here with Leo." Whitney faced Andie. "And this is Beth."

The woman pressed a strand of blond hair off her face. "You wouldn't mind?"

Andie smiled. "I'm a preschool teacher, he's older than my students, but I wouldn't mind."

"I want the green one!" Evan shouted. Andie gave a little start, not realizing he'd followed her. Before any of them could react he raced back to the table, grabbed a green dreidel, and created a light show over to the corner.

"He's a handful. You don't have to," Beth said.

Andie shrugged. She'd take children handfuls over the adult version any day. "Not a problem at all."

She joined Evan in the corner and settled on the floor. He'd already begun spinning. When the dreidel stopped, he picked it up again, not even checking to see what it landed on. She let him play, spinning her own, ending up in a spinning war. Evan laughed every time their dreidels bumped into each other and the sound warmed Andie's heart. Children laughing had to be the best part of her day.

It sparked to life the dream she'd been working toward before her father got sick. She loved her job, but she wanted the option for more. To help more people, like her father had. She'd begun the process of getting her master's in special education so she'd be able to better serve the students that needed the most support. The degree would expand her knowledge and give her new methods for being the inclusive teacher she strived to be. She'd gotten accepted and had started planning for juggling work and school. Caring for her father had changed all of that. She had no regrets. One day, when the timing was right, she'd begin the process again.

Across the room, Leo set up a large menorah—not quite as large as outside, but still impressive in the room. He'd rolled up his sleeves, strength showing in his arms and shoulders as he worked.

Child laughter and Leo to watch. This might be the best night of Chanukah yet.

* * *

"Uncle Leo!"

That was the only warning Leo got before Millie threw herself at him and he had to scramble not to drop the kid. Millie hung on, arms and legs wrapped around him.

"Hey kiddo, you okay?" He shifted until he had a good grip on her and could straighten.

She disentangled herself and slid to the ground. "Yup." She looked around the room, where kids had already dived into food and games. Their laughter and chatter a symphony in the background. A symphony that meant he'd have a harder time hearing. The things he did for his niece. "Where's Andie?"

Leo laughed and pointed to the dreidel table. After Andie's success keeping Evan entertained, she was a natural shoo-in for leading some of the dreidel games.

"Oh, she's pretty." Millie crossed her arms and stared up at Leo. "Did you make any more wishes?"

Leo copied her stance. "I didn't want to abuse the magic."

Millie nodded as though they were having a perfectly reasonable conversation. "But what if there's something you really want to wish for?"

"Then I'll consider it."

Millie nodded again. "I'm going to bug your girlfriend."

Leo flung out a hand, grasping Millie's shoulder. "She's not my girlfriend."

"Isn't that what you wished for?"

"I wished for a date, not a girlfriend."

"Then maybe you know what your next wish should be." At that, Millie skipped off. If she said anything it got swallowed up by the room.

Leo blew out a breath, hoping Andie's move wouldn't be too much of a hardship for his niece. He already knew it would be one for him, no sense having two members of his family sad.

The dreidel table looked like chaos to Leo but tell that to Andie. She needed a circus top hat and a gold medal with how expertly she played ringmaster to two separate games simultaneously. She handed out dreidels to one group while monitoring winnings in a second and didn't even bat an eye when Millie came right up to her.

He got close as Millie stuck out her hand in formal greeting to Andie, catching the end of what she said, ". . . Leo's niece."

Andie chuckled. "Hello Millie. Your uncle has talked a lot about you."

Millie beamed.

Leo placed two stern hands on his niece's shoulders. "Haven't you been talking about Mrs. Wiseman's sufganiyot?"

"Oh, it's ready?" At that, Millie took off for the jelly-filled donut treats.

"Where are you stationed?" Andie neatened the center pot for one group, handed out gelt to the other, and still managed to have a conversation.

She made his head spin in wonderment and awe. "How are you doing that?" Leo asked.

She looked up. "Doing what?"

"Ringmaster of a three-ring circus."

She chuckled, collecting a wayward dreidel that had fallen to the floor. "Oh, gimel, good land!" She handed it back and facilitated the next turn, before facing Leo. "I teach preschool. This is nothing."

A strong sense of something pushed against his sternum at this amazing woman. He wanted to rub the spot and managed to resist. This woman, she got to him in so many ways. She had a calmness he rarely felt, especially in an environment like this. He'd have ten children yelling at him if he tried to take over.

"Still think I should work for Amazon?" Andie teased.

He doubted she'd let this one go. At least he agreed he'd deserved it. "We've already discussed that I don't. They don't pay you enough."

Andie chortled. "Welcome to the real world." She picked up one of the candy gelts and placed it in his hand. "You earned this one."

He relished in the feeling of her hand against his, missing the skin-to-skin contact that lasted far too briefly. "I'm, uh, on the Maccabee sword-fighting station."

She leaned forward, looking to that corner. "I think you've got your own three-ring circus to assist with."

He tore his gaze from hers and to the small crowd of kids trying to inflict damage with foam swords waiting for him. "I believe you are right."

Leo walked away to the sound of Andie's laughter, but he didn't make it to the sword station before getting interrupted by Whitney.

"I meant to ask, how are things going with the business? Jodie is so worried your father will sell it outside of the family."

Leo longed for one of those foam swords to be jammed into his side. The polite answer would be to say everything was fine, but Whitney already knew too much. "It's still a battle, and my oil is running out."

Whitney shook her head. "Forgiveness is a virtue often over-looked. You are a respectable man who has atoned for the past."

Tell that to Glen. "Respectable person doesn't equate to success-ful business owner."

Whitney placed a hand on his shoulder. "And yet, you're the only non–parental unit here helping out."

"Andie is even less related to the children."

"And she's here because of you."

Whitney took off at that and Leo could only shake his head. It didn't matter what someone said to him. Unless they had the perfect item he could fix up, they needed to be talking to his father about forgiveness.

Leo had tried, in many different ways. But one could try only so much on their own. Progress needed two willing parties.

With that sobering thought, he headed into the Maccabee sword battle.

* * *

Forty-five minutes into the party, Andie stood and stretched. She'd been replaced by one of the other volunteers, who dived into the position like a seasoned parent. Around the room mayhem ruled, as kids ran from activity to activity. The menorahs in the room had already been lit, one large electric one and two small candle versions burning into the night.

Leo remained at his station, and Andie couldn't help but scoot to the side to watch. He held a foam sword in each hand, dueling two laughing kids at once. He let them both stab him in the side, trapped their swords with his arms, staggering backward.

He collapsed to the floor, foam swords curving as they didn't have the structure to stand on their own. The two boys high-fived each other and left, not checking on their victim.

Andie made her way over and held out a hand. "Wounded in battle, I see."

Leo grasped her hand and let Andie pull him to a standing position, using his legs to propel him upright. She'd done more work to lift a willing three-year-old. "Many times over, in fact. Those Maccabees know how to fight."

Andie lingered a finger over his palm and finger as she let him go. "Got battle scars that need tending to?"

Leo smirked. "Plenty."

More kids arrived and he left her, attending to his next set of victors. Andie stayed and watched, unable to find anything else as entertaining. Leo wouldn't know these students well, he was here for Millie, and yet he jumped into the fray like someone who truly loved and appreciated kids. It brought an image to mind of him with his own children, playing around like this on a normal night, couch cushions tossed around and sounds of laughter ringing through the home.

The life she wanted. She often had visions like this of herself and kids, but never of another adult. He fit into this dream, this happy family she craved. But his life was here in Massachusetts. And her future was in Ohio.

Now she needed a moment to put everything but Chanukah out of her mind. And a bathroom. She slipped out into the hall, not wanting to bother anyone. The noise of the room dwindled, her ears relaxing in the quiet echo of the hall. She picked a direction and started walking, coming to a corridor with a set of doors along the wall.

The rooms inside were dark, but curiosity had her peeking in. The set up felt like a classroom, but the chairs and table were far too small for the tweens in the other room. She checked in on another room, with alphabet letters hanging on the walls, along with artwork from very young students.

It looked like a preschool, but maybe this was a spot for kids during services. She shook it off, back to hunting for a restroom, when a bulletin board came into view. And at the top of the board: Preschool Notes.

She was right. The temple had a preschool.

"Are you looking for something?"

Andie turned with a slight jump, finding Whitney standing before her. "I'm sorry, I was looking for the bathroom and got distracted."

Whitney's smile was warm and open. "You teach preschool, don't you?"

"I do. Little Friends."

Whitney's smile fell. "Not the one closing?"

"The very same."

"What are you doing next year?"

"I'm looking for a new job." Sure, she had an offer on the table, but it wasn't a done deal yet. Besides, maybe Whitney would mention a lead she could pass on to Sarah.

Whitney glanced at the rooms behind her, then at Andie. "Meredith has the cloud room and she's pregnant. With twins."

Andie studied Whitney's face, wondering where this conversation was headed.

"She's not returning after they are born."

Andie waited for Whitney to say more, but the woman simply stared at her.

"Are you implying you're hiring?"

"I am."

"Why tell me?"

"Because I've seen you interact with a very energetic five-year-old and holiday-hyped bigger kids. If you bring half that energy to your preschoolers, anyone would be lucky to have you on their team."

Andie's cheeks warmed at the compliment. She held out her still-dyed hands. "Projects before beauty, am I right?"

Whitney laughed. "I'd love for you to send me a resume." She went over to the board, untacked a business card, and placed the card in Andie's hand. "And the bathroom is around the corner. Meant for adults, not the little ones. You don't want that one."

Andie chuckled. "Thank you." The card warmed her palm as she followed the directions and entered the bathroom.

There she leaned against the wall, mind whirling. She already had a job lined up. A good one. One that she hadn't seen, hadn't been able to set foot into and get the true feel and vibe of the place.

All options were good options. Before she could overthink things, she used her phone to email Whitney her recently updated resume. More options, just in case, she told herself. They'd have plenty of qualified applicants, or a teacher who changed her mind and wanted to return to work after her twins were born.

Like the oil that looked enough for only one night but burned for eight, the end of the story was not always known in advance. So, she'd keep her options open and be prepared for anything.

CHAPTER ELEVEN

Leo collected the swords as the teachers called the kids to head back to their classrooms. Eager students did not have to be told twice, not with the promise of lighting their own candles and exchanging presents in their future.

He headed over to check on Andie, discovering he wasn't the only member of his family to do so.

It took him a moment to register Millie's voice in the loud area, once he heard the word "lights" he knew exactly what she was up to. ". . . the entire street is all lit up!" Millie jumped with enthusiasm.

"That must make it difficult to sleep."

Millie shrugged. "Doesn't bother me. Uncle Leo, you should take her."

Andie looked over as Leo joined them. "Millie says they are the best around."

"They are, how do I put this . . . It takes an extra half hour to visit my sister this time of year because of it." His brother-in-law took the phrase "keeping up with the Joneses" to heart when they moved to the street, adding Chanukah magic to the neighborhood.

"Bring her tomorrow night, I'll have Dad make cocoa."

"Millie! Your class is waiting for you!" Whitney called out.

"Oops," Millie started running away but said over her shoulder, "See you tomorrow!" And then she left the function room.

"I think your niece decided our plans for tomorrow," Andie said.

Leo faced her, the rest of the room fading away. "I can sway her if you have other plans."

"Wouldn't want to disappoint Millie." Andie shifted closer. "Or you."

"Yes, wouldn't want to disappoint Millie. Or me."

Andie chuckled. He wanted to lean forward and capture her lips, in a house of worship with children around or not. She broke their spell first, clearly smarter than him, and collected dreidels and gelt from her table.

"Something tells me I'm not disappointing you," Andie spoke low, but he managed to hear her, helped by his gaze lingering on her mouth.

"Not the slightest."

"Even if I didn't join you tomorrow?"

"Even then, though I'll just give Millie your number."

She headed for the boxes where all the items were being stored and he followed. This woman continued to amaze him. Her willingness to interact with him aside, she'd given up her night to be here.

"Thank you for coming, I hope you had a good time."

Andie beamed. "Of course."

"Not too tired of being with kids all day?"

Andie sorted the dreidels and gelt into separate containers. "Nope. I have my moments, believe me. But kids don't have the same agenda that adults do. Making a difference in their lives for even a short time is a wonderful thing." The light hit her cheeks as she talked. She glowed, inside and out. He had no doubt she made a difference wherever she went. She'd already made a profound impact on him. She amazed him, between her determination and dedication, it spoke to him on some base level.

"You're incredible," he said before he could catch himself.

She bumped hips with him. "You're not so bad yourself." How this wonderful woman saw something special in him, he'd never begin to figure out.

They got sent into separate directions to continue with the cleanup of the room and didn't get a chance to connect again until they settled into Leo's cold car. He blasted the heat as Andie rubbed her mitten-covered hands together.

"So Millie wasn't exaggerating about all these lights?"

Leo shook his head. "It is quite the to-do. I'm actually surprised you haven't heard about it."

"When people talk about lights to visit . . ."

"Yup. Jodie's street is one of them."

"Oh boy, that must be a bit much at times."

Leo backed out of the space, thinking of how well his brother-in-law managed to catch up with his neighbors. "They make it work."

"Cryptic response."

Leo stopped with the car in drive, leaning over the console. "You'll see tomorrow night what I mean."

Andie licked her bottom lip. "I guess I will."

Leo forced his attention forward, before he dared kiss her in the temple parking lot with his foot on the brakes.

He made it onto the main road when his phone rang, Dean's name popping up on his console. He slid a glance to Andie. "That's my brother and business partner, I should answer it."

"By all means."

Leo clicked the button, connecting the call. "Dean, you're on speaker, what's up?"

"Speaker?" Came his brother's staticky voice. Great, bad connection, that did not bode well for hearing. "Oh, the Chanukah party. . . . Andie is there with you? Hi Andie!"

Leo's cheeks grew warmer than the heater attempted to make his car. He dared a look at his passenger, finding an amused look on her face. "I, uh, might have mentioned it."

"And so did Millie . . . and over again. In typical Millie fashion."

Andie laughed. "Having met your niece, I can see that."

Leo tried to figure out if he should feel awkward about any of this, but his passenger was relaxed and at ease. The streetlights that played on her face gave him no reason to be concerned. He kept his focus on driving and decoding his brother's voice.

"I know this isn't why you called." Leo wanted to get them back on track before Dean gave him reasons to be concerned.

"Yeah, right. . . ." He didn't know if the connection was bad or his ears. Maybe his passenger heard Dean, maybe she didn't. But this wasn't her responsibility.

"Repeat that."

"I said I think I found it."

Leo turned on his blinker. "It?"

"The item that will . . . and save the business."

Leo blinked into the night, part of him hoping this truly was the miracle item they needed. But experience made doubt heavy and larger than life, and he knew he couldn't simply believe.

Not after the last phone call they'd had like this, the one where Dean had mentioned a find and Leo had heard it wrong and gave Dean the go-ahead to spend far too much money on a complete flop.

A car honked behind him, and he realized he could have taken his turn and quickly caught up. He swallowed his concerns; he knew Dean regretted it as much as he did. "What did you find?"

"A Persian rug, I'm guessing eighteenth century. It's faded but with a good cleaning could be worth a pretty penny."

Leo chewed that over, letting the car and phone line fill with silence. It had potential, in either direction. His skills didn't extend to repairing rugs, but they had a dry cleaner they trusted with that task. More importantly, Dean knew rugs better than he knew furniture, and that had been part of the problem with the flop. "What's your assessment of it?"

"Really?"

Leo didn't have to check on Andie to feel her staring at him. He called Dean his business partner, not his little brother that works for him who's opinion he didn't automatically want. Leo scrubbed a hand down his face. Apparently, his dad wasn't the only Dentz bad at trusting the younger generation.

He made a mental note to fix it, regardless of the future outcome of Dean's find. "Yes, really." He tried to convey more than his words did and didn't know if a choppy cell phone connection would work.

"It's, ahh, got some fading, as I mentioned, and a few of the wool threads fraying in one corner. But it's in good shape for its age and reminds me of similar items from Iran that have been heating up on the market."

Leo nodded, though Dean couldn't see him. The assessment proved why Dean didn't follow Leo into restorations. Leo wouldn't be able to pick out a potential rare find in rugs. But Dean knew to focus on the areas outside of Leo's strength. The fact that they had different areas to excel in made them an excellent team. "It's not costing an arm and a leg is it?"

"It's not. And I'm not using the business card."

Leo mulled that over. Showed Dean's confidence in the product. Or fear over another mistake. Perhaps a bit of both.

"Bring it into the shop, we'll take a look at it tomorrow."

"If I'm right, then all our troubles are over, brother."

"Don't forget we have to impress Dad, and he prefers to live unimpressed."

They disconnected, and Leo braced himself for whatever Andie thought of that interesting call.

"So that's your plan to save your job? A rug?"

Leo glanced at her, expecting some slight that he would have well deserved for how their Chanukah started. All he found was curiosity on her face. "Yeah. If we find something that brings in business and money, something valuable enough to garner attention, then he'd have no choice but to sell to us."

"You hope."

He snorted. "Yeah."

"Because he still sees you as a reckless teenager getting into trouble?"

Leo wanted to brush it off, agree with her, and downplay the whole thing. But Andie was moving anyway. "More like reckless teenager that cost thousands of dollars in damage by wrestling with his brother rather than be a responsible sixteen-year-old."

"I'm sorry, the phrase 'responsible' and 'sixteen-year-old' don't always go hand in hand."

Some of the weight eased off his shoulders. "Still. I accept the blame for this. I knew better, I just had a chip on my shoulder."

"As teenagers often do."

"I thought you worked with preschoolers?"

"I do. But I have a general interest in childhood education, and those teen years leave a mark."

"Oh?"

"No 'oh,' I'm just an observer and I've seen some great kids do stupid things. It's all part of learning. Tell me Leo, did you learn from this past experience?"

"Absolutely."

"Then it had its benefit."

"Tell that to my dad." He gripped his gear shift, digging his fingers into the leather.

Andie reached over, covered his hand with hers. "Your father should have realized that years ago. I wish I had a magic word that would change him, but people don't always allow for others to grow and err and be human. I hope this item your brother found helps."

He let go of the shift, entangling his fingers with hers. "Thank you. Truly."

She gave his hand a squeeze. "Like you wouldn't speak up for others if you might be able to help in some way?"

Don't move to Ohio. He swallowed the words. They would help him, not her. It didn't matter how much her support meant to him. It shouldn't, not from a neighbor. But he wanted to bottle her up, keep her nearby. He wanted Dean's find to be big enough that he could give Andie the world. "I would. You're amazing, Andie."

She let go of him, cold air replacing where her hand had been. "Just calling it like it is."

He'd made three major mistakes in his life. The first was letting damage occur in the shop at sixteen. The second was the miscommunication with Dean. The third was not making his move on this special woman earlier. If he'd acted even months ago, they could be spending Chanukah together as an established couple, and he'd be helping her find a new job nearby. Or moving with her to a new adventure.

* * *

Leo walked Andie to her door. She'd call him a gentleman, but considering they were neighbors, the move made complete sense on multiple levels. She didn't want the night to end. More time with Leo tempted her more than she'd thought it would. It even topped her Thursday night ritual. Thursdays had long ago identified themselves as her crash day because most nights she devoted time to class preparation. The end-of-week exhaustion crept up on her and a little R&R on Thursdays became her go-to, one she looked forward to. Especially the week before winter break, when less prep was needed and more rest required.

Only now she had a reason to want a little something different added to her Thursday night plans.

"Thank you for helping out with Millie's Chanukah party." Leo leaned against the wall, his full attention on her.

"Thank you for inviting me. I had fun." More than she'd expected. "I still have my candles to light, and a bit of a Thursday night ritual, if you'd like to come in?"

Leo pushed off the wall. "What kind of ritual?"

Her confidence faltered, wondering if sharing her quirky habits was her best move. Too late, she'd already put her foot in the door. "By Thursdays I'm usually wiped and ready for the weekend, so I've made Thursday a movie and popcorn night. Fair warning, I very rarely stay awake for an entire movie."

Leo rubbed his chin in consideration, though Andie suspected he didn't have much to consider. "Will I have a say in this movie option?"

Andie collected her key and turned to her door. "Perhaps." She unlocked her unit, opening the door wide. "What do you say, Leo. Up for starting a movie we might not finish?"

She meant due to falling asleep, but a second, sexier meaning hung in the air between them, vibrating the molecules in their personal bubble. His brown eyes deepened, focused on her, wrapping her up in a bit of Leo magic.

"I'd love to start a movie with you, Andie."

She entered her apartment only to find her guest hesitating at the threshold. "Is something wrong?"

He shook his head, a soft chuckle escaping his lips. "Debating with myself. You mentioned popcorn, I often make chocolate-covered popcorn for movie watching, want me to get the supplies?"

"Salty and sweet? I'm not going to complain."

He grinned, eyes shining. "Then I'll be right back."

He headed down the hall and she settled in. Coat and purse on their respective hooks. A few wayward items put away. Her cozy home somehow felt light and airy. Tonight, it wasn't a retreat for one. No, tonight it was meant to entertain two. Excitement and potential filled her up, made this holiday all the more special. Most years, the week flew by, too many other life duties getting in the way. But this year she'd savor it and create lasting memories. At least her last holiday season in Massachusetts would be a memorable one.

She tapped out six candles and had them set in the menorah by the time her door creaked open and Leo joined her. He closed the door behind him and the space grew impossibly cozier. He'd removed his jacket and carried a bowl with all his supplies inside.

"Does your snack take long?" she asked.

He set the bowl on her kitchen counter. "Not long, a few extra minutes for fresh popcorn, that's all."

"Then let's light the candles so you can get working."

He moved next to her, not touching but close enough she somehow felt his body heat and she wondered if she needed a match or just the combustible energy between them. She pushed that silly thought aside and grabbed her matches, lighting the shamash. They said the prayers as she lit the other five candles. Soon teal candles glowed with high-arching flames, lighting the night, taking an ordinary Thursday and making it special.

Even more so due to her evening companion. Giving him a second chance was truly the best Chanukah decision she'd ever made.

Leo placed a hand on Andie's back. "I'll get started on our popcorn." His fingers dipped down her back, leaving at her waist, creating a trail of goosebumps.

The sexier reason for not finishing a movie grew more and more enticing.

She shook it off and helped collect the additional supplies he needed. Soon oil sizzled on her stove, the first few kernels popping to life.

"Oil. It would seem homemade popcorn is rather fitting for Chanukah."

Leo chuckled. "So it would."

"But we don't think that way, do we?"

"Of course not. Because fried latkes and jelly-filled dough are more memorable than corn."

Andie considered that and found no fault. "I suppose you're right."

"As a wise man, I'll take that win."

Andie laughed as the kernels rapidly popped.

"Millie would point out that popcorn wouldn't have been an option when the Maccabees were around."

Andie's fondness for Millie grew. "She would be right."

The popcorn sounds continued to bounce around them.

"What movie are you subjecting me to?" Leo asked.

"Oh, it's subjecting now?"

"Your home, your tradition, your rules."

He expertly shook the pan on the stove, strong arms showcased in his green button-up. He might be taking over her stove, but he held onto the mantle of guest, never trying to overstep her like others might do.

It warmed her more than all the fire elements in her home.

"Well, it is the holiday season, so a holiday movie would be ideal. Sadly, I can really only think of one mainstream Chanukah movie: *Eight Crazy Nights*."

Leo used two hands, holding the pot cover as the popcorn reached up to the rim. "It's a shame after all these years that there isn't more. But commercialism is certainly the theme of the season."

Andie nodded. "That it is. Things are changing, but very very slowly."

Leo dumped the popcorn out onto a baking sheet. "Is there a holiday movie you gravitate toward?" He collected a microwave bowl and filled it with melting chocolate, adding a hint of oil.

Andie's cheeks warmed. "There is one I love. No rhyme or reason why, it just always brings a smile to my face."

Leo placed the bowl in the microwave. "Which movie is that?"

She debated changing it up to something more sophisticated, or romantic, but ended up being her true self. "*Elf*."

Her microwave beeped and Leo removed the bowl, stirred it, and put it back in. "That one is a bit of a classic."

Andie laughed. "Probably because of people like me."

"What do you like about it?"

The smell of chocolate mixed in with popcorn and candles and Andie wanted to bottle up this smell and make it last. "There's an innocent youthfulness to it, one I often see with my students. A reminder that belief can be a powerful thing, and the true magic of a holiday season is in the actions of others."

Leo stirred the chocolate one last time, then used a fork and drizzled it over the popcorn. Andie's mouth watered. "That is true. A bit like how I'm encouraging Millie in the magic menorah fantasy."

Andie nodded. "Exactly. Santa Claus isn't real. And while I am a big fan of how Chanukah gifts come from parents and loved ones, there's something so beautiful about the holiday spirit. When the adults don't ruin it."

Leo laughed. "Oh, you mean all the fighting over the best gifts." He collected the bowl he'd brought over, and dumped the finished popcorn in.

"Don't even get me started on how attitudes go both directions around this time of year." She reached out, collected one chocolatey popcorn. Sweet and salty bursting on her tongue. "Oh, this is good." She grabbed another. "You might have me changing up my Thursday habits."

Leo's smile lit his eyes and thoughts of anything other than this moment, with this man, faded. The curve of his lips called to her, made her want more than she had time to fully enjoy. Before she could think twice, she placed a hand on his cheek, kissing him. Her lips lingered against his, and she absorbed his taste into the sweet and salt.

"What was that for?" he asked. "Not that I'm complaining."

She laughed and made her way to her couch. "A little appreciation of my Chanukah partner." She settled down and he joined her, the popcorn on the coffee table in front of them.

"Thank you," Leo said.

Andie paused with her remote in her hand. "For?"

He gestured between them. "For this. For spending Chanukah with me. I've been focused on work and only work for so long, I'd almost forgotten how to take a break and smell the candles, so to speak."

She shifted; the TV screen forgotten. "I get that. I truly do. And I agree, this is nice." A pang of sadness hit her, that this wonderful feeling of something new starting would be a flash in the pan, not growing into anything more than a nice memory. She'd find a special spot for it, because nice memories were good to have. A reminder that the holidays do hold adult magic.

Leo leaned forward and Andie met his lips, tasting the sweet and salt of the popcorn on him, also with the flavor she was starting to learn was Leo. His face held a slight scratch of late-day stubble, and she let it prickle her fingers. A different kind of magic existed here, in this kiss and the connection two people could make.

The kiss ended, and Andie licked her lips. "Should we start the movie before the popcorn gets cold?"

"As the lady wishes."

CHAPTER TWELVE

Forty minutes later, as children cheered and Buddy yelled "Santa!" on screen, Leo realized Andie had fallen asleep. Her head had been nestled into his shoulder for most of the movie. He hadn't thought of *Elf* as a movie to cuddle with, but he refused to complain. Andie's breathing had slowed to a soft rhythm, her weight pressed against him. Even the chaos on screen hadn't gotten a shift, peep, or change in breathing.

Careful, in an effort not to wake the sleeping woman on his shoulder, he reached forward, next to the empty popcorn bowl, where the remote lay. He had to stretch his fingers but managed to grasp the end and collect the item, then turn the movie off.

The apartment grew silent, the last remaining embers of the candles simmering in the menorah, and Andie slept. He guessed she slept hard and he guessed he would, too, if he had her job.

Now he faced a bigger problem: what to do? He reached into his back pocket, pulling out his phone, going to the person he always went to when he needed dating advice.

Leo: Got a minute?

The fourth candle extinguished before he got a response.

Jodie: For the brother who put my kid in such a good mood, of
course!
Jodie: Millie will not stop talking about how wonderful Andie is.
And she somehow has it in her head you two are coming
over to see the lights tomorrow.
Jodie: So tell me, dear brother, is it true?

He would have scrubbed a hand down his face if he wasn't losing
feeling in his fingers from Andie's position.

Leo: Yes. But I've got more important things going on.

He started typing his situation, but his sister sent a response
before he could finish.

Jodie: What did dad do this time?

He erased what he wrote, retyping his response.

Leo: Nothing. This time. Though Dean might have a lead.

Again, he started typing what he really needed, but Jodie texted
before he could finish.

Jodie: Oooh, what did Dean find?

He backspaced, again.

Leo: Can you hang on a minute? I need help.

Jodie sent an emoji with a zipper over its lips and Leo quickly
typed out what he needed for a third time.

Leo: I'm over at Andie's. She invited me in to watch a movie with her, but she's fallen asleep. What do I do?

Jodie: Wake her.

Leo put his phone down, and nudged Andie. She curled off his shoulder, snuggling into the side of the couch. He stretched his tingling fingers and used both hands to type.

Leo: She's not waking.

Jodie: I suspect you don't want to wake her.

Guilty. Andie looked so peaceful. He wanted to curl up behind her, sleep with her in his arms, and knew that was far from being a potential option.

Jodie: And I know you won't respond to that. You leave, dear brother. Make sure her lights are off and her door is locked and you leave a note.

Leo: On the couch?

Jodie: This isn't Millie or Little Orphan Annie, you aren't going to change her clothes or tuck her into bed, not even if you've seen her bed already.

Outside the winds picked up, the final candle extinguished, and the woman beside him slept.

Leo: But it's cold.

Jodie: Look, I get it, you like her and want to stay. But find a blanket and go home.

He sighed, knowing his sister was right, on more than one point.

Leo: Okay.

Leo: Thank you.

Jodie: I look forward to meeting this
woman who has you in knots.

He wanted to respond but figured it best to leave it alone. He stood, stretching out his hand to wake it up the rest of the way, and checked out Andie's living room. No blankets, nothing warm. Well, checking out her bedroom was different than putting her there. He made his way to the open door, peeked inside. Unmade bed, small pile of clothes on a chair, and a desk that probably had a laptop under all the papers.

Leo chuckled. Andie's living room was clean but lived in, her bedroom a bit of a tornado. It somehow endeared her to him. The two sides of her, a different part of her creating each situation. He wanted to understand those parts.

At the foot of her bed he found a haphazardly folded blanket and snatched it. In the living room he draped it over her, tucking it around her body. She murmured and he leaned forward, trying to hear if she made noise or spoke words, but didn't get any confirmation.

"Good night, Andie." He brushed her hair back, pressing his lips to her temple. Hoping, somehow, that his kiss would wake her when everything else didn't.

She slept.

It was for the best. Andie was obviously tired. And even if he wanted to make the most of their limited time together, this wasn't the way.

He turned off the lights, made sure the oven was off. Then he let himself out, locking the bottom from the inside since he didn't have her keys.

The hall felt extra lonely and he heaved a sigh, shoving his hands into his pockets, making a slow trek back to his own apartment. There he stood in his dark living room, staring at the streetlights. An itch, a tick, something simmered below the surface, settling in his foot and the steady tap against his wood floors. Unsettled was the best way to describe his mood. He needed sleep, should force himself to bed, or at least begin to wind down for the night and trick his brain into sleep. His limbs wouldn't move. All he could think of was Andie. That led him to her desk, and the time didn't matter—he knew what he needed to do.

Without a second thought he grabbed his keys and left his unit, taking one more glance back to Andie's, just in case, before taking the stairs two at a time.

He had a desk to work on, a very special Chanukah gift for a very special woman.

* * *

Andie startled awake when her alarm went off, knowing immediately something was different. For starters, her alarm sounded softer than usual. That combined with her contorted position in a small space that did not resemble her queen-sized bed had her lifting her head, blinking her room into focus.

Her living room.

The previous night came back to her: Chanukah party, popcorn, movie, and the last thing she remembered was thinking Leo's shoulder looked mighty comfortable.

Humiliation seeped in. She fell asleep on his shoulder, didn't she? Yup, she must have. She pulled the blanket up, sleep fading from her vision. The blanket hadn't been here, she didn't keep blankets in her living room. Leo had thought to cover her. Her heart tugged at the action and she held the blanket to her, gave herself a moment to appreciate the man and the care, before letting it go. She didn't have time for heart tugs in her morning.

Andie stretched and investigated her living room. No signs of Leo. She rose and went into her bedroom; he wasn't there either. Of course he went home, not like he lived far away. Still, she collected her phone, taking another precious few moments from her morning routine, and found a message waiting for her.

Leo: Hope you slept well. I didn't want to move you when you
fell asleep. Let me know if we're still on for tonight.

There went the tug in her heart again. She checked the time he
sent the note, wondering how quickly she really fell asleep.

Two am.

Huh. The movie wouldn't have lasted that long if they'd finished
it. She glanced around again and there were no signs Leo had lingered. Was her neighbor a night owl and she didn't know it? Myster-
ies she might never solve.

Andie: Sorry I conked out on our movie, though I did warn you.
Andie: And yes, we're still on for tonight.

She held her phone to her, ignoring how that tug had grown. Just
the holiday magic, nothing more. She set her phone to charging and
got ready for the day.

* * *

Bang. Clatter. Crash.

Leo woke with a start, the loud noises reverberating in his head.
He brushed the sandpaper from his cheek and pushed in his hearing
aids, stretching out the kink in his neck.

"Well look who it is, sleeping beauty burning the midnight oil."
Dean picked up the box he'd dropped and walked over, examining
the item Leo had used for his bed. "Andie's?"

Leo nodded, stretching his neck in the other direction. He
investigated where he'd placed his head and moved the rag that got
turned into a pillow. The desk looked good. His face, probably not
so much.

"I thought you went to Millie's Chanukah party together?"

Leo yawned. "We did. And then started a movie. She fell asleep
and I came here."

Dean nodded, studying the work Leo had put in. "Looks like you made some headway."

Sleep clung to him, and he felt like a year's worth of gunk crusted his eyes. His ears itched, not used to having the hearing aids in all night, and he bet his batteries would need to be charged before the day was out. His internal clock insisted it had to be deep in the night, but sunlight poured in through the windows, and Dean very rarely came to work early. Or stayed late. He didn't get the thrill of putting in long hours with rewarding results. The restoration process was a slow one, needing time in between the steps. Leo had arrived last night to discover the cleaned wood had dried and he went about inspecting the desk. The marks were gone or significantly reduced, to the point he called it character rather than a defect. He had checked on the wobbly leg again and replaced a pin, stopping the wobble. The desk stood straight and secure. He'd been prepared to find an area that needed more work than the others, checking extra for them. All he found was that beneath the busted drawer, wobbly legs, and stains, the piece had been well loved and cared for.

Except for the polish used, but he'd make sure that never happened again.

All in all, it made him smile. It meant Andie had taken care of it, as her mother had before her. He understood that antiques weren't for everyone but liked it better when he had a place of common interest. Especially since antiques were very much his life.

So he'd gotten to work, cleaning a few more areas because he couldn't help himself, ensuring that anything left behind truly fell under the "character" heading. And at some point, he had fallen asleep.

"Hey, what time is it?" Leo scrubbed a hand over his face, willing himself to wake up fully.

"Ten of. Why?"

Ten of. No time to get ready for work, he'd have to make do with a bathroom clean up. Leo stretched. "Give me a few minutes and I'll be ready for the day."

Dean waved him off, heading to the front. "Take an hour. Go home. Shower. I've got this."

Leo opened his mouth, ready to interject, but Dean hadn't stopped moving. Another day, Leo would have protested, undermining his brother's worth. So instead of not learning from the past, he made sure all the pieces were positioned to dry, then left out the back door to do just as Dean had instructed.

* * *

"You fell asleep while watching *Elf*? Who falls asleep while watching Will Ferrell be silly?"

Andie picked up her sandwich, chewing instead of responding to Sarah. They sat in the teacher's lounge, grabbing lunch in between the two sessions.

"Why watch *Elf* anyway? There are plenty of sexier holiday movies." Sarah wiggled her eyebrows, before turning back to her soup.

"I was enjoying Leo's company. If I wanted to get him in the bedroom, I would have invited him there." Not that the thought hadn't crossed her mind. She figured she'd start the facade and stop the movie and see where the night went from there, not that she'd fall into such a deep sleep she wouldn't even know he left.

Sarah stirred her soup. "Well, what are you waiting for? You said you wanted a Chanukah fling, not a long-distance relationship."

Andie sighed. Relationships were meant to be built and see what, if any, potential existed. This thing with Leo was the first time she'd tried something different, and old habits died hard. Or perhaps relationships were in her blood, the way she'd been built. "I'm still here for a few more months, I don't need to rush anything. If it happens, it will happen organically."

"You're no fun." Sarah blew on her spoon and took a bite.

"Relax, I'm seeing him tonight. Chanukah isn't over yet."

A large gust of wind made a strong whistling sound enter the room. Sarah groaned. "My morning kids were spooked by this noise; I was hoping the winds would die down by the afternoon."

Andie's students had reacted the same way. "I told my students it was due to how busy the elves were finishing up all the gifts."

"Oh, Oh! That's clever. I'm stealing that," said Naomi, one of the other teachers sitting at a different table. The lunchroom was small enough that conversations normally crossed between tables.

"Me too," said Sarah.

Andie was going to miss the camaraderie here. "Go right ahead and use it. If the students have friends in other classes, it'll be all the better."

A chorus of agreement floated through the room before everyone resumed their previous conversations. Andie took another bite of her sandwich, finding Sarah staring at her.

"What?" Andie said, covering her mouth as she still chewed.

"You looked sad for a moment there, why?"

The room held student work on the walls, staff notifications, and a countdown to the end of the year. The *final* year. "I'm going to miss this and everyone here."

"Yeah, I know. But you'll find something similar, if not better, in Ohio."

Andie thought about the temple, and the spur-of-the-moment sending of her resume. "I might have another option."

Sarah leaned forward. "Oh?"

"The temple I was at for Leo's niece's Chanukah party? They have a preschool on site and were impressed with how I interacted with the kids." Andie mulled that over, odds were, it was a pleasant compliment, nothing more. "You should apply."

"When they are so clearly enamored with you?"

"How do you get enamored by one sentence?"

"Did they ask you to apply?"

Andie chewed on her bottom lip. "Yes."

"See. Enamored."

"And they may be just as enamored with you when they meet you." Sarah would be her top choice for teacher if Andie had kids.

Sarah chuckled. "Okay, send me the details. I applied to an elementary school the other day to expand my options."

Andie had been about to take another bite, but instead put her sandwich down. They'd met with the joint goal of working in preschool and until now neither had strayed from that objective. "But you like the little ones."

"I know. I do. But I also like eating."

Another reason why this situation stunk more than a bathroom accident. "Agreed." Andie's cell phone rang, and it took her a moment to recognize the sound as hers. She pulled it from her pocket, staring at the number on the screen.

"Who is it? Lover boy?" Sarah asked, leaning forward, her shirt nearly sliding into her soup.

"No. It's local. Maybe it's about one of the jobs I applied for?"

Sarah's eyes grew wide. "Oh! Answer it! Answer it!"

Andie pushed her chair back and answered as she made her way into the quiet hall. "Hello, this is Andie."

"Hi Andie, this is Gwen Hoffman, the director of the temple preschool."

Andie nearly gulped in some air. "Hi Gwen, nice to meet you."

"The feelings are mutual. You made quite the impression at the Chanukah party."

Andie blushed and became very aware of how echoey the empty halls were. She dipped into Sarah's classroom, since it was closer.

"I know Evan well, he used to attend the preschool before entering kindergarten, it took a special person to be able to meet him on his level."

"I'm sure kindergarten has changed things for him."

Gwen laughed. "You're humble, I like that. And I've seen Evan many times since he graduated. He is still quite the handful."

"I believe the children that are handfuls are the ones expressing some unmet need. It's all about figuring out what that need is. Once you meet it, most of those misbehaviors stop."

"And now I see exactly why Whitney raved about you. You teach preschool, entertained a rowdy kindergartner, and effortlessly transitioned to managing tweens. Do you intend to stay in preschool?"

Andie settled on Sarah's desk. The short answer was yes, the long answer involved more education and options. "Yes. I mean, I accept I'm young and life might pull me in different directions. But I like helping the young minds, shaping them and preparing them for future success."

"'The success of the future starts here.' That's our slogan."

Andie tried not to cough. "I wasn't aware of that."

"I didn't think you were."

Andie wasn't sure she could hear a smile over the phone, but if she could, she heard one now.

"Your program is closing, I understand."

Andie looked around the room and all the artwork Sarah's students had completed so far. It tugged at her, made her want to wrap the entire school in bubble wrap and preserve the magic they created here. "It is. We've tried to save it, but no luck."

"That's a shame, we need more preschools, not fewer. But that's why I'm working on expanding my program."

"So you're not only filling one position?" She let the fantasy unfold. Sarah and she could both find the same new job and stay together.

"For now, it's the one. Like your program closing, it all comes down to dollar signs. I'm working on mine at the moment, and I'm hopeful but cannot guarantee anything."

That crushed her fantasy, but not completely, this phone call was still about her potential prospects. "I understand."

"I imagine it must be difficult to keep morale up."

Andie settled into a more comfortable position. The clock on the wall warned her not to get too comfortable. Her time to chat dwindled fast. "It is. We're trying our best to save the school, but it may not be in the cards. So, we all put on our best smiles and make this year count for the students."

"You said *all*, what do you specifically do in your classroom?"

"I'm building a foundation for my students' future education, so that they have the tools they need to carry them wherever they go. I don't know where they'll be next year, or if they'll even have a class. But I know when they leave me, they'll have what they need to be successful."

"Spoken like a person with a teacher's heart."

Sadness gripped her at losing this program and separating these students, but Gwen's comment filled that hole—that after such a short conversation she would see something like that, enough to mention it. "I wouldn't be in this career if I didn't have it." Voices echoed in the hall. "Gwen, I'm sorry but I need to prepare for my next class of the day."

"I won't keep you. I just had to talk to the woman who Whitney kept gushing about. I'll be in touch."

"I know it's the holidays and all, but can you give me an idea of when I should hear more?"

"We are closed next week, but you should hear something before the New Year, if not sooner."

Gwen disconnected the call before Andie could ask for more details. Andie clicked to the home screen on her phone. "Did that really happen?" She chuckled, shoving her phone into her pocket. It did happen, and now she needed to wait and see what, if any, results would come.

The classroom door opened and Sarah hurried over. "So?" She bounced on her sneakers.

"It was one-part casual conversation, one-part interview."

"Ooh!" Sarah's face lit up.

"And they're planning on expanding so . . ."

"Yup, give me the details. I'll jump on that if I'm not in direct competition. They seem to love you anyways. Calling you after one day?"

Andie rubbed her warm cheeks. "I apparently made an impression at the Chanukah party." She couldn't believe it. She'd just been there, being her authentic self, not thinking of employment options or anything beyond Leo and Millie and having a good time.

"The best way to open doors to new opportunities."

Her happiness took a momentary nosedive. "But I've got the Ohio job."

"Options are good, Andie!"

Options meant decisions. It meant taking a leap in one direction or another at a time in her life when her heart felt truly torn. "Options are only good until I need to make a decision and don't know which one to choose."

"Are we talking about Leo at all? Tell me we're talking about Leo!"

Andie pushed off Sarah's desk. "I need to get back to my classroom." The last thing she needed was this new thing swaying her career decision. She had to do what was right for her, end of story.

"Stalling!" Sarah yelled as Andie walked past.

"I'm not basing my decision on a guy I've started to actually know for less than a week." She exited the room, not allowing Sarah a chance to respond. Deep down, she knew Leo was part of the desire to stay in Massachusetts. But it didn't change the fact that, currently, she had only one offer on the table, and she had no intentions of passing it up.

* * *

Showered and filled with sustenance that didn't consist of the snacks kept in the backroom, Leo arrived back at the shop. The sun was high in the sky in defiance to the strong wind echoing through his windows and rocking the car.

A nap would have been smarter than the large coffee he'd grabbed, but he wouldn't sleep. He couldn't sleep when work called to him. Or rather, work called, but all he heard was the sweet whisper of Andie's desk.

More than the woman, it was a challenge. A chance to do something for someone who would actually appreciate it. The hum in his veins wouldn't sleep, not until he'd finished the piece.

Or at least checked on the drying process. He needed to remember refurbishing required time and patience. Attending to other things in the shop, and his evening plans, would be the necessary distraction. And he'd take a night out with Andie over fixing anything. Except maybe his chance at more than a brief holiday fling with her.

Leo scrubbed his face, his whiskers scraping across his palm. He hadn't shaved, not yet at least. He slapped his cheeks, needing a strong kick in the pants.

The first brisk rush of air as he exited his vehicle did the trick. It nipped at his skin, slipped under his clothes, and proudly held a finger up to the hot fiery sun. Leo clutched his coffee, turned up his jacket lapels as the wind snaked into his clothes and rustled against his hearing aid microphones, and hurried inside the building.

The workroom was closest. Excuse or not he didn't care. Instead of going up front, relieving Dean, getting admonished for not bringing his brother a cuppa (really should have thought of that), he headed to the back corner where Andie's desk lay.

Leo set down his mug, shucked off his jacket, and began inspecting his late-night work. It looked good, really good. It wouldn't need much, possibly only one coat of shellac would revitalize the wood. His fingers pressed against the wood, the wood sticky to touch. Not wet, but not fully dry, either. He'd set a heater up in the area to hurry along the process.

He could do more. This quick touch-up would bring the desk back to life. But he saw little signs of further wear and tear, and wanted to take it all apart, fix it piece by piece, before putting it back together. No time for that now, but perhaps he'd mention it to Andie. If she liked his work, maybe she'd let him play more.

And yet, the extra challenge, the chance to do more work on this desk, to make it worthy of the woman it belonged to, gave him a surge that made him forget about his lack of sleep. He'd leave it up to her and use this energy to make even this small fix-up the best possible.

"I knew I'd find you here."

Leo jumped at Dean's voice. "You scared me, you need to stop doing that."

Dean crossed his arms. "And you were supposed to go home, get refreshed, and come back here."

"I'm back here."

Dean gave him a look and then took a pivot. "I dropped the rug off with our cleaner."

Leo studied his brother's face, but all he found was a carefully constructed nonchalance. "And?"

The nonchalance faded. "It's going to get a good clean, but she doesn't think it's as good as I hoped."

"It'll still catch us something."

"Oh, for sure, we'll still turn a profit. I would have liked an extra set of zeroes in the equation."

Leo nodded; on this they were on the same page. He picked up his coffee, taking a sip.

"Hey, where's my coffee?"

Leo pressed his palm on the sturdy work bench. "I got two hours of sleep with my cheek pressed into wood and you expect me to remember coffee for you?"

Dean tsked. "Grouchy. Can't have you helping customers today. Best you stay back here before your scruff game upstages mine."

Leo rubbed his chin. "I'm not grouchy."

"He says grouchily." Dean crossed the room and placed a hand on Leo's shoulder. "I'm telling you to work on Andie's desk. I've got the front."

If Leo's brain was doing more than banging stones together, he would have figured that out. "It still needs to dry."

Dean raised his eyebrows. "All of it? I know you; you've got more tinkering to do."

No, not all of it, he had work he could do, shellac to get started on. Dean gave him the option to stay back here for a day and work on something not related to the future of Dentz Antiques. And he could trust Dean. More than he realized.

"I'm sorry if I've underestimated you."

Dean blinked at him and he saw the twelve-year-old under the stubble and bags under his eyes. Dean wasn't a kid anymore, none of them were.

"Where did that come from?" Dean finally asked.

Leo gestured to the grandfather clock, then around the space, where some memories hung around like ghosts.

"You hear those plates like an annoying echo?"

Leo quirked a smile. "All the damn time. My tinnitus loves it."

"I bet."

They'd been through a lot, but they'd been through it together. Leo felt the weight of it on his shoulders. But Dean had grown up and his shoulders were strong enough to carry half of the load.

"There's no one I'd rather be my partner in this business."

Dean turned to him. "Really?" Stubble or not, his face morphed into a bit of childhood innocence. Regardless of age, the man was capable and, like Leo, had done his best to prove his worth time and time again.

"Yes. Really."

Dean shuffled a foot against the concrete floor. "There's a small antiques store twenty minutes from here. Hasn't been around long, doesn't have the best supplies. They're closing down, selling. It wouldn't be much of a leg up in the world, but it could be a start."

Leo mulled that one over. He'd been so focused on keeping Dentz Antiques he hadn't truly explored his other options. But he wasn't the only Dentz in this game. "We still have our name and our years here, regardless of Dad."

Dean nodded. "And we learned from the best."

"Gramps." Leo chuckled. Then scrubbed a hand over his face. "Let's get through the holidays, then you and I will talk."

"Deal. Now focus on Andie's desk."

He'd been so focused on his plan A, he hadn't realized that his brother worked on a plan B. They really were a good team. "Thank you."

Dean nodded, heading away. "Next time remember my coffee."

Leo chuckled and took a large gulp of his caffeine before getting back to work.

CHAPTER THIRTEEN

Cars had been backed up for miles. On a normal day, Andie tried to avoid traffic like the plague. To have this delay be something people willingly ventured into just to see Christmas lights had her a bit perplexed. Sure, she'd enjoy a few she saw along her journeys, when she wasn't feeling Grinchy and left out of the holiday celebrations. The suburban area had its fair share of lights, but Leo assured her this wasn't the main attraction.

Up ahead, through a tree bending with the wind, the sky lit up as though they approached the city. "That's a lot of light," Andie said.

Leo chuckled. "Just you wait."

"All I can think is, if that's not a city, then the electric bills must be through the roof."

Leo laughed harder, the sound mixing with the wind whistling against the windows. "Astronomical. Jodie's threatened divorce over it a time or twenty."

Andie turned away from the lit sky and red brake lights ahead of them. The light cast a glow over Leo, one that created the type of ambience she'd want to snuggle closer in. "So the lights aren't her idea?"

"They are David's baby. And he's extremely proud of them. Then Millie was born and became enamored with not only the lights but also the representation of her holiday and Jodie's grumblings grew less forceful."

"Millie must think this is normal."

Leo flicked on his blinker, like all the cars ahead of them. A chorus of red turn signals mixing in with all the house and yard lights. "She complains about the lack of decorations the rest of the family has. And considers the explanations flimsy excuses."

Andie continued to be charmed by Millie and with Leo's relationship with her. "She's got spunk. I like it."

"She's a handful. She's going to change the world. But not before aging her poor parents."

"The best kids do."

Leo turned onto the street, and red and green lights exploded into view. This first house had alternating lights lining every angle of the roof, windows, doors, and arches of the home's exterior. The lights continued down, lining the front pathway.

"Wow," Andie said. "That's impressive."

Leo held up a finger. "Wait. This is called trying to keep up with the Joneses and not quite succeeding."

Andie gawked at Leo, and the sexy curve to his lips.

"You're missing the view." He turned to her, locking eyes, and in the midst of Christmas wonderlands and slow-moving traffic, Andie wanted to lean in and kiss the amusement off his face.

He broke eye contact and she forced her gaze to the street. The cars had slowed to almost a crawl, people parking where they could and walking. The next house had decorations in white lights and more blowups in the yard than Andie had ever seen: Two Santas—one in a sleigh with reindeer—three snowmen on the snowless grass, a tall gingerbread man, two Christmas trees, and a North pole. The blowups danced in the wind, adding charm to the display, even if the chance of ending up on a neighbor's lawn was highly probable.

"I didn't even know that many blowups existed!"

Leo barked out in laughter, startling her from the view.

"Hey, what?"

He held up his hands. "Sorry, sorry. Just wait. Each house attempts to top the other." Hands back on the wheel, he glanced at her. "I'm enjoying your commentary. I said some of the same things the first time Jodie dragged me here."

"Was the wind adding to the ambience then?"

"Not like this." The car rocked from another gust, but Andie had grown used to it throughout the day.

They passed a house with a yard filled with candy canes, making a maze on the front lawn. Several kids raced through the maze, with parents standing off to the side. Another house had a tropical theme, which included blowup pine trees and Christmas fish. Andie had never seen Christmas fish before and could hardly believe they existed, but there they were, flapping in the breeze. Another had more Disney Christmas items than Andie saw on her December Disney World trip as a kid. She had to admit, each house had its own outrageous character and charm, topping the one before or after it in its own special way.

Leo rolled down his window and the sounds of *Jingle Bell Rock* floated in, syncing with the lights on one rock 'n' roll–themed house with a large tree in the yard that had a cord and not roots. Luminescent beams danced in tune with the music, and Andie found herself bopping along, beyond enchanted and wishing she could bring her students along.

"This really is something, huh?" Andie asked, sure a note of wonderment was in her voice.

Leo didn't answer. She wanted to shake her head, of course her voice would be too soft with all the sounds. She touched his shoulder and repeated herself when he looked her way.

"Yup. I couldn't believe Jodie and David wanted to move here, but apparently David had plans even before the first December."

Andie tried to think of what he could possibly do to make Chanukah match. Sure, there were options here and there, but at its root Chanukah was a minor, unimportant holiday; meanwhile, Christmas held religious and celebratory weight. "How does he mesh with all of this?" Andie waved a hand, at both sides of the over-the-top street that probably starred in a movie or two about feuding neighbor lights.

"You'll see."

Leo turned on his blinker again and Andie looked ahead, where blue and white became the dominant attraction, the blue gleaming brighter than all the red and green from the other homes. Leo waited until walkers and cars passed before he pulled into the driveway, and Andie turned in her seat, the seat belt struggling to hold her still. The front walkway had a blue and white arch, welcoming visitors into the Chanukah Wonderland. The invitation worked, as several walkers ambled inside to see more. Blue and white lights covered the house, the walkway, the trees, anything it could find. A large dreidel spun next to an oversized polar bear in a blue sweater holding a dreidel. More dreidels lined the pathways, three large menorahs stood tall and proud—one blowup, two not. Animals dressed in blue and wearing yarmulkes chilled on the lawn. Leo exited the car, and Andie followed, Chanukah music playing in the air, the blue and white flashing in time to the music.

Andie's jaw dropped open in awe. She swept her gaze back and forth, catching some new delight each time, completely enamored. "This is amazing!"

"My brother-in-law aims to please." Leo stepped up beside her, yelling over the music. He held out a gloved hand. "Shall we?"

Andie put her own covered hand in his. The wind picked up, blowing her hair and scarf, but she hardly felt the cold. Together, they slowly walked around, taking in the view. The setup had larger-than-life gelt and presents, and the music changed from one Chanukah song to another, in both English and Hebrew. Andie had never felt more represented than she did in that moment. She wanted to bottle it up and send it to her younger self when she felt left out during December.

Andie rose up on her toes, angled toward to Leo, hoping he could hear. "I wish I had something like this to see as a kid. I wouldn't have felt as lonely."

Leo pulled Andie into a side hug and she stayed there, in his warmth and the blue lights, until the front door opened.

"Uncle Leo!"

They broke apart as Millie raced toward them, not wearing a jacket, and flung herself at her uncle.

Leo let out an "oof" but managed to catch her.

"You made it!"

"Of course we did. Andie deserved to see this."

"It's the best house on the whole block!" Millie leaned back, smiling at her father's hard work, the wind whipping her hair around.

The door opened again, and a woman a few years older with a strong resemblance to Leo came out. She wore an open coat and carried a pink one. "Millie Jane Bernstein."

"Uh-oh." Millie slid out of Leo's arms. "Sorry, Mom."

The woman came over, holding open the jacket, and Millie slipped inside. "It's much too cold and windy to come out here without a coat on." Her gaze tracked to Andie. "Hi, I'm Jodie, this one's mom and that one's sister. I've heard a lot about you." She held out her hand.

"Jodie," Leo muttered.

Andie reached out her gloved hand and shook Jodie's ungloved one. "Nice to meet you. This is quite the display."

Jodie leaned back toward the house. "David! Leo's new girlfriend likes your display."

Andie felt her cheeks burn, even in the cold wind. Beside her Leo shuffled his feet.

Jodie smirked. "Sorry, it's what big sisters do." She flung an arm around her brother.

The music began another loop.

Leo ducked out of his sister's grasp. "I'm going to take Andie on a walk to show her the rest of the houses."

"You're coming back though, right?" Millie glanced up, batting her eyelashes. "Dad's going to make his famous hot chocolate."

Leo turned to Andie. "The only thing more impressive than the decorations is his hot chocolate, you don't want to miss it."

A gust of wind burst through, ruffling jackets and pushing around the inflatables and lights. Andie shivered. "I suspect hot chocolate will be a nice warm-up after the walk."

They waved and Leo took Andie's hand as they walked to the next house. Couples and families did the same, and they ended up in a slow stroll between two parties. Fathers pushed strollers, mothers carried small children. People laughed with the familiarity of family; by blood or choice. It made her think of Leo with his niece, and now with his sister. Love existed there. All Andie ever got from her extended family were unpleasant looks, or a half-hearted pat on the back at her father's funeral. Leo's family truly cared for each other. What Andie wouldn't give to have the warmth of family to visit, and that had nothing to do with shivering a bit in the cold night air.

"You have a nice relationship with your sister and her family." She wanted to know more about what it was like, the unconditional love from many people.

A blowup Santa ho-ho-hoed from amidst a pile of wrapped gifts.

"She's a pest and a thorn in my side, but we're family."

Family. Spoken like anyone would know what that meant, the love and annoyance of a sibling. Andie tugged her coat closer around her, not in defiance to the wind. "I always wanted a larger family and siblings." Leo had been helping ease the loneliness of this time of year, but seeing his happy family cut through the fog.

"I'd say I wished for the opposite, but that would undermine your pain." He stopped beneath a tree covered in white blinking lights. "Come here." He reached out and pulled her in, sharing his warmth with her.

"You don't have to—"

He put a gloved finger against her lips. "I know. I want to. Besides, I can hear you better this way." He glanced up, the wind blowing his hair around. "I'd love to say something grand like you can share mine, but I know that's foolish for what we are. All I can say is that you are welcome here, with me and mine, at any time. And someday some family will be very lucky to include you in their fold."

Andie often worried that would never happen, but standing there, in the midst of lights and music and people and cars, looking at how Leo's brown eyes sparkled like the tree behind him, and Andie knew, down to her core, that he somehow spoke the truth, her truth.

"Thank you." She rose on her toes, pressing her cold lips to his equally cold ones. They warmed with the contact, the chill and wind momentarily forgotten in the embrace.

Leo pulled back. "Come on, let's continue our journey and then defrost with hot cocoa. Maybe I can even get David to light a fire."

Andie shivered as she lost Leo's warmth. "A fire sounds delightful."

* * *

An hour later they all sat by the fire, warm cups of hot chocolate topped with toasted marshmallows. Leo tucked a still-shivering Andie into his side, kicking himself for not returning sooner.

"This is really good hot chocolate. I'm impressed," Andie said. Leo resisted the urge to lick the marshmallow off her lip, and nearly groaned when her tongue snaked out to catch it.

"Told ya," Millie said. She sported a marshmallow mustache and didn't seem to care.

"David, relax. If the wind topples anything over it's going to topple it and countless other items along the street," Jodie said.

The entire room turned to where David stood, holding back the curtain, staring out into the night while his own cup of hot chocolate waited by the fire.

"I don't need a dreidel to end up in a creche and be mistaken for a baby Jesus."

"Daddy, no one will ever think that a dreidel is Jesus."

David sighed and let the curtain fall back into place, joining the family and setting himself up on the ottoman closest to the fire.

"I have never seen a display like yours, David." Andie placed her mug on the coffee table, then snuggled back into the love seat she shared with Leo. He wrapped his outstretched hand around her shoulder, cuddling her further into his side. "To be fair, I've never much checked out Christmas lights on purpose, so this entire evening was something new."

She turned to Leo, eyes filled with something. He swallowed. Her expression made her words take on a heavier weight, as though she'd cherish this night and experience for years to come. And it hit him just like every other time, he didn't want to be a memory, or a footnote, he wanted to experience these moments with her again and again.

Too many thoughts, too many feelings, and only his failure to act quick enough to blame.

"All right, Millie, it's bedtime, time to say good night," Jodie said.

Millie glanced back and forth between all the people in the room so fast her hair swirled around her. "Awww, Mom! Uncle Leo and Andie are still here!"

Leo saw his opening and knew his sister would thank him. "We'll be leaving soon," Leo said. "And you'll see me tomorrow at Grandma and Grandpa's to celebrate Chanukah with our family."

"And Andie?" Millie batted her eyelashes, all pure innocence that wasn't innocent at all. "Will your girlfriend be joining us?"

Andie sputtered over a sip of her cocoa and Leo rubbed her back. While he'd love to bring Andie and introduce her to the rest of the family, he knew even her being here had "premature" written all over it.

"I don't think Grandma would appreciate an unexpected guest."

Millie rocked on her feet. "Andie isn't unexpected. I told Grandma."

Leo barely held in a groan. Andie glanced at him, and if he read her right, part amusement and part fear lit her gaze. The amusement got to him, as though this thought he deemed outlandish might hold potential. As though Andie's mentions of wanting more family life might actually be soothed—he hoped—by seeing his in action.

"I'll have to discuss this with Andie."

"I can wait."

He shot a look at his sister and brother-in-law, but they both avoided eye contact. He'd remember this. He faced Andie with something akin to hope filling his lungs. "If you don't have plans, would you like to come to the Dentz family Chanukah gathering, where my mother is apparently expecting you, at no notice."

The range of potential reactions were enormous, and they mounted in his head as he waited for Andie's response, no longer able to even guess her expression.

"Please, Andie! Uncle Leo's never even brought a date and Uncle Dean has!"

Leo closed his eyes, dropped his head, and wished for death. Hope dashed in a flame.

A hand on his knee had him cracking a lid, finding Andie smiling at him. "I guess I better say yes then. I wouldn't want to disappoint the family."

"Yay!" Millie ran over, flung her arms around both Leo and Andie, before racing off up the stairs to get ready for bed.

"You don't have to be roped into this," Leo said softly to Andie.

She sipped her hot chocolate. "I know. I'd like to see what the rest of your family is like. And help you finally bring a girlfriend to the holidays."

A half chuckle, half groan worked its way up Leo's throat.

"Don't complain, that kid has your back," Jodie said.

"She also is a puppeteer and gets her way."

"Blame Jodie for that." David poked the fire.

"I am raising a strong, ball-busting woman who will one day rule whatever business she gets into."

"Right."

Leo shifted to the end of the love seat. "You two can have this fight after we're gone."

Jodie waved a hand. "We've had this fight many times, we'll have it many more. It's called 'marriage.'" Jodie smiled at David, though, and he smiled back.

I want that, Leo thought. And he'd thought it for years. David had stepped into Jodie's life and supported her and loved her. They clashed and bickered and always came back together. Jodie knew David would always have her back and she'd always have his.

Leo had been too focused on work, thinking he'd have time for that later. And now, with the deadline nearly down to the wire and no answer, and with Andie moving far away, he could be starting out the new year with truly nothing.

But not yet. He still had more time with the woman beside him. And he'd do his best to enjoy it.

CHAPTER FOURTEEN

"Am I partially blinded by David's street, or are there really no lights on in this area?" Andie checked out the houses on both sides of the car, finding one dark abode after the other. The night sky blended into the buildings and trees. No Christmas lights, no lights spilling out from windows, only the headlights and faint glow of the moon.

Leo pointed ahead. "Considering that traffic light is out, I don't think it's just the effects of David's street."

Andie focused on the hanging traffic light, swaying in the wind, illuminated only by headlights bouncing off the metal. "I guess the high wind warning wasn't kidding." The headlights picked up some fallen branches.

"Hopefully it's localized and not widespread."

"One can only hope. I think David will cry if the power goes out."

Leo chuckled, she checked on his profile, illuminated by the dash. "You catch on quickly. He'll cry more about any damage to his inflatables than about a random power outage, assuming that it doesn't cause any power issues when it comes back on."

"And what makes you cry, Leo Dentz?" Andie shifted in her seat, more focused on her companion than whether any of the homes had power.

He sent her a look that she couldn't place, but somehow, and she didn't comprehend the why, it made her toes curl. "Damaged antiques."

"But you fix antiques."

"Damaged antiques that I've already fixed."

"Is that a hint to be careful with my desk when you've finished with it?"

He straightened in his seat. "That desk is going to be solid. You won't be able to damage it." She'd hit a nerve, and his pride, and why did that just endear her to him more?

"I think a hacksaw would beg to differ."

Leo turned on his blinker, a slight shake to his head. "I'd be worried if I didn't already know how much it meant to you. You won't damage it, at least not on purpose."

Truth. The desk held a special place in her heart, a way to keep her mother's memory alive. She'd cherish it for as long as she could.

"Hey, lights are on."

Andie snapped to, taking in the lit street and glow of holiday and inside lights adding to the night. "On our street, as well. That's fortunate."

"Fortune, or foreboding?" Leo's voice dipped low as he parked in the back of their building. He turned to her, arm against her backrest, leaning in.

"Are we turning this into a holiday horror story now?"

Leo's face blanched. "What? No. I . . ." he dropped his head. "I was trying to set the mood, and not in that way."

"No attackers lurking in the dark, ready to cut the power and blame it on the wind?"

Leo pulled back.

Andie laughed. "Sorry. I'm not all crayons and fingerpaint and ABCs."

"I guess not." He turned off the car. "Better that way."

They exited the car and headed up to the building, the wind making itself known and flicking hair, jackets, trash—anything it could find—about.

"This wind got worse since we left," Andie said. They hurried ahead, Leo holding the door open for her, stepping into the warm lobby.

Both shook off the cold.

"That was event—"

Leo's words cut off along with their power. The lobby plunged into darkness, the steady hum of the heater and the elevator halting. With her vision cut off, Andie's throat constricted, and the first beads of worry rose to the surface. Needing something, or rather someone, to latch onto, she reached out and clutched Leo's arm, amazed she found it on her first try.

"Hang on," he said, fumbling with something, and then his phone cast a glow in the darkness.

Andie breathed easier seeing their shoes and the floor. "I'm sorry I joked about attackers in the dark." Really sorry, now that her anxiety ran rampant and her skin prickled with the unknown of what surrounded her.

Leo pulled her in, holding her close. "Come on, maybe it's temporary and it'll turn on by the time we get upstairs."

She could only hope. They passed the elevator, heading to the stairwell, following the light of Leo's phone up the four flights. Andie kept one hand on the wall as they climbed through the dark space. "Shouldn't there be emergency lights?" Andie asked.

No answer came from behind her.

Andie stopped and turned.

Leo shined the light toward her face. "Did I miss something?"

Andie pointed. "Shouldn't there be emergency lights?"

Leo angled the phone up, to the dormant security light on the wall. "Should have been."

"This has all the makings of a horror movie," Andie grumbled.

At their floor, they exited into the even darker hall. Andie shivered. It wasn't cold, not yet at least, but the dark made the night feel eerie. As though anything could jump out from any corner. Not a thought she'd ever had in their building. She tried to control her breathing, tried to remind herself that the only difference was the power. The thought brought no comfort.

"You okay?" Leo shined the light so he could see her face.

Andie shielded her eyes from the glare and tried to smile. "Yes." She never really liked it when the power went out, not alone at least. During the last power outage she'd gone and spent the night with her father, it didn't matter if he had electricity or not. "I had been thinking of asking you in, but under the circumstances it's grown more than a simple thought." She grimaced. "I'm not exactly a fan of power outages."

Leo pulled her lapel close. "Whatever you need, Andie. I'm here."

She breathed him in, nearly chest to chest. And even though the glow of light made it very obvious the power was out; Andie no longer felt the effects of the wind or the dark. She knew how he tasted now, knew it would make her dislike of outages somehow less. "I need you to kiss me."

"You never had to ask." He crushed his mouth to hers, the light shining away as something crashed to the floor. Probably his phone. Definitely his phone. She didn't need light, not at the moment. She wrapped her arms around his neck as his hands banded her waist to his. They lived inside their own little bubble, blocked off from the rest of the world, and exactly what they each needed.

Well, at the very least what she needed, and judging by the complete commitment from her partner, she held confidence in it being mutual.

She pulled back and he groaned. "I need my keys, we're still in the hall."

Leo's phone had landed with the light shining up, showing off his long eyelashes as he blinked. Andie watched as realization slammed back into him. "I, uh, forgot."

That made him adorable. And sexy. Sex-dorable? No, that's bad, she'd have to check with Sarah for better opinions if she remembered.

Andie quickly unlocked her door, opening it wide for Leo to follow her inside. Her shades let in a sliver of the moon's glow. Without any other ambience it felt cold, rather than sexy. Leo caressed her arm but Andie held up a finger. "Give me a moment."

She took out her phone, accessing her flashlight app, and moved about collecting candles that were not meant for her menorah. She had a thing for candles and easily found tubs of various sizes, and fragrances, and placed as many into her arms as she could manage. Now was the time for light, not deciding which smells would go well together. She snatched her candle lighter and then froze. Where to set up? Was her bedroom too forward? Would they even get to her bedroom? Should she want it to be that obvious?

"Need any help?"

Leo's voice broke her from her overthinking. Living room. Candles could be moved. With her arms nearly overflowing, and her phone trapped under her chin, she turned to Leo. Without a word needed, he came to her and took her phone and most of the candles.

"Quite the selection you've got there."

"I like candles." And they came in extra handy at times like this. She set up two in her kitchen and lit them. "And not just around Chanukah."

Leo held one up, studying the name. "Vanilla cupcake, nice."

Andie took it from him, setting it on her coffee table. "I like things sweet." She glanced over her shoulder. "Like you."

Heat from the flame soothed her cheek and Leo stepped closer, bringing more warmth to the cold, powerless night. "I can be not sweet."

Her belly clenched.

He cringed. "Sorry, that sounded wrong."

Andie laughed. "See, sweet." She set down the items in her hand and rose to his height. "And I liked what you said." She kissed him then, in the glow of fewer candles than anticipated, meshing her body to his. They both still wore their coats, and she had the sudden urge to get the coats and much more off, now.

But it was too soon and still far too cold. Instead, she pulled back and resumed lighting candles.

"You're an amazing woman, Andie."

She tossed her hair over her shoulder to look at him. "Why is that?"

The glow of the flames danced across his face, illuminating a look of wonder and affection. "I just like everything about you."

It made the moment feel different than it should, more meaningful than neighbors taking comfort during a Chanukah power outage. A charge of electricity between them, strong enough it should have turned the power back on. And Andie didn't care. Because she liked him, too—the only thought that truly mattered.

She lit two more candles, then joined Leo where he stood. He'd removed his coat, and she tossed hers on a chair. "I like you, too."

He pulled her to him, claimed her lips, and she kissed him back, savoring his taste, the subtle sting of his late-day shadow, along with the candle smell in the air.

If anyone ever asked her for a perfect night and a perfect first time, she'd think of this night, whether it got there or not, power outage and all.

His hands rested on her hips, lightly gripping the fabric of her shirt. Tame, innocent, but hinting at restrained tension.

Andie licked at the seam of his lips, and he let her in, tangling tongues. He tasted of cocoa, yet he was the one groaning, tightening his grip, pulling her flush against him. She wiggled against his hardness, insides clenching as anticipation ratcheted up several notches.

157

Leo pulled back. He pressed his forehead to hers, breathing heavily. "I need you to be very clear about why you invited me in. Use small words if possible, I'm not sure I'm thinking straight."

Definitely sex-dorable. She placed her hands on his cheeks, holding his head to keep his eyes locked on hers. "I want you to spend the night. In my bed. With me."

"Good, because that's all I can think of."

He crushed his mouth to hers, showing her some of what he'd held in. It created a tug straight through her, made her want more than she could remember wanting from anyone else. His hands slid from her waist to her rear and he squeezed, nearly setting off a tiny rocket through her.

This time, she broke the kiss. "Couch or should we move the candles to the bedroom?"

"I'm not going to notice a damn thing except you."

There went another tiny rocket. She could become spoiled by this man. He'd taken her bar and threatened to set it higher than it had been before. It might create problems for the next guy, but she'd deal with that later. His kisses and words and touch were too good to miss and she fell back into him, wanting to kiss him all night.

No, scratch that. Only part of the night.

His hands slipped under her shirt, just barely. Goosebumps erupted, the good kind, and she pressed her chest into him, trying to relieve the pressure, desperate for his attention. But Leo stuck to his pace.

Andie tried to follow it, but she'd gotten promises of things to come, and she wanted to explore it all. "Is there a problem?" she asked.

"I don't want you to be cold."

Oh, oh. This man. What was she going to do with him? "I'm so turned on I don't think I feel temperature."

His lips curved into a sinful grin. She nearly licked him. "In that case . . ." He reached forward and collected the bottom of her shirt.

Even with all the go-ahead she'd given him, the man paused, not moving forward until she gave him a single head nod. Then he managed to pull her shirt up and off without leaving her tangled.

At the sight of her lace bra, his Adam's apple gave a big jump.

"My turn."

Andie slipped his buttons from their holes, revealing a lightly muscled chest with a smattering of chest hair. Leo's shirt soon fell to the floor. They reached for each other, pressing skin against skin, both losing the cool, smooth vibe of earlier. One of Leo's hands slid up her side, and around, until he brushed against her pebbled nipple.

The next time the power went out she was definitely remembering this, and the feel of his hand against her. The dark night had suddenly become her favorite thing. She nipped at his lip, showing her appreciation. His groan snaked through her and then she meshed her mouth to his, their hands exploring, and if the wind made any noise outside, Andie didn't notice. She pulled him to the couch and he covered her body, pressing into her, creating their own personal self-heated cocoon. How could he have thought she'd be cold? Not with them together.

Though tangled on the couch, they somehow managed to remove more clothes, lips barely stationary. There was skin to explore and taste, pleasure to be shared and had. A moment pure and sexy, a union of two souls.

By the time Leo grabbed a condom and slid inside, Andie was practically panting his name. The first push was magic, the second divine, and then it was only the rollercoaster of pleasure, the climb to the peak, the drop, the climb again, until they both lay sweaty and sated in each other's arms.

"I don't know about you, but this is the best power outage ever," Leo said into the crook of her neck.

Andie laughed and held him closer. "Happy Chanukah, Leo."

He lifted his head, kissed her forehead. "Wrong types of candles."

She chuckled again. "You got something better?"

He shifted off her, until they lay side by side facing each other. "Thank you for giving me a second chance."

She brushed at a lock of his hair. "Thank you for proving I should."

He kissed her then, soft and sweet in contrast to before, and somehow making her yearn for more.

CHAPTER FIFTEEN

Leo woke to light filtering into Andie's bedroom. Hope that the electricity was back on had him going from sleepy to alert, only to realize the sun created the glow. The electricity status was still unknown. A slight smell of candles lingered in the air from where they burned and were blown out prior to sleep. The temperature was also a question, as the warm body curled up next to him was all the heat he needed.

Andie slept with her head on his shoulder, her hair tickling his neck. One of his hands was trapped under her and tingly, but he didn't care, not with her soft breath against his neck. The sunlight danced across her face, accentuating the curve to her cheeks and the few freckles on her nose. Her beauty tugged at him, deep in his chest. The more he got to know her, the more he liked this special woman who'd agreed to brighten his Chanukah.

The tingling in his hand increased and as much as he didn't want to move from this position, ever, he knew he should. Leo lifted his head, taking in the area, and the clock on the nightstand behind Andie, dark.

For all he knew it hadn't worked before the outage. He continued to look around, not finding any signs of electricity. How many hours had it been out? The present time unknown, the sun his only clue, and he'd never learned how to easily tell time that way.

At least it was Saturday, and he already knew neither of them had to work.

Leo used his non-numb hand to nudge Andie's smooth shoulder. "Andie, I think the power's still out."

Andie groaned and burrowed her head into Leo's shoulder. She shifted enough that he was able to stretch out his numb hand. Instead of returning blood flow, he clutched her naked waist. What he would give to wake up every morning like this.

"Andie. We need check on the power."

She lifted her head, blinking awake. He waited for regret over the night they'd shared to cross her face. All he got was a slow, sleepy smile, and he barely resisted kissing her silly. She spoke, but he didn't have his hearing aids on and only a soft mumble of noise made it to his ears.

He shook his head and leaned in close, angling one ear closer to her. "Repeat that."

"Morning. Power?"

Leo pointed behind her. "Your clock is dark, is that normal?"

Andie turned to the clock, then sighed and lowered her head, snuggling in. Another mumble of noise vibrated against his chest.

"Still can't hear you."

She lifted her head, eyes more alert. "Sorry. Not normal."

"So we're still in the dark." Which meant he couldn't charge his hearing aids. He had some power left in them, but he'd never had to test it out in this situation before and didn't know how long that would last. Between that thought and his hand still lacking blood flow, he found it hard to relax and fully appreciate the moment.

Andie didn't move. Leo hated the thought of losing the warm and cozy feeling, but the bad kind of tingles deepened. He shifted his hand but couldn't get full blood flow achieved.

"Problem?" she asked and he somehow managed to hear her.

"I've got about two drops of blood left in my hand."

"Oh!" Andie scrambled up, freeing his hand, not seeming to mind that she gave him the best view. Leo moved his hand in front of him, using his other to wake it up. "That bad?"

He wasn't sure how his hand wasn't limp. "Not too bad."

Andie chuckled. "Liar." She took his hand, massaging it in hers. She sat next to him, blankets fallen off, and raised his hand to her lips. "Feel this?"

He saw it more than felt it, only a light flutter of her lips, which had to be the saddest thing he'd ever experienced. "Not really, but it looks good."

Andie glanced down at herself. "I bet." She took one of his fingers and sucked it into her mouth.

Leo groaned. "My hand is still numb, but the rest of me isn't."

Andie's smile was part sin, and if Leo could bottle this moment he'd never leave. She straddled his waist, running his hand down her neck, over the swell of her breast, before cupping it around her. "How about that?"

"I can't tell where the tingly is from. Come here." He sat up, claiming her mouth, collecting her other breast in his non-tingly hand. Andie rubbed against him, arms around his neck. "This has to be the best Chanukah morning ever."

Andie chuckled and pulled back, but not enough to remove his hands. "Do we need to figure out the time?"

"The power is out, we'll figure it out later."

"In that case." Andie reached over, grabbing the box of condoms they'd opened the night before. She sheathed him, then resumed her position, this time taking him deep inside.

"I will never have a better Chanukah than this," Leo groaned.

Andie kissed his neck, rubbing against him. "It certainly has a very adult flair. Maybe we should have tried strip dreidels after all."

At least, he thought that was what she said, he couldn't focus. Leo grasped her hips. "Later." He thrust up into her until her head fell back, until the tingles traveled to his toes instead of his hands, until she cried out in pleasure.

Andie's head went to his shoulder, body still shifting against his. And once again mumbled.

"I haven't got my hearing aids on; you need to stop talking into my chest."

She angled to face him. "I don't mean to forget."

He nearly laughed. "Most people do."

She frowned. He leaned down and kissed her. "It's okay."

"No, it's not fair."

He let that go. "What did you say?"

"Oh. I claimed you made the power outage happen on purpose, didn't you?"

Leo ran a hand down her back. "I'm nowhere near that smooth or plotting. And we've already established the menorah isn't magic."

Andie raised her head, laughter dancing in her eyes. "So you did wish for this?"

"I didn't, but if I did, I would simply have wished for you." Too much, he revealed too much, but her lips were curved as she kissed him. She began moving, a slow and steady rhythm he never wanted to leave. He met her pace, building her up, setting her off again before he followed.

They curled up together, breathing heavily, and Leo knew in that moment he could love her. If only the universe didn't have plans against them.

Andie reached one hand out of the blanket, running a finger over the curve of his ear. "Tell me if I'm not loud enough. How long have you worn hearing aids?"

"I can't tell you if you're loud enough if I can't hear you."

She waited him out, staring up at him with those brown eyes.

"Twelve years." He swallowed. "I was sixteen."

He watched her face, waited to see if recognition would kick in. It didn't take long. "Wait, wasn't that when you had an issue with your father and the business?"

"I got sick a month later, but yeah." Sixteen had been a very bad year for him. First, he missed the party, then he had the incident at the store with Dean. Then sick enough to miss school, to battle fever after fever and the ear infections that wouldn't quit. To the world not being loud enough anymore and having to accept a new reality with a disability.

Andie placed a hand over his heart. "I'm sorry, that must have been rough."

He shrugged. Not wanting to get into it. "It's who I am." It had taken time, and he'd gone through a lot of anger, but if he'd been that sick and only lost some of his hearing, then he had a lot to still be grateful for.

"Okay, what time is it?" Andie separated them and reached for her phone. "Five percent battery and nine a.m. I need to see if my power bank is charged." She snuggled back to him.

"You don't seem at all concerned about the power."

"It's out. We can't do anything until it comes back on. I do my best not to sweat the small stuff."

He could learn a thing or two from her. "You are wise beyond your years."

Andie laughed. "I'm also too refreshed to care. I never sleep in this late, teacher's curse. Thank you."

"Nah, the power outage messed you up." Yet he wrapped a hand around her. His fingers went back to tingling, but he didn't care.

She kissed his shoulder. "You don't give yourself enough credit, do you?"

He let the question hang in the air, sensing a strong amount of truth in her words. He'd been denied credit time and time again with his father, all due to one major mistake. Perhaps that affected him in more ways than he thought.

He'd deal with that later. "Are you still going to want to come to the party, even with the power out?"

"Do I want to stay here where it's cold outside of the blankets or do I want to go someplace warm with food. Hmm . . ."

Leo really could fall for this woman. "My mom tends to serve a late lunch and wants people over beforehand."

"So we need to move?"

"I'm afraid so."

"I'm meeting your family without a shower?"

She was beautiful with or without a shower, but he wasn't about to mention that. "Who do we know that might have power? I can check with Jodie." Even an hour to charge his aids would hopefully allow him to make it through the day.

Andie shifted off Leo. "Let me find my charger. It just so happens I have a friend who very rarely loses power."

* * *

Twenty minutes later, Andie sat near the coffee shop window, while Leo got their food. She'd thrown her hair back into a ponytail, and felt an odd combination of satisfied and frumpy. At least Sarah had power, she'd be able to wash off the frumpy. The satisfied might be a different story.

"One egg sandwich and coffee with cream, no sugar." Leo placed the bag and cup in front of Andie, before putting down his own items for himself. He'd powered up his hearing aids and put them on, explaining that while they didn't have full power, they would do until he could charge them.

"And did I hear you ordering a sugary latte?" Andie leaned forward, amused for some odd reason, but not surprised.

Leo lifted his mug and took a sip. "Yup."

"Sweet tooth."

He grinned at her, one filled with heat. "Extremely."

Andie reveled in the warmth of the establishment, of the cup in her hands, and of the man sitting across from her. Somehow her Chanukah had gone from hard to celebrate to one she would never forget.

"Are we going to be late?" She took a bite of her food.

Leo unwrapped his own sandwich. "Nah, we'll be fine. Mom isn't rigid on time, and I already explained about the outage." He took a bite. "She offered her shower, just so you know."

Andie paused and had to force herself to swallow. "To someone she didn't even know about until Millie said something?"

Leo remained very focused on his sandwich. Chatter from other coffee shop patrons hit her ears, along with the whir of machinery.

"Leo?"

He sighed and looked up at her. "I might have mentioned my neighbor once or twice before."

Andie studied Leo. Her friendly hot neighbor, who'd always flirted but didn't take it further until now. The way his cheeks pinked easily. Her new friend was shy. And she'd bet he'd thought about their potential for as long as she had.

"Well, I'm glad they feel comfortable with my joining their celebration."

"Andie, you don't—"

She cut him off. "I know I don't have to come. I want to. And I don't want to disappoint Millie or anyone else." And maybe some not-too-small part of her wanted to be enveloped into a close-knit family gathering, to see how the other kind lived and loved and laughed.

He reached a hand out, covering hers. "Thank you. They can be annoying, though."

"Aren't all Jewish families?" She didn't understand how some people made annoying little traits a reason to stay away. She'd take her father's open-mouthed chewing, or overly cautious behavior, any day to have him back. And she didn't let those moments bother her when he was alive, she simply let those annoyances add to the love.

Leo nodded. "You've got me there." He took a bite, chewed. He took his family for granted, as most did. "So tell me about your friend."

"Sarah? She's a fellow teacher at my school."

He paused, then swallowed. "So she's also looking for a new job?"

"Correct."

"Is she moving away, too?"

Andie leaned back into her chair. "She hasn't found anything yet."

"That sucks."

More than he knew. Sarah was a fantastic teacher and belonged in the classroom. "It does. We met in college, and you can thank her for the strip dreidel idea."

He'd been about to take a bite, but instead he put his sandwich down, elbows on the table, leaning forward. The table shifted in his direction. His eyes lit with a challenge and it reignited the spark deep in her belly. "But we haven't played strip dreidels."

Andie copied his stance, though the table didn't dip back her way. If they were back at her place she'd crawl across to his lap. "Yet. Play your cards right and maybe we'll give it a try tonight. There are two nights left of Chanukah."

"We can't play dreidels outside of Chanukah?"

"Nope. It's in the torah."

Leo shook his head, a smile on his face. "It is not, and no one will mind."

The mood shifted, away from playful flirty banter. "Are you suggesting we spend time together after Chanukah?" Something akin to hope swirled inside. She might be on borrowed time, but the thought of enjoying Leo for more than the holidays was tempting.

He swallowed and she followed the motion. A nervous gesture? She dared to think his thoughts mirrored hers. "Yes."

Her pulse kicked in a way that had nothing to do with the caffeine. "I'll be moving soon." Though the temple preschool job came to mind. Would it be a better match, or a foolish one?

"I don't care. I like spending time with you. And if you'll allow it, I'd like this to continue as long as it can. What do you say, Andie?"

She suddenly needed a different drink than coffee. Leo brightened her life, no denying that small but potent fact. Still, now wasn't the time to start something new when she already had an end time stamped in place.

Leo leaned back, picking up his sandwich. "Just, think it over. You know where I live."

She did. And she feared the end result would be awkward hallway encounters. Was it better to flirt and wonder about the potential, or to have experienced it and lost it?

Andie forced those thoughts aside. She'd worry about that after the holidays.

* * *

The ramifications of showering at some stranger's home hit Leo about two seconds before the apartment door opened. Awkwardness seeped in and he understood why Andie had balked at showering at his parents' house.

"I'm so happy you have power!" Andie said when Sarah opened her door.

Sarah stood several inches shorter than Andie, with straight dark brown hair past her shoulders, wearing a "their, there, they're" sweatshirt. She propped a hand on her hip, studying her guests in a way that had Leo resisting a squirm. "Well, don't you two look cozy."

Andie glanced back at Leo, and he tried to cover up all of his uncomfortableness. Just another normal day in his life, nothing unusual about showering at a stranger's apartment. Nothing at all. "Bug me about it later, we have a Chanukah party to get to."

Sarah stepped back and let Andie and Leo into her apartment. Andie dropped her bag to her feet while Leo kept his on his shoulder. Why, he had no clue. Pretending not to be awkward had never been his strong point.

Andie pointed over her shoulder, in a direction that Leo guessed the bathroom would be in. "You want to shower first?"

He would have showered with her, but that would only have happened if they were at one of their apartments. "Ladies first."

Andie shrugged, picked up her bag, and headed down the hall. "Towels in the closet?" She called over her shoulder.

"Yup. You two can share."

Andie stopped and glared at Sarah.

"You gonna tell me you didn't spend the night together?" Sarah's smile claimed an innocence her words contradicted.

Andie opened her mouth. Closed it. Opened it again and then turned back down the hall. If she managed to say anything, he didn't hear it.

Sarah laughed. "She's too fun to tease." A finger pointed in Leo's face. "Don't abuse that."

Leo raised both his hands. "Not my intention at all."

Sarah studied him from head to toe, no shame. "Okay. I'll buy it."

Sounds of water running through the pipes filled the unit.

"Want something to drink?" Sarah headed to the left, into a small kitchen.

Leo followed. "Uh, sure."

Sarah filled a cup with water, then propped a hip on her counter, handing it out to him. He took it and stepped back. "Andie's had it rough. It's nice to see her out with others."

Unsure what to do, Leo drank his water. Small talk had never been his thing outside of work, and this one posed an extra challenge. Sarah scrutinized him, and he had to accept it on behalf of Andie.

"Her dad was her world, and when he died, a piece of her did, too. Andie is the kindest person you'll ever meet, with the biggest heart, and she has so much love to share. But her family is gone."

He nodded, absorbing Sarah's words. Not that he didn't know most of this, but hearing it from someone close to Andie meant something. "Why tell me all this? I'm just her date for Chanukah."

"Hmm. Are you? Because for years I've heard about her hot neighbor. Even when her dad was very sick there were stories about how this neighbor, you, brightened her days when she needed it the most. So tell me, Leo, are you just an eight-night wonder?"

He placed down his cup before he dropped it. "She's taking a job far away and moving." He wanted more; but her plans didn't allow for it. A week wouldn't have him on bended knee, but he wanted to see where this attraction and chemistry went.

"Sure. She might be. But I've watched enough rom-coms with her to know there's often a way."

"As the movie fades to black and you don't know how or if they actually succeed."

"Hmm, a realist. She could use some of that."

"Is there a reason for this interrogation?" Because he was about to start squirming like a kid being lectured.

"I like you. I like the way she smiles when she talks about you. And the way you're staring longingly after her. Plus, I'm all for giving her reasons to stay local."

"I would never ask her to give up a job for me." He would think it, sure, but not ask.

"Ah, see, that just makes me like you better." The water stopped chugging through the pipes. "Go, check on her, I'm sure you want out of this conversation."

He did. He didn't want to be so eager and transparent, but he was. So, as calmly as he could, he left Sarah's kitchen and grabbed his bag.

Then he returned and found a spot to set up his hearing aid charger and pop the hearing aids on. Much like Andie, Sarah didn't react beyond positive curiosity.

Down the hall, he found a closet, then the bathroom, and knocked. "Andie, it's me." He pressed his ear against the door, realizing he probably should have knocked before taking off the aids.

"I'm almost finished, come on in."

He opened the door. Andie stood in only her bra and underwear, scrunching gel into her curls. "God, you're beautiful," he said before he could stop himself.

"I'm half naked, of course."

He walked over to her, placing a finger under her chin. "I don't deny the view is spectacular, but so are you, just you." He kept revealing more of his cards than he should, unable to have the control he so desperately needed around her. Her cheeks were rosy, lips bare, and he leaned in, kissing her, wanting to be the reason she stayed instead of moved but knowing he'd never be able to live with himself for that.

"Shower is a bit fussy, the pressure likes to change, but it's warm."

"Noted." He collected the items he needed from his bag, then stripped, setting up the shower.

He turned when he felt eyes on him. Andie stood, one hand in her curls, not moving. "What?"

Her lips curved. "Maybe I get why you called me beautiful earlier."

The desire to cross the room and drag her into the shower grew strong, and she probably knew it. Not at Sarah's apartment, when they were already running late for his parents' house. Still, Sarah's words rang in his head, and even if he risked messing things up, he needed to try.

"Has this been a good Chanukah for you, Andie?" Unable to help himself, he grasped her waist, bringing her close to him.

She let go of her hair, placing cold, sticky hands on his shoulders. "Yes. Yes, it has been."

"So why should it stop just because the menorah is put away?"

Her eyes grew wide. "I, uh . . ."

He knew better than to risk things and stumble all over himself. He kissed her forehead. "At least consider it. I've enjoyed this week with you and all I've ever wanted was to make you smile. I meant what I said earlier, I don't want to stop."

She cocked her head to the side. "You're standing here naked and I'm nearly naked."

"That's just a perk."

She ran her hands down his back.

"I don't think my back needs your gel."

Andie laughed. "You're about to get into the shower."

He didn't know if she deflected or was just being herself, but he needed her to know he was serious. "I'm nowhere near done with you."

Her cheeks curved in a smile.

"As long as I can make you smile, I'm going to."

He feared if he stayed there longer he'd ruin something, so he let her go and climbed into the shower. The water ran over his head when he heard the curtain shift. He blinked the water away, finding Andie looking at him.

"Just so you know, I like making you smile, too."

He had to swallow. "Noted. Now go before I drag you back in here under the excuse of needing to hear you better."

Andie laughed as the curtain closed. Leo let the water rain down on his back. He'd give this woman the world if she gave him the chance.

CHAPTER SIXTEEN

Leo pulled up to the two-story Colonial he'd grown up in and cut the engine. Beside him, Andie took in the gray siding with bushes along the front of the house. Out on the front lawn Dean and David played what appeared to be keep-away with a ball and Millie in the middle. His niece jumped high, but the men were taller, with arches to their throws.

"Do we need to save your niece, from her own father no less?" Andie asked, eyes on the three playing on the frosted lawn. She'd taken the time while he showered to dry her hair and he didn't begrudge her the gumption.

"Nah. Millie can save herself."

Andie turned to him.

"She's been known to fake an injury or two." She'd been five years old and limping from a hurt ankle, though mysteriously the injured ankle had switched from left to right.

"They aren't touching her."

"Doesn't matter."

"I'm equally impressed by that girl and glad she was never one of my students."

"I know the feeling." He angled over the center console, getting close to Andie. "Are you ready? They don't bite, this is just a fun afternoon for all of us."

Andie's brown eyes shone and she placed a hand on his cheek. "I'm ready." She kissed him, still in view of his brothers and niece, should they check on the adults lingering in the car. Short, innocent, but there, and for a moment he forgot he wouldn't be bringing her here for more family get-togethers.

He still leaned toward her when she opened the door, a brisk burst of air snapping him back to his senses.

"Oy, the wind hasn't quite died down yet, has it?" Andie asked when Leo joined her.

He turned up her jacket collar. "Not yet."

"Andie! You made it!" Millie ran away from the ball sailing over her head, flinging her arms around Andie's waist.

"Hey, what am I? Chopped liver?" he asked, amused by his niece.

Millie laughed and wrapped herself around him instead. "Nope. Because you brought Andie."

"Since you made such an impression on my kid, wanna play?" David asked.

"You mean do I want to toss the ball so Millie can't get it? Or do you need a taste of your own medicine?"

David had been tossing the ball into the air and catching it, he stopped tossing it. "It's all good fun."

"No, Daddy, it's not." Millie turned with a flip of her hair, facing Andie. "What's your plan? I want in."

Andie's cheeks rose with amusement as she squatted down to Millie's height. Then the two looked up at him. "Whose team are you on, Leo?"

"Yeah, Uncle Leo, whose team are you on?"

"He's on the man team, that's which team," Dean called out.

"That's sexist, Uncle Dean!"

Dean stood taller. "You don't split up into teams of boys and girls at school?"

"Sometimes, and I point out that not everyone's gender is as simple as that and it's unfair to make us all pick."

Leo felt a swell of pride for his niece. *Never change, kiddo.* "I'm on this team, sorry guys."

"Wimp!" David called out.

Leo raised his eyebrows. "You want me to get my sister?"

David dropped the ball and held up his hands in a peace offering.

Leo bent, to join the huddle with Andie and Millie. "So how are we gonna win?"

"The answer is very simple." Andie grew quiet, making eye contact with each team member. "We don't let them get the ball."

Millie squealed. "I like it!"

"They're tall and fast," Leo said. Dean was taller than him, David shorter by a hair, he'd be the only one on the same vertical playing field.

Millie was not swayed. "And we're short and equally fast. What's the saying? They go high, so we go low?"

"I'm not short. I don't think that's what the saying is supposed to mean."

Andie waved a hand. "Whatever, you both follow me, right?"

Millie nodded. "Right!" And as if someone had blown a whistle, she took off across the lawn, to where David had picked up the ball, and expertly snatched it from him before he had a chance to react.

"Hey," David yelled, before taking off after a laughing Millie. She headed straight for Andie, and passed the ball in an underhand toss that would make any football player proud.

Andie took off in the opposite direction. Dean wasted no time going after her so Andie tossed her ball, a low one again, to Leo.

And because Leo played ball with both of these men more than once, he found himself chest to chest to chest with his competitors.

"Millie, we found the weak link of your team," Dean called.

"Weak link, my ass," Leo said.

"Ha ha, he thinks he's got us."

Leo kept changing position of the ball as the men tried to knock it from him, meanwhile they were so focused on him, they didn't notice the ten-year-old sneaking over. And since Andie said the name of the game was to go low, Leo hurled the ball between David's legs, where Millie caught it and ran toward the house.

"You prick," David muttered, taking off after his daughter.

Andie jogged up beside him. "Nice one!" She raised her hand for a high five. He meshed his hand to hers, but wrapped his fingers down, holding her.

Ahead of them David decided to simply catch Millie and swung her around in the air. Millie laughed and the front door opened, Leo's mom standing there.

"Are you children ready to come inside or do I not get to meet the lovely Andie?"

Andie's cheeks pinked, and Leo lowered their hands—still clasped—to tug her toward the front of the house. Everyone had moved inside except for Leo's mother.

"Mom, this is Andie. Andie, this is my mother, Gayle."

Andie held out a hand. "Nice to meet you."

Gayle trapped Andie's gloves in her bare hands. "Trust me, the pleasure is all mine."

Leo then watched in horror as Gayle wrapped an arm around Andie's shoulders and led her inside.

"Leo has never brough a girl home, not since high school, can you believe that? I'm his mother, I deserve to meet his girlfriends. I deserve for my children to settle down and get married."

"Mom." Leo cringed. He should have known this would happen. Especially since his mother spoke loud enough for him to hear.

"Oh, hush. You let me enjoy this moment. I waited long enough for it."

Andie glanced back, her face saying, "it's okay, I've got this." And while Andie surely knew Jewish mothers even without knowing her own, he still worried that Gayle Dentz would be a different threat altogether.

* * *

Andie's first impression of Leo's family home was cozy. The outside said typical New England middle-class family, manicured lawn with the right number of bushes. Cookie cutter without being cookie cutter. The inside, in contrast to the keeping up with the Joneses exterior, claimed one simple fact: love lived here.

Stairs divided the living room and dining room, with pictures climbing from the first floor to the second. Wedding pictures. Baby pictures. Graduation pictures. Andie spotted Leo in a few, at least she thought she'd correctly identified him.

A plush carpet led the way into the family room, where a fire glowed in the fireplace. A round coffee table sat in the middle, with a couch, love seat, and two loungers lined around it. Pillows welcomed backs and sides. A plant stood tall in one corner and presents, wrapped in blue and white, were piled in a different corner. There were more pictures on these walls, displaying school events and childhood artifacts.

Yes, love lived here.

Andie's father had pictures and items of hers cherished on his walls and shelves. He'd taken them with him in each move and she now had them in a box, because no one except a parent framed a drawing from a six-year-old. Well, parents and teachers. Andie put up a picture or two, but for just herself it felt strange. The images belonged in a parent's home. Like here with the Dentzes.

"You have a beautiful home, Mrs. Dentz," Andie said. She'd been brought over to the couch and sat next to Leo's mother.

"Oh, hush. None of this formal 'Mrs.' stuff. Call me Gayle." Her tone demanded no questions and Andie suspected that's how she once kept three children in line.

"You have a beautiful home, Gayle."

Gayle laughed and pointed to Leo, who sat in the lounger across from them. "You have good taste, my boy."

Dean sat next to Leo. "Only with this one. You should have seen the others." He made a scared face and Leo jabbed him in the side, without pulling his punch based on how Dean curled inward.

Gayle patted Andie's knee, stealing her attention back. "So how did you two meet?"

Andie slid a glance to Leo, but he was busy whispering to Dean. "We're neighbors."

Gayle waved a hand in the air. "Oh, I know that. I want specifics, all I've ever heard is 'some woman in my building.' Some woman, huh, you're here, that's more than 'some.'"

Andie swallowed a laugh. It was one thing to flirt with Leo over the years, another to learn he'd wanted more, and quite a different level to hear it from his own mother. "Well, I live next door, so I'm not really sure what the very first meeting was. Elevator rides, mailbox meetings, parking lot passes, we got to know each other bit by bit."

It sounded right, felt right, but from across the room two brown eyes landed heavily on her. She'd snagged Leo's full attention. "Andie moved in around the end of summer, probably before the school year started, now that I know you better. She was struggling with a box, trying to get it into the elevator. You were probably hot and sweaty and frustrated but looked like some fierce warrior ready for battle and absolutely beautiful. I stepped in to help, because the job really needed at least three hands—not that you weren't capable. And I felt like the luckiest man alive that the empty apartment next to mine would be yours."

Andie's mouth dipped open, staring at Leo and his words that made her heart flutter. She wanted to say he made it up for his mom's benefit, but the memory clicked, and lingered. He told the truth and somehow remembered their first meeting.

"Aww, that is adorable. Dean, slap your brother," Gayle said.

Dean did as told, shrugging at Leo's "what the" response. "Why?"

"Sure, you hit first, ask questions later," Leo muttered.

"I follow Mom's orders first, ask questions later."

"Because it took you far too long to make your move after that lovely meeting." Gayle said.

The moment should feel awkward. The pestering, the prodding, the weight of a relationship to be more that simply wouldn't. Andie waited for the unease to work in, but all she felt was comfort. Peace. This family loved hard and long, and every member should be happy to be a part of it. Perhaps that's why Andie was there, to ensure they did not forget the special gift they had.

And maybe she needed to experience what she'd always wished for, at least for a single day.

"Sometimes the wait makes it all the sweeter, and the timing needs to be right." Andie feared she misspoke, the way Leo's expression shifted, from light and playful, to serious and something else. Because timing was not on their side, not if she moved, and this little slice of heaven she felt here would become a fleeting memory.

"Come on, Grandpa!"

From the entry into the rest of the house, the back of Millie's head appeared, pulling on the hand of an older gentleman with white hair and a striking resemblance to Dean.

Millie stopped near the couches. "This is Andie!" She held out both hands, as though presenting some prize.

Andie rose and held out her hand. "Pleasure to meet you."

He shook her hand, but said nothing, the temperature dipping in the room. His focus wasn't on her, it was over her shoulder, to Leo or both his sons, she didn't know.

"Oh, Glen, put business away for one day, would you? It's our chance to celebrate with our family."

"Yeah, Grandpa. It's Chanukah!" Millie bounced on her feet. Glen angled his head down at his granddaughter, the grumpy frown fading, replaced with a kind smile.

Millie turned, beaming at her uncles. A dangerous combination: a child aware of their own superpowers.

Gayle nudged Andie's shoulder. "That child could change diplomatic policies with an eyelash flutter."

Amusement warmed Andie, and filtered out, though she managed to keep it quiet. She focused on the pictures above where Glen sat, one of her favorite things about family homes.

"The baby making the silly face is Leo." Jodie entered the room, clearly catching Andie's gaze.

"Which one?" Leo shot back.

"You were all adorable children who took an occasional bad photo." Gayle laughed.

"I don't take bad photos." Millie placed both her hands under her chin, hamming for an imaginary camera.

"My grandbabies never do." Gayle somehow managed to eye all her children at once. "Should I be so lucky to get more."

Jodie snagged a seat on the armrest near her father. "Told you, the factory is closed. Focus on your single sons."

Andie remained very still. On one hand, she loved the comfortable family banter. On the other hand, she did not want her parental status to get roped into this conversation.

"No focus here. This is the first time I've brought someone to Chanukah." Leo held a relaxed position, as though his words truly would be enough for his mother.

A Jewish mother. Andie doubted he'd win.

Jodie leaned forward. "Exactly. First times mean something, don't they?"

Leo put his foot on the floor.

Gayle raised her hands. "I'm not here to scare off our newest guest. And don't worry middle child of mine, you get a few more plus ones before I start questioning."

Leo locked eyes with Andie. "This was a bad idea, my apologies."

Andie noticed he didn't look the least bit upset. Which was good, since she didn't feel any remorse either. "You'll have to make it up to me sometime."

"Deal."

Millie hopped to the center of the room, hands rubbing together. "Where are the dreidels, I have more gelt to win."

CHAPTER SEVENTEEN

Leo thanked his lucky stars that even with the power outage and Andie distracting him in the best possible way, he still remembered to grab his gelt for the day. Granted, the small pile fit easily in his coat pocket, so not nearly the challenge his niece—aka current champion—enjoyed.

Which led him to a much bigger conundrum: how to count Andie into this game. He reached out and snagged her arm as the family moved into the dining room, her big brown eyes large and questioning back at him, and equally as enticing. Dreidels and gelt and family slipped from conscious thought and his focus became Andie's lips and beauty. A slight bend and her lips could meet his. Christmas had never been a thing he wished to call his own, but what he wouldn't give for the excuse of a mistletoe.

"Everything okay?" Andie smiled brightly up at him, not helping his brain getting back on track.

Get it together, Dentz, your baby pictures are on this wall.

"My family takes dreidels very seriously."

"I gathered that."

"And plays with real gelt."

"Real as in . . .?"

"Not candy."

"I might have some loose change in my purse."

Leo chuckled, unable to hold it in. At Andie's furrowed brows, and how adorable were her furrowed brows, he held up a finger and made his way to the front entry hooks that housed all their coats. Before Andie could reach for her purse he pulled out the felt bag he'd stashed there. "Hold out your hands."

Andie did as directed and Leo dumped the one dollar coins into the palm of her hand. Her eyes grew wide, followed by a laugh escaping her plump lips. "Oh my."

Leo nodded. "Yup. Let's go see the ringmistress and figure out a plan."

The gelt went back into the bag and he placed a hand on each of Andie's shoulders, steering her into the dining room. The family had all gathered around the round table, bags of gelt and favorite dreidels making their way to the surface. Voices rose over each other, always creating a challenge for him to hear, and Leo prepared to use his lungs to get important details settled.

"Oh Millie," Leo called out, "how are we going to incorporate our newest member?"

Millie glanced up from counting her stash, a finger tapping against her lip. Leo realized then with no small amount of horror the ditch he'd stepped into. There he stood, hands on Andie's shoulders, presenting her to his family for the first time, incorporating her into their long-standing game—as though she'd be a bigger part than this single day.

His thoughts veered off course when Millie hopped up. "I've got it. Shin rules." She glanced around the room as though this made perfect sense to anyone else but her. "Everyone, put two in to help Andie get her start."

Millie sent Leo a wink and he winked back.

But Andie backed out of his grasp. "I don't need to take your money, maybe I have a few ones I could use." She tried to escape, but the only one who garnered more attention and control than Millie spoke up.

"You will do no such thing. Millie's idea is perfect and hardly a challenge for most of us." His mother deposited two coins into the center, giving his family a look that challenged anyone to be a chazir.

Leo grasped Andie's hand. "Come. Enjoy. This is mostly for fun. Cutthroat fun, but fun."

Andie's tight shoulders relaxed away from her earlobes and she gave his hand a squeeze. "Okay. I guess I'm starting with fourteen coins."

Possibly more than he had in his pouch, but he'd let her take the lead from last place.

Everyone settled in around the table, dreidels being tested and chosen. Gayle brought over a bowl of chips and a tray of Christmas candies.

Millie clapped her hands once for attention. "Standard rules. Shin means two in. Every round you add one to the center pot. We spin to see who goes first. Last gimel standing wins." She held her dreidel in front of her and everyone followed, Leo nudging Andie to join in. Then they all spun, dreidels bumping into each other like bumper cars, his father's dreidel going off the table.

"Default! Spin it again, Grandpa."

Glen's chair squeaked and he let out a groan as he collected his dreidel. "It landed on gimel."

"Nope, we've got to see it."

"Gimel shimel, that was a nun," said Dean, who sat next to him. "You need glasses."

"Maybe you do, you're the one in expensive contacts," Glen muttered, spinning again.

"Nope, got my eyes checked just last month."

Glen landed on a hay, not joining Andie, Millie, and David with gimels.

"Non gimels are out. Gimels, try again!" Millie bounced and sent her dreidel into a loopy spin, where it collided with Andie's, both sputtering to a stop. David's kept going, and he held up a hand blocker to keep it from falling off the table.

The end result yielded no gimels.

They all spun again, this time all three dreidels meeting in a miniature rave, before wobbling, landing on a shin, nun, and gimel.

"Andie is our first winner," Gayle said.

Andie blushed, but didn't back down, taking her dreidel and spinning it one more time. It bumped into the center puddle of coins, before falling with hay up.

"Half, not bad," Millie said.

Andie collected the pile, her tiny stash growing. "I'll take it."

Play continued clockwise around the table, personal piles growing and shrinking. Luck was not on Leo's side this Chanukah, as his pile faced imminent extinction. He spun with one final hope of remaining in the game.

The dreidel sailed right off the table, streaking in between Dean and Glen.

Dean glanced down from his leaned back on two chair legs position and shot both hands in the air. "Gimel!"

Cheers rose up and relief filled Leo. He leaned forward, ready to collect his winnings, stopped short by his father's voice. "It landed out of bounds." Glen glared at Dean. "And was not a gimel."

Dean's chair banged back to all four legs. "I know you need reading glasses, and gimel and nun can be confusing, but that," Dean flung a hand toward the ground in between them. "Is a gimel."

"Which is still out of bounds. You always did anything to cover for your brother, didn't you?" Glen said.

A hush fell over the room. Leo's jaw clenched hard enough to break a filling. The tightness of Dean's jaw telecasted the same. Leo was the perpetual troublemaker. Dean, on the other hand, was only good for being Leo's shadow. They had equal blame in the issues they'd had with the store, and yet it was all Leo's fault and Dean needed to extricate himself from the issue.

Leo had been the older one, and in charge. He'd already spent years trying to get rid of the negative self-association.

"Glen, it's Chanukah." They all turned to where Gayle gave her husband a not-so-friendly glare.

"Rules are rules and need to be followed."

Andie shrunk in her chair next to Leo and more than this age-old issue being brought up any chance his father got, he hated the timing of Andie being here. He had hoped the novelty of bringing someone home would have his father playing nice. He should have known better. It wouldn't have lasting effects on Andie, she'd be moving soon after all, but the odds of him ever bringing home another date dwindled. If he managed to fix his craptastic dating record.

Across the table Millie sat extra quiet, her bottom lip stuck out by a hair, shoulders squared back. Millie had a good relationship with her grandfather, and yet he knew that look in her eyes—she planned to step into the fray, for her uncle's sake.

Leo unclenched his jaw. He didn't need his ten-year-old niece fighting his battles, even if her negotiating skills were beat by no one. "Dean, toss me my dreidel. I'll spin again."

"But Uncle Leo—"

Leo held up a hand, cutting Millie off. "It's okay. Good sportsmanship is always worth it." He finished his words while looking at his father, a sneer slipping through that he couldn't quite tame.

Dean bent and tossed the dreidel. Leo caught it easily and spun it again, eyes on his father. Glen looked unphased, another moment in his life where his sons disappointed him.

Everything always Leo's fault, right down to his hearing loss.

The dreidel clunked to a stop and the room remained silent. Leo tore his gaze from his father to his dreidel by the center pile. Shin. He took his remaining two coins and tossed them into the center. "It's taken a few years, but you all have finally beat me. Deal me in again sometime." He scraped his chair back and headed away from the dining room, with the need to get away from dear ole dad.

* * *

"Well done, Dad, that was just epic." Dean clapped. "You can't even hold it in for one Chanukah, not even when he's brought a date."

Andie's cheeks burned. She hated family conflict, hated that most of her memories of her extended family involved a fight, or two. She'd never forget the last time she'd been around them, before her father had died. She'd caught him in a heated conversation, hidden in the corner with her uncle. He admonished her father for working with the homeless. Proclaiming that he'd failed his daughter, and that was why Andie worked in a preschool. She'd feigned sickness shortly thereafter so they could leave. Her father had been saddened by the encounter. He always held out hope for others. In Andie's mind, they'd done nothing to earn that hope.

Leo's family had been so warm and open and welcoming. She'd known there were issues with his father, but knowing it and witnessing it were two different beasts.

"Rules are rules," Glen said. "Something you two boys need to learn."

Dean placed an elbow on the table, leaning into his father. "Rules are meant to be broken. And we know the rules. We've been punished for longer than the recommended jurisdiction."

"You nearly folded the business."

"And here it is, still standing all these years later, even with the two of us working there. Yet, you'd rather sell or, in your words, fold it, than give us a chance." Dean stood, bumping the table, jostling the contents, and heading out of the dining room. Andie wondered if he was going after Leo, but Dean went out the front door, opposite of his brother's direction.

"Excuse me," Andie said in her soft teacher voice. She didn't need to be here for this. But she could go after the reason she was here in the first place.

"Oh Glen, you are going to make those two leave and never come home. Learn how to let people grow from their mistakes," Gayle said as Andie left.

"Those two haven't learned."

"Dad, the only person who hasn't learned is you. Come on, Millie, let's give Uncle Leo some gelt to play with next time."

Andie was tempted to stay and hear what came next but let the voices fade to the background as she tried to figure out where to find Leo. Following his path led her to the kitchen. The open space with island and table for the whole family to fit at didn't give many additional escape options. Only the backyard, which held no pissed off and hurt man stomping around, and a hallway.

The hallway brought Andie to a half bath and then a worn room that at one point must have been a playroom, and perhaps still was for Millie. On the tan couch sat Leo, elbows on knees, head in his hands.

Her heart went out to him. Cracking a tiny bit on his behalf. To live under that much pressure, she couldn't fathom it. The man she was beginning to know tried his best to do good. And yet he'd been held in place, stuck in a past that no longer defined him.

"I'm sorry you had to witness that," came his rough voice.

Andie hadn't realized she'd been seen. She ventured into the room, sitting beside him. Leo straightened, though his face remained strained. "It's all right. Families are families. They are complicated and sticky and don't always know how to be there for each other."

Leo scoffed. "That's an oversimplification of the truth."

Andie shrugged. She didn't want to get into it, saw no point. She might have missed the warmth she'd witnessed earlier, but she also didn't have to deal with the theatrics. Life was too short for drama, especially from those you loved. She'd rather keep her circle small than welcome in that kind of animosity on a regular basis. And did just that after her father's death, when greedy hands came stretched out with false claims of promises of property, rather than offers of support.

Perhaps she asked for too much; it's not like Leo chose his particular baggage. She'd had this dream of family for so long, amplified with her father's death. She had time, youth still on her side. No sense giving up a dream unless she met a person who made her forget about the rest.

Leo let out a sigh and placed his head on her shoulder. It tugged at her, deep down, beyond organs and atoms. For a moment she could envision it, putting up with the bad for the good. Putting up with the conflicts to be the one there to soothe the aches and stings. That's who Leo needed. His family still had some of the balance hers had lacked. He needed someone to help pick him up and dust him off when others pushed him down. Beyond the rest of his family caught up in the mess. An urge deep inside wanted to be that for him.

She'd unpack that another time. She angled her head, leaning it against Leo's. The thought emerged, of accepting potential opportunities. The temple preschool job, and Leo in her life. It meant staying, turning down Ohio but keeping the area she'd called home, her local friends, and places where her father's memory still lingered.

Yes, there would be conflict, but also love, so much love. Did she really need to judge Leo's family based on one bad seed? No. She didn't. Especially as, somehow, she wasn't running. Imagine that.

"What can I do to make it better?" she asked.

Leo's soft chuckle vibrated against her shoulder. He shifted and they both straightened. "I'm amazed that didn't send you running for the hills."

How odd, his words mirroring hers. "I'm no stranger to drama."

"Yeah, but you don't like it."

Had she mentioned as much? She couldn't remember. Either his memory worked better than most or he read her with ease. Both notions somehow soothed her usual responses. "You're right, I don't like it. Doesn't mean I can't support my date for the day when he needs it."

Leo leaned back, hands going into his hair. "I've done everything I could to prove myself to that man, to make up for my teenage misdeeds. None of it makes a dent. He'd rather sell his father's business to someone else when both his sons want it than to let bygones be bygones."

Tension rose back in Leo and Andie tried to work it out. "His loss."

"Sure. His loss. But come January, Dean and I may be looking for new jobs or careers."

"And your years of experience won't count for something? Or how about your customers, I'm sure you each have some that prefer to work with you."

He looked her way, the first sparks of hope flickering. "What are you saying?"

"Life is never black and white. It's scary when a door closes, but sometimes that door has to close in order to open up something new and better. Look at me, I'm losing a job I love in an area I love, yet a new opportunity has presented itself, and I know this journey will be an experience." Two new opportunities, the inside voice whispered, but Andie left that locked up tight. One offer was official, the other was not. She would not count chickens before they hatched.

"I suppose you're right. I wanted Dentz Antiques."

"I'm sure you did. And while the outlook is certainly murky, it's not a done deal yet."

The twitch of his eyebrows suggested hope wouldn't be easy for him. "You're saying to have hope? After that?"

"I'm saying that life has been known to throw more interesting curveballs than that."

Leo stared at her, eyes wide and incredulous. And then, a slight shake of his head, a laugh, and a relaxing of his furrowed brow. He hauled her to him before she could react, chest to chest. "I'm so glad you're here," he said into her hair.

She wrapped her arms around him, holding him close. The "same" stayed in her head, but from her heart beating against his, she suspected he didn't need to hear it.

CHAPTER EIGHTEEN

With everything going on, the last thing Leo expected to dominate his mind was the fact that Andie smelled good. Great, in fact. The kind of smell he wanted to bottle up and keep with him always. Because he cared for her, more than he should.

The thought should have had him breaking apart and shifting to the other side of the couch, or the house, instead he nuzzled in, pressing his lips to her neck. Her sharp intake of air only spurred him on and he took a nibble, then a lick, turning her into putty in his hands.

"Does this make you feel better?" her breathy voice asked.

"You make me feel better. Come here." He needed a filter gifted to him for Chanukah. Since that was as likely to happen as the menorah having real magic, he turned them until his lips met Andie's. Hunger came through in how she pressed into him, devoured him, and suddenly nothing else mattered. Certainly not when Andie straddled him there in the den they all used to play in as kids. Sure, he'd had a date here, or two, but never like this. His teenage self would give him a few high fives around giddy laughter.

"Is this what you want?" Andie asked, pressing her soft center to where he strained against his jeans. He could only groan and kiss her, be lost in her.

Why hadn't he brought a date home earlier? This sure beat dealing with his father. As Andie kissed down his neck he knew the answer, Millie's doing or not, there hadn't been anyone he wanted to bring home before Andie.

He collected her rear into his hands, squeezing, pushing her harder into him to their mutual gasp. He debated how much they could get away with when Andie scooted off him.

"I think Millie's checking on us," she whispered into his ear.

He now understood why he never tried this before, at least after he'd lost hearing. Andie smoothed her hair and wiped her mouth. Leo crossed his legs, uncrossed them, and tried again, before finding a position that would not give his niece nightmares.

"There you are!" Millie bounded into the room.

"Here we are." Did his voice still sound too husky? Judging by how Andie snapped a look at him, he probably did. He cleared his throat. "What's up, kiddo?"

"We've collected some gelt for you. It won't be fun to play without you."

Suddenly he didn't need to worry about hiding body parts. "Millie, you know that isn't necessary. I can buy my way in if needed."

"Andie didn't have to buy her way in, and that gimel should have been yours." Millie plopped down on the couch, wedging between them.

"Thanks, kiddo." He shifted to give her room. "Sorry for messing up Chanukah."

Millie shrugged and left it at that. Not the first time she'd witnessed similar, and it wouldn't be the last. It sent a fresh wave of anger through him. Glen could have as many issues with his sons as he wanted, but Millie was innocent and deserved not to have her childhood marred by things that transpired prior to her birth.

"Uncle Dean went outside. It's cold, I don't think he grabbed his jacket."

Anger morphed into concern. This day had him on one roller-coaster after the other. Dean must have had the same need to blow off some steam, without the sexy date to level him out. Brother or not, he needed to be there for his partner.

Leo found Andie's eyes over Millie's head. Barely, kid was getting tall. "I'm going to go find Dean."

Andie nodded. "I'll stay here. Millie can keep me company."

His niece nodded and Leo wanted to pull them both into a hug for being in his life. Wrong time, wrong place. He slipped out of the room, avoiding the dining room and sharp sting of voices. He knew every creaking board, every visible locale. The Dentz siblings were not only skilled at sneaking out, but they also shared tips and tricks that he'd thankfully memorized prior to sixteen. Leo wondered how Millie had caught Dean, but he suspected Dean didn't care who saw him leave. Leo, on the other hand, wanted to get outside unscathed.

He ducked into the living room, and then glanced around the staircase into the dining room. His mother, Jodie, and David chatted, not paying much attention to their surroundings. Even if they did, Leo suspected they'd let him be. The wall coat rack ahead of him perched next to the front door that hadn't latched closed, cold wind seeping in. Leo grabbed his jacket and Dean's, and made his final escape, ensuring the door closed behind him.

Dean hadn't made it far. His large frame sat hunched on the front steps. Leo draped Dean's jacket over his shoulders and sat down next to him, shoving his arms into his.

"That one moment in time must play on a freeze frame loop in that man's head," Dean said.

Leo stared out into the yard where he and his siblings had played ball and built snowpersons. A hill to the side had been perfect for sledding and biking into the street with abandoned care. Those were the memories he wanted to keep and cherish, not the endless sound of ceramic breaking. "Well, I guess we all have that one in common."

Dean picked up a stone, tossed it to the grass. "There's a difference between guilt and remorse and holding a grudge long enough to destroy a family legacy."

"I don't even think he remembers the story straight anymore. He claims we cover for each other, when we've been working together to try and make up for my mistake."

Dean straightened. "It took two of us to fight."

Leo nodded. Old habits were difficult to break. "Right. Our mistake."

"I'm sorry."

"You're not the one who has to apologize."

"Maybe not, but it can start with us."

"A new Dentz Antiques. We won't let him destroy what Grandpa built."

both brothers stared at the yard. A leaf blew past and somewhere a dog barked. They'd grown up, made their own peace with the past. Now they could both weather the storm, and together it wouldn't wear either of them down.

"Brothers and partners. The next generation."

Dean's head gave a sharp turn in Leo's direction. "You mean starting fresh?"

It scared him, starting from scratch would be a lot of work. But it meant they could finally get out from their father's disapproval. "I do. We'll sit down and talk numbers and details. January second sound good?"

Dean smiled wider than Leo had seen in a long time. "January second, January second . . . I don't think I have a date that day."

Leo shook his head and bumped shoulders with Dean.

"January second is perfect."

He held up a fist, and Dean bumped it. They let the silence consume them, sitting side by side on the front steps like they'd done so many times before. One way or another, they'd make it through to the next stage in their professional lives, even if it meant starting from scratch.

* * *

"Did Uncle Leo show you the magic menorah?" Millie asked after Leo left them alone.

Andie made sure her smile said "friendly" and not "beyond amused by this firecracker." "He did."

Millie's hand went over her mouth. "I'm not supposed to say it's magic, am I? It might ruin his wishes."

Her large eyes appeared genuinely worried, and Andie reached out and touched her shoulder. "I'm sure whatever he wished for is fine. People make wishes on birthday cakes and everyone knows."

Millie exhaled and lost an inch in height. "Oh phew. Because he really likes you and needed the push to finally do something about it."

Andie's smile slipped, but she caught it, unease crawling up her spine. What would Millie think when Andie left? Hopefully in a few months it wouldn't matter, but Andie made a mental note to warn Leo nonetheless, because their split would have nothing to do with Millie or wishes.

Until then, Andie did what she did best: redirect. "Do you like wishes?"

"Yup. But only when they come true."

"What would you wish for?"

"On a birthday cake or menorah or shooting star?"

Andie's training and experience in childcare meant she knew "aren't they all the same" wouldn't necessarily be the right response. "Do different types require different wishes?"

Millie nodded and sidled closer, as though imparting a great secret of the wish sort. "Of course. Birthday cakes are for wishing for something good for the year ahead or for an amazing birthday gift. Shooting stars are rare chances to fix something in your life in need of fixing. Menorahs, on the other hand, that's newly discovered magic, makes it very special. Chanukah is about miracles and something lasting longer than it should. So a wish on a menorah should be the same, wishing for a miracle to last."

This kid was too smart for her own good. Andie wanted to sit there longer and explore Millie's mind. She got why the family found her so endearing, and that had little to do with her being the only grandchild. That wonder contrasted with a deep disturbance in her gut. Most of the family were thinking big relationship thoughts since Leo didn't often bring home dates, the kind of thoughts that led to wedding bells and many more gatherings to come. And even with those far-fetched thoughts for what Andie and Leo truly meant, they would all understand that not all relationships are built to last. Millie, on the other hand, thought it was because of how he made the "wish." Wishes don't allow for error margins of moving halfway across the country.

Andie had the sudden urge to defuse the situation and the fantasy but knew she couldn't. This wasn't her child or even family member. If Millie was her student, she'd change the subject completely. And perhaps that was all she could do here.

"How's everyone in the dining room?" Andie asked. Not the best conversation swerve, but she'd roll with it.

Millie shrugged and hopped up. "Gramps is mean to my uncles, everyone else gets on Gramps's case. It happens." She left the room and rather than be alone, although preferable to drama, Andie followed.

They found the dining room lacking any level of theatrics, and Glen had left fortunately, or unfortunately, considering his sons weren't there. Millie bounded over to her parents. Andie found herself being scrutinized by the matriarch of the room.

"I'm sorry you had to witness that," Gayle said.

Andie carefully took a seat next to her. "It's okay. Life happens, right?"

Gayle shook her head. "This is an old battle that should have been finished years ago. I don't know what to do to rebuild the relationship between father and sons."

Andie knew the polite thing to do, but she didn't want to be polite. She wouldn't be back here again, so no reason to hold back. "In my experience, the only person who can begin the rebuild is the person holding onto the drama and refusing to allow growth in."

"Are you blaming my husband?" An edge sketched into Gayle's voice, but Andie held her own.

"I'm sharing what I've seen with my own extended family. How people held so tight to the pettiest of disagreements and destroyed a family from within. I'm not saying what happened here is petty. But I've seen people react to things that happened before my lifetime as though it was yesterday." Like her father moving her mother far away for a job opportunity and staying away until after Andie was born and her mother had passed. As though the death was his fault for moving. So rather than welcoming them back and cherishing the new family member, they held blame high and above all else.

Gayle glanced around the room, a single finger tapping the table. "You might be wise beyond your years like our Millie here."

Andie smiled, a genuine one. "That's a compliment I will gladly take."

Gayle covered Andie's hand with her own. "I'm glad Leo has you then. He could use someone levelheaded and kind, especially after days like this."

Andie wondered how she ended up here, in the midst of her own situation, and how her departure might make things worse.

"And I still have hope. Glen is a good man. One who needs a swift kick in the rear, but he's good. Underneath it all he's got his father's words in his head, stirring the pot."

"Oh?"

"My father-in-law once struggled to let his own business go. He questioned if Glen could handle it and Glen had to prove himself again and again. Not dissimilar to what Glen is doing to Leo and Dean. On top of those repressed emotions, getting older is hard."

Andie thought of her father, who hadn't been an old man, but aged faster than his years. "We're not immortal. And sometimes that can be a hard pill to swallow."

Gayle studied Andie. "Like I said, wise beyond your years."

"My father was sick for a while before he died. His future plans—anything from retiring to seeing me married and meeting his grandkids—all taken from him. And he knew he'd lost it and had to face his own mortality head on."

"Leo got very sick not too long after the incident. So sick that Glen and I worried, as parents do. And then Leo started having trouble hearing and Glen, oh Glen, he blamed it on a teenager's attitude long after we all realized it was more than that. The sickness, the hearing loss, it should have been enough to bury all this drama."

Andie's heart went out to Leo. To be dealing with everything with his father, and being sick, and then a disability, it couldn't have been easy. It gave her more appreciation for the man he'd become.

"I suspect Glen has a lot of his own emotions to work through that don't involve Leo and Dean."

"Yes, I like you."

"Are you writing this down, Mom? Or recording it?" Jodie asked.

Andie's cheeks burned; she should have realized the quiet meant that they had listeners.

Millie popped up. "Let's video it! Oh! We can do a reenactment!"

David put his hands on Millie's shoulders and quieted her down. "Not the right time for that, kiddo."

Millie pouted.

"I think it will be better coming from me than Andie. But don't you worry, I'm making mental notes." Gayle winked at her granddaughter, tapping her temple. "Come on, let's bake some cookies, what do you say?" Gayle rose and held out a hand, Millie took it and skipped out of the room, dragging Gayle with her.

"I never got a chance to thank you for helping with the Chanukah party. Millie had a blast." Jodie switched to a chair closer to Andie.

"My pleasure. I like kids."

"That's right, you're a preschool teacher."

Andie nodded.

"Don't you get sick of kids, then?" David said.

Jodie shot him a look.

Andie could only laugh. "Believe it or not, I don't."

"Millie had a great preschool; I know the good you do."

Andie took that to heart. She loved kids, loved supporting their early education. And to have it appreciated meant more to her than Jodie could know. "Where did Millie go?"

"Our temple. They have a preschool there. That's actually how we got connected with the place. Best decision ever. They nurtured and encouraged Millie, handled her rough spots easier than I could."

An odd flutter hit Andie's stomach. "We don't all have a knack for that, but the ones who do are golden."

"And from what I hear you are that type of gold, if not platinum."

It felt good, the accolades. She wasn't in her job for awards or fame or money. But knowing she did good would never get old. "Am I being buttered up?" Andie turned around.

"I'm just thankful for people like you."

"So you really liked Millie's preschool experience."

"It was more than that. It was the environment between classes. All the teachers were warm and loving, they gave the kids a good educational foundation. The kindergarten Millie went to had her bored after that."

I want that, Andie thought. *I want to be part of that kind of legacy.* The Ohio job could have that, or she could be the one to bring that element there. But stepping into a team already on that path, it meant magic.

Perhaps Andie did believe in wishes herself, or at least some sort of magic. The magic of childhood. The magic of a teacher who took the time to connect with kids on their level. The magic of having support and like-minded coworkers.

She mulled that over. If the preschool at the temple offered her a job, she could stay local, not leave Sarah and her other friends behind. She could stay in touch with Leo, see where their spark went.

"You okay?" Jodie asked.

Andie snapped out of her thoughts. "I am. Sorry. My school's closing so I'm looking for a new job and the way you spoke about Millie's education, that's what I hope parents of my students will say."

"If what I've seen is any indication, I'm sure they will."

Which meant Andie could do her own form of magic anywhere. But she wasn't sure she wanted just anywhere.

CHAPTER NINETEEN

"What do you mean you're going to the store?" Gayle's stern voice echoed into the room like a clatter in a quiet library.

Andie froze, her dislike for conflict making her squirm.

Jodie's eyes grew wide, mouth setting into a firm line. "Not again," she muttered before pushing her chair back and heading to the kitchen.

Andie stayed in her seat, now alone in the dining room. Part of her wanted to follow the action and see what she could do about it. That thought, so new and foreign, she blinked into the room, stumbling over these new yearnings. She typically stayed away from the commotions, her students were the exception she allowed in.

"The McFaddens are my best customers; they need a little Christmas miracle," Glen said from the kitchen, matching his wife's voice.

Stay where you are, Andie, stay right where . . .

"But Grandpa, we need our own Chanukah magic with you here."

She didn't even think, Millie's voice propelling her into the kitchen where the girl gave her grandfather doe eyes, looking up at him with a bit of cookie dough on her lips.

Glen knelt in front of Millie. "Want to know where the money for those Chanukah gifts of yours comes from? Customers like the McFaddens."

"You sound like we celebrate Christmas. It's not about the presents."

Glenn stood sharply. "So I should return your gifts."

Millie reached into the empty bowl, swiping a finger of leftover dough. "I like gifts, but I would rather you be here."

"Listen to the child, Glen," Gayle said, voice not softening one bit.

"Business is business, Gayle."

"It's Christmas Eve, Glen. McFadden should be with his family today. He can bother you after the holiday."

"It's Christmas Eve and he needs a gift."

"Not your problem."

Husband and wife stared at each other with unyielding eyes.

"You don't act like a man about to retire."

Andie hugged the cabinet near the entrance. Unease threatened to consume her, but now that she'd entered she couldn't leave the car crash happening before her.

Glen backed up. "When I retire it will be a different story." He took a step toward his wife, but she crossed her arms, effectively erecting a bubble around her. He grimaced and turned. "I'll be back for dinner. In fact, I'll pick up the Chinese."

He left through the back door, the bang of his departure the only sound in the room. It echoed straight through Andie, a horrible vibration.

Gayle put a hand on her head, taking in the room until her eyes landed on the non-family member. "Andie, darling, I am so sorry this is the impression we are making on you. This is turning into an interesting year." Her gaze turned soft and pleading. "I promise you this is the abnormality."

Andie smiled, though she had trouble believing that. From everything Leo had said, the rift between father and sons had been built into a fortress over the years.

"Should I get Leo and Dean before they see the car?" David asked.

Gayle sighed. "Yes, that would be wise."

David passed Andie on his way to the front.

"I know this doesn't work for us, but Grandpa needs coal in his stocking." Millie stabbed a finger into the bowl.

Jodie took her own finger swipe. "Kid's right. What's the Jewish equivalent?"

"There is none. We don't work that way," Millie said.

"No presents when the family likes to exchange gifts." Gayle's eyes glinted dangerously.

"Oh no, Mom?"

Gayle's grin matched her eyes. "Come on, help me find and hide all of your father's presents."

"Yes!" Millie jumped up and ran ahead of Gayle into the family room.

Jodie shook her head. "I'm going to echo my mother here and apologize. Do not judge Leo by the rest of our mistakes."

Andie wanted to comment on that request being a difficult one, but Jodie had already left, and Andie didn't have to defend anything. She might not even be here to see if father and sons ever managed to figure it out and make amends.

More importantly, she'd seen how this kind of conflict drives apart a family. She didn't know how they'd held on for as long as they did, but she knew the end result.

At least, she thought she did, but she couldn't deny how much they all loved each other, despite the drama. That said something, and a part of her yearned to explore the emotions more, dive in and see where it went.

Strange thoughts, being pulled in despite drama, not something she would have ever thought she'd be tempted by.

* * *

"We should probably head back inside," Leo said. The cold wind had found a way under his jacket and he refused to shiver next to his younger sibling who still hadn't zipped his.

"Cold, brother?" Dean asked casually. Where Dean had always been a furnace, Leo easily turned into an ice locker.

Leo shifted, trying to get his jacket closer to him without being obvious. Judging by the laughter beside him, he failed.

The front door opened behind them, and they both turned, only to be distracted by the garage opening.

Leo and Dean lost interest in the door, angling to see the car pull out of the house. Family rules meant the cars lined up blocking their mother's car, not father's.

The one-year-old Lexus came into view, window rolling down. "Going to the store. McFadden needs a favor."

Dean turned to Leo and rolled his eyes.

"In other words, McFadden forgot it was Christmas, or to get his wife a gift, and now is desperate for a favor to keep him out of the doghouse?" Leo understood business, but he fully planned to put his family first. There were no emergencies in antiques.

"McFadden is a long-term, high-paying customer. It's good to keep a customer like that happy."

"A customer like that is a pain in the ass." Dean ignored the glare Glen sent. "But more importantly, McFadden likes his antiques and we've treated him well. He'll be back regardless of today. In fact, he might start respecting you more if you said, 'Sorry, I can't. I'm with my family' once in a while."

Glen's face changed into a red tint. "This is why you two will never succeed in business. And why you don't deserve Dentz

Antiques." Final shot fired, he rolled up the window and continued down the driveway, leaving them in his exhaust dust.

"*He* doesn't deserve Dentz Antiques."

Leo and Dean looked behind them, where David stood, no jacket.

"I know, I'm the outsider. But I've heard stories about your grandfather and been around long enough to know Glen's distracted and not thinking straight."

Leo stood, brushing dirt off his rear. "And he's not going to realize that in time to make a difference."

"One day, when Dad is very old, he will regret these moments." Dean also stood.

Leo patted Dean's shoulder. "I like your optimism."

"But yours is gone?"

He thought about Andie and the refreshing way she had hope in the world. Pure and unburdened by life, even though she had ample reason to be. He needed that, needed more of it in his life, to remind him of the good. "Mine broke when even my sickness didn't bring Dad back around."

"Well, feel better. They're hiding your father's gifts inside."

Dean snorted. "Oh man, I need to get in on that action." He sprinted inside. "Is there gift theft going on?" his loud voice carried out, followed by female laughter.

"Hey, your Andie, she's really something," David said.

Your Andie. Leo liked the sound of it. Too bad it wouldn't be true. "Yeah, she is."

"She broke down Glen's issues and brought it into the light, in favor of you and Dean. Don't let this one go." David nudged Leo in the side and headed into the house.

Leo didn't want to let her go. But he didn't know how to convince her to stay.

Inside Millie stood by a pile of presents on the coffee table, having procured a clipboard and holding it in hand like a tiny CEO.

"Listen up family! The mound before me is all of Grandpa's gifts. But he's being a Jewish Grinch and no longer deserves them."

"Grinch or Scrooge?" Dean asked.

Millie tapped the end of the pen to her chin. "Scrooge. Definitely Scrooge. Anyway, we are going to split up and hide his presents throughout the house. Everyone will have paper and will create a scavenger hunt clue so he can find them."

Jodie held up a finger. "But he will only get the clues if he decides to play nice."

Millie nodded, brown hair sliding across her face. "Right. If he's somehow visited by three ghosts before he gets back, he'll get help. If not, he'll have to find them on his own." Millie scrunched up her face. "None of these expire, do they?"

"Who cares?" Gayle laughed. His affection for her swelled. His mom truly was his saving grace. She continued to love and support her sons through the incident and beyond, keeping them emotionally healthy. She'd been the first to realize he wasn't copping an attitude when he couldn't hear, been the one who went to battle to get the issue diagnosed, and been the one to support him in his new, quieter world. Without her, well, he didn't want to think about it. And knew without checking that both his gift and Dean's were special for their mom.

Millie handed out papers to everyone and David found a handful of pens and pencils. Boxes and bags were grabbed, the pile on the table quickly diminishing. Before he could stake his claims, a soft hand landed on his arm.

He faced Andie, saw her mouth moving, but couldn't pick out a word. He shook his head and angled closer to her.

"I have no idea what I'm doing," Andie said.

He took in her rosy cheeks and sparkling eyes and wanted to kiss her right there, in front of everyone. "Stick with me then, I'd like the company."

She beamed and they collected the final three gifts from the table. Footsteps and laughter fanned out throughout the house, mostly on the first floor. Leo wanted to take Andie's hand, but both of theirs were full. Instead he nodded his head toward the stairs and she followed him to the second floor. He turned to the right, but Andie went forward into the room at the top of the stairs—the bathroom—sticking her head inside.

"Would it be mean to put one in the shower?" Her lips curved and he really needed a taste.

"Yes, do it!" called Dean from down the hall, Leo guessed in Dean's childhood room.

Andie laughed. "You're the worst encouragement."

Dean backed into the hall. "I'm the youngest, what do you expect?"

"You two could be trouble together," Leo muttered.

"Shouldn't that be fun and not trouble?" Andie glided past him into the bathroom, brushing against him when she didn't have to.

"Oh, I like her, you're going to have to keep her." Dean chuckled and shook his head, disappearing into his room.

Leo had to admit, Andie fit in as though she belonged. A true part of the Dentz family unit. Maybe her easy rapport with Dean and everyone meant she sensed it, too. If so, then Leo had a starting point to truly winning her heart this Chanukah.

*   *   *

Andie pulled back the shower curtain. Inside was a typical shower setup with bottles and soap collecting on the ledge, nothing inspiring there. Until she spotted the sponge hanging by a hook. She only held a single box, so she turned to Leo.

He leaned casually against the counter, filling up the space with his relaxed stance, a warm smile on his face she guessed was just for her. Helped by the love and support of the rest of his family, even with the drama. Leo and Dean had both been cut down by their father, this scavenger hunt revitalizing them and preventing the day from completely souring.

Imagine that. If Andie's family had shown a fraction of the love over their conflicts, she might have had plans beyond Leo this year.

"I know where to put that one." She reached out, plucking the small bag from his hand, and settling it on the hook. "It'll be enough out of the way to not get too wet should it not be found."

Leo stepped behind her, looking over her shoulder. For a moment, she forgot about hiding gifts, focused completely on the strong body against her back. "I like it. And it's his fault if it gets wet."

She chuckled and stepped back, forcing her mind on the task. Hide the gift and then . . . oh, the clue! The paper was tucked in Leo's arm and she pulled it out, pressing it against the wall. "Let's see," she spoke as she thought. "If you want this gift, you'll have to get clean."

Leo snorted. "Love it."

Andie beamed.

"Should have known Ms. Ikea Scavenger Hunt would be good at this."

It warmed her that he remembered a silly little fact like that about her. "I never claim to be good, but fun, that I can do."

"Fun is appreciated." He locked eyes with her, the temperature rising as though a hot shower steamed up the room and fogged the mirrors. The tension a living wire between them, pulling them closer, ready to fuse the connection.

Leo cleared his throat. "I know where the rest should go." His voice was deep and scratchy, and it lit a path across Andie's skin.

"Lead the way."

She followed him out of the bathroom, down the hall to a closed door. Leo opened it and led her inside. Andie had the impression of a clean room, a bit generic, before her back hit the now closed door and Leo's mouth met hers.

Andie dropped her gift, paper, and pen, linking her arms around Leo. His mouth was insistent on hers, swamping her senses, creating that delicious tug deep down in her core. She wrapped a leg over his hip and he angled into her, pressing his hardness against her soft center, wrenching a moan from them both.

"I can't get enough of you," he said, then continued kissing her.

She licked his lip and he groaned again when she retreated. "You've barely had me."

His eyes were hazy as they met hers. "I'll say that in ten or twenty years or more." He kissed her again, not letting her respond to those deep words, not letting her retreat with his hands on her hips, pulling her to him, giving her a moment she didn't want to end.

Her fingers played with the tiny strands of hair at the nape of his neck, her mind torn between giving in to pleasure and thinking too much. She couldn't get enough of him either and couldn't imagine this little slice of heaven ending. No one had ever felt like this; this fire and connection. Her father always said sometimes you just knew. It could be a friend or a meaningful acquaintance or a love, but the soul knew this person would be important and continue to be a meaningful person to hold onto.

She wanted to hold on. To Leo, and surprisingly to his family. They welcomed her in, made her feel like she somehow belonged, and had a family again—something she'd always wanted. Life didn't seem to want to let it work, but all the decisions were still hers.

Leo pulled back, pressing his forehead against hers. "As much as I'd love to take this further, now is not the time."

She ran a finger down his jaw. "Later. We might need to generate more of our own heat with the power out anyways."

He kissed her again, this one soft and sweet, with an underlying hint of steam. "That we know we can do."

He pulled back to analyze his room. "I could probably just leave these two on the bed, he'd never find them." And yet he moved about, studying options.

Andie let him, new questions running around in her mind. What if she turned down the Ohio job? She'd lose her only guaranteed job offer. But there was the temple prospect. And if she stayed, she'd have the support of her friends regardless of the tight job opportunities.

She breathed in deeply, air filling her lungs and feeling that fullness in her heart. She'd have Leo as well, and not in a long-distance scenario. Something felt right here. As though she'd finally found where she belonged.

No rash decisions, even though her thoughts and emotions tempted her to jump right into this man's arms. She'd think it over some more. But at this moment in time, she wanted to stay.

CHAPTER TWENTY

Leo placed a tall and thin gift on his shelf in between two of his woodworking trophies from high school. "Dad never looks here, so this will be extra confusing," he said.

"So what's the clue? Talents of my middle child I'm ignoring?"

Leo turned to find a sly smile on Andie's face, tongue planted in cheek.

"Or is that too harsh?"

"It's harsh. It also works." He held out his hands and she handed over the paper and pen so he could add the clue.

That left them one final gift to hide.

Andie collected the gift from the bed. "If I may?" She bent, her dark-jeans-covered rear sticking in the air, enticing him with her soft curves to the point where she could have lit his room on fire and he'd think the heat emanated from him. Only after she stood did he realize she snuck it under his bed, barely visible by the bed skirt.

She wiped her hands together. "This I call 'where dust bunnies sleep.'"

Leo snorted. She charmed him, from the tip of her nose to the bottom of her soul. "You are something else, you know that?" He wrote down her clue, proud of this woman, even though he had no right to be.

"We teachers need to think on our toes." She rocked on her feet, a shift in her as swift as the wind. Some of her enthusiasm diminished, her light dimming, and he had to fix it beyond anything else.

He put down the paper and pen. "Hey, what's wrong?"

Andie pressed her lips together, eyes flitting from one corner of the ceiling to another. The seconds passed and he waited her out, giving her the time she needed to process whatever had caused her shift in behavior. When he thought for sure she wouldn't answer him, she finally spoke. "What do you know about Millie's preschool experience?"

Of all the possible things she could have said, he never would have guessed that. "Um, I guess it was good. The temple has a preschool, so that's where she started her education."

Andie nodded and he somehow guessed this wasn't new information.

"But you knew that."

"I did. Jodie told me." She clasped her hands together, wringing them.

He reached out, covering her hands with his. The connection hit him, as it did each time they touched. Only this time he hoped he could bring her some peace from her troubles. "Is something wrong?"

"No." She turned one hand around to grip him, freeing her other and flailing it as she spoke. "I found out about the preschool while there for the Chanukah party and was invited to apply. They called me yesterday and it turned into an interview. A good one at that."

Hope had never hit him this fast, and he nearly stumbled backward. Instead, he gave her hand a squeeze and swallowed the rest of his emotional reaction. "They offered you a job?"

"Well, no, not yet at least. But it's an option, potentially, and local . . ." She bit her lip. His head might be spinning from the new information, but he still had to fight not to lean forward and soothe the sting.

"I thought you accepted the Ohio job?"

Andie's hair swished as she shook her head. "No. Not yet. I planned to, soon, because it's a good job offer and there aren't any other prospects."

"Now you have a prospect."

"Right. And . . . more people in my tiny world that I'll miss."

It boiled up inside, the desire to ask her to stay. The selfish need to keep her as an important member in his life. "I'll miss you, too." It didn't count as a grand gesture or a request, not that he intended it to. This had to be Andie's decision. He wouldn't have her regret something because of him. Letting her know she meant something to him—that he could do.

"What are you going to do?"

Andie shrugged. "I don't know. I think I have a big pros and cons list to make for each."

"I'd like to be a pro, and a con, in the appropriate categories."

"And which categories would that be, Leo?" She brought her hand to his neck, resting it there, bringing their bodies closer together.

"Which ever one reduces the chances of me getting a bad neighbor."

Her laughter cut short when he kissed her, hoping to relay the rest of his sentiments through his lips and not his vocal cords.

"Uncle Leo! Andie! Are you finished?" Millie's voice broke their fog.

"Not nearly finished," he grumbled into Andie's neck, her laughter bouncing against him.

"Later. For now, I believe you have uncle duties to attend to."

He wanted to stay in this position for the rest of the day. Heck, the rest of his life. And before he could overthink it he blurted out. "What are you doing New Year's?"

"Are you bringing up a second holiday while we're still celebrating the first?"

"Yes." Thoughts of Andie in his bed on the New Year would not go away.

"You are something. How about this: I have tentative plans with Sarah. Let me check in on those after Chanukah and see what we can work out."

"Okay. This doesn't change the pro/con placement does it?"

Andie's sweet laughter hit him as she turned to the door. "No. Not yet, at least." She winked over her shoulder. "I'm going to use the bathroom. I'll meet you downstairs."

Leo took a minute to compose himself before joining the family.

* * *

Andie checked her phone while going to the bathroom, force of habit and all that. She scrolled through her email, deleting all the marketing junk decked out in red and green and sporting this or that deal, pausing when she found an email from her potential Ohio employer.

"Did they make my decision for me?"

She finished up, and quickly washed and dried her hands, before checking on the contents.

Dear Andrea,

I wanted to thank you again for meeting with us virtually. It occurred to me in our excitement over what you'll bring to our center, I didn't go over the benefits package in full. Please find those missing details attached. Let me know if you have any questions. And we look forward to hearing your response.

Sincerely,
Natalie Wright

Andie leaned against the counter, curious despite her dueling options and building desire to stay local. She opened the document, scrolling through the pages. Basic time off, health benefits, though she noted a few areas stronger than with her current employer, or any she'd seen. Then she hit a new area that had her forget how to blink. The heading read: continued education benefit.

"No way."

This couldn't be real, and yet excitement built as she speed read the details. Tuition reimbursement, time off for classes, an entire plan with the continued education of their staff in mind. She could go back to college and get her master's without it putting her further into debt. This alone would more than make up for the expense of moving.

"Is this place for real?"

She stopped reading and took in her environment, Leo's family bathroom. Baby blue paint on the walls, white tile in the shower with a blue floral curtain over it. A few worn parts to the corner of the sink and on the floor, showing years of a family being raised here. They had welcomed her in and accepted her, giving her a glimpse at a future she so desperately wanted. And yet, the offer in her hands gave her another path, matching a different set of dreams and goals. A strong divide built inside. The Ohio job had always presented as a good opportunity for her, a chance to grow in her career, and this option solidified it. Yes, she had reasons to stay, but not professional ones. She still had a few more days before she'd hear anything from the temple.

A crossroads appeared before her, both paths holding potential. Professional versus personal growth. She wanted to peek ahead, get a glimpse of the outcome, and settle back and know which way to go. Life didn't work that way, not with both sides calling her forward.

She checked the document again, searching for a loophole, something to make this amazing benefits package less than amazing, and found nothing. Not even a smidge of a reason not to take on this opportunity. All she found were reasons to not pass. This wasn't simply her next job; it was one that would help shape her future and give her job security.

Laughter echoed up the stairs from the first floor and a stab of guilt hit her. Prior to seeing the email her pro/con list had been nearly set, now the table had been flipped, and the contents rearranged. Somehow, she needed to go downstairs and not have "existential crisis" stamped on her face.

She exited out of the email and switched to her phone app, clicking on Sarah's face. "Come on, come on, pick up!" She muttered. She needed her bestie more than she'd needed a warm shower this very morning.

"Everything okay?" Sarah asked in way of greeting.

"Would you move for an excellent benefits package?"

"Hell yeah, I would, but that doesn't explain this frantic phone call while you should be cuddling on a couch with your new flame."

Andie sighed and updated Sarah on the email. When she finished she could hear a pin drop on her friend's end.

"Is this place for real?" Sarah finally said.

Andie had to laugh, though it felt bordered on hysterical. "I asked the same thing."

"If you don't want it, I'll take it. We'll do a romcom switcheroo. They've only seen you on zoom, they'll never know the difference."

"But then I'd lose my bestie and a fantastic opportunity."

"Do they want two for the price of one?"

"We'll never survive on the price of one."

"Boo. You're right. But boo."

Andie leaned back, head meeting the mirror. "I've been hearing amazing things about the temple preschool. Leo's niece went there. I think it could be a really good match and allow me to stay close to you and him. But . . ." She worried her lip between her teeth.

". . . but the odds of them having a benefits package that even begins to compare is highly unlikely."

"Exactly. What do I do?"

"Well, I doubt they're expecting an answer right this minute. Relax. Enjoy Chanukah with Leo and his family. You started seeing him thinking that it would be temporary, what's changed?"

What's changed? That really was the question. Andie's heart wanted to stay. After such a short time of really getting to know her neighbor, she felt this deep connection, one she wanted to hold on to. Add in the family downstairs and he represented the potential personal life she craved.

Too soon. This was simply a glimpse at a potential. And right now, all she had were potentials, on the professional and personal front. The only guarantee was this amazing offer already on the table.

She hadn't expected it to hurt, but she couldn't deny the slight tear in her heart at leaving. There'd always been one there, now adding in Leo and the Dentzes, it had more than tripled in size. For all the good the Ohio job came with, it also brought the pain. She couldn't go after one without losing out on the chance of the other.

* * *

Down on the first floor, Leo intended to join the women in the living room, but he got pulled in by Dean and David huddled together in the dining room.

"What's going on here?" he asked, joining the group.

The two welcomed Leo into their huddle. "I want in," David said.

Leo waited for that to make sense, but nope, his brother-in-law stared at him, arms crossed, not even flinching. "In regards to . . .?"

"Dean was explaining your plan, to start your own business since Glen isn't thinking clearly. I want to help."

Leo couldn't stop it, his eyebrows tried to touch the ceiling. "You have a full-time job and limited knowledge of antiques."

"He's got a full-time job that pays well enough to light up his house like the overachieving Maccabee."

David jabbed an elbow into Dean's side, not looking at the man.

Dean doubled over, rubbing the spot. "It's true! Your electric bill has an extra zero to it than mine!"

"You live in an apartment."

"Potato, potahto."

Leo crossed his arms, waiting.

"Silent partner. For more reasons than one. I'll help fund your startup capital. We'll develop a contract fair for everyone."

Leo mulled that over and had to make sure the facts were all on the table. "Silent from Jodie?"

"Nah, she's in. Antiques mean a lot to all of you."

"And your catch?"

David didn't even flinch. "None. I'm in a position to help, I want to help."

Leo shared a look with Dean.

"This is good. You and I have the skills and knowledge. We know we can manage a new business. This will give us the cushion we need to start strong and stay strong. Dentz Antiques two point oh."

"We're not calling it that."

"I'm not suggesting we call it that. What do you say?"

Leo looked back and forth between the two. It was sticky, stickier than this never-ending feud he had with his father. David was family, and family had each other's backs. On the other hand, David was family, and any potential problems came with risk to the family unit. He'd been there for all of them since he started dating Jodie and he was more than a brother-in-law, he was a friend. Leo trusted him.

"Are you sure about this offer?"

"Yes. Look, why don't we meet up the first week of January. Glen would have made some sort of decision by then. We'll talk plans, see if we can agree."

"New businesses are not cheap."

"Neither is his light feti—"

Dean stopped talking when David wrapped an arm around his head, covering his mouth, silencing him. "As your brother kindly points out, I have the funds."

A vision formed, a new place, a different version of Dentz Antiques. Leo could focus more on restoration. Dean could sell. With careful planning they'd pay David back for whatever he contributed. They could take on retro items as well, attract more buyers.

It could work.

Leo held out his hand. "Let's talk in January and make sure everyone really thinks this through. I won't have another business move of mine split this family."

David grabbed his hand and shook. Dean wrapped both of his hands over the others. Yes, they'd make a good team. All three of them.

CHAPTER TWENTY-ONE

After a splash of water to her face, Andie managed a normal-looking smile in the mirror and did her best to shove her emotions down. Regardless of anything, her future plans didn't affect enjoying Chanukah with the Dentz family.

She hadn't stepped two feet into the living room before Gayle patted the cushion next to her. "Oh, Andie, come here."

She obliged and sat next to Gayle, noticing the woman had an oversized book with family pictures on the pages open on her lap.

"What's this?" Andie asked, knowing she barely had to ask.

Gayle smiled wide. "Oh, just a few pictures of my children."

A few seemed to be more than an understatement judging by the thickness of the book, and pile of five more on the coffee table.

"This one is all Leo. He was an adorable baby." Gayle passed the book to her, and it landed in Andie's lap with a weighted thud. The not-too-subtle hint loud and clear—*look at how adorable your children will be.* Children that would never exist if Andie moved. What she wouldn't give to not be dealing with this internal crisis during Chanukah.

Still, she did her duty, flipping through the pages, aw-ing over the pictures. Leo really did take good baby pictures, even the one with him in the kiddie pool, crying, while a slightly older kid that Andie assumed was Jodie splashed nearby.

The photos were filled with family and love. Even a few with Glen tossing a smiling baby Leo in the air. Before conflict tore a hole in this family.

"Mom? What are you . . . No. Put those back." Leo came right over to the couch, hands out, ready to snatch the book from Andie's lap.

Considering she'd landed on the naked bath photos; she couldn't blame him.

Gayle snatched the book before her son could make contact. "It's my right as your mother to share these of my middle child."

Leo grasped the bridge of his nose. "You mean it's your right to embarrass your son. At least skip over the bath pictures!"

Gayle sent Leo a shrewd look. "I doubt I'm showing her anything she hasn't seen."

Andie's cheeks burned. If it hadn't been for the power outage . . . No, probably not, though tight timing nonetheless. She expected him to stomp off, leave, or try and barter with his mother. Instead, he sat down next to her.

Surprise had her staring at him, even as the book landed back in her lap.

Color shined on his cheeks, but warmth blossomed in his eyes. "I might as well know what you've seen rather than guess."

She couldn't help it, she leaned into him, nudging his shoulder with hers.

Leo reached out, flipping through some pages, before opening it up to one that held a few year's worth of Halloween pictures.

"Oh, trick or treat." Gayle sighed. "I miss those days. I've got Millie now, and it's wonderful but different."

Andie stopped focusing on the conversation. Leo hadn't let go of the page and she realized he pointed, right to a photo of a younger Leo wearing a white shirt under an open jacket, a beige belt, tan pants, and holding a lightsaber.

Andie laughed. "Not much of a *Star Wars* fan, are you?" She jabbed his side.

He tapped the photo. "Focus again."

Andie retrained her attention and noted the shorter boy next to Leo in black pants, white shirt, black vest under a black jacket holding a gun, and a girl dressed in white with the signature Leia hair.

"Dean is the *Star Wars* fan. He convinced us all to dress up with him."

"So you're saying don't suggest a movie night with Dean?"

"Might be in your best interest."

Andie chuckled and realized she'd inserted herself into a future photo album somehow. That potential movie nights with Dean and Leo were an option. That she'd get to see Millie dressed up next year. That the rightness of this family meant more than the bonds they shared with each other.

She turned the page, made sure she reacted to the photos for the mother and son bookending her on the couch. Even as her heart wanted to claim this spot as her own, the benefits package lingered in the back of her mind. This spot on the couch wouldn't guarantee her continued employment and education. Many families had albums like this, but she knew it simply wouldn't be the same.

For now, she really did think Leo had been a cute kid.

* * *

Something had changed. Leo knew it down to his core, though what could have changed between having Andie in his arms and panting against the door and now, he couldn't fathom. None of his family members were upstairs to say anything to her, and he doubted a bathroom trip could create this sudden crater-wide distance he felt in her. On the surface, she smiled and laughed and engaged. But he knew her better now, caught that the smile lost some of its fullness, the shine in her eyes somewhat dimmed. Subtle, so subtle he tried to convince himself he overthought things as usual and needed to breathe.

His gut insisted it wasn't an illusion.

So when his mother finally ended his torture session and left them alone he wasted no time in leaning into Andie's ear. "What's wrong?"

The shock in her eyes proved he read her right. "What do you mean?"

"Something's off. Did my family do something?"

"Oh no, it's not that." She worried her bottom lip in her mouth. "I just got an email from the Ohio job following up and got distracted."

He studied her and the curls falling down the side of her face. Her chin held high, almost begging him to question her. But she spoke the truth. Not all the truth, he knew that. And he had no right to push. "Anything I can help with?"

One side of her mouth curved. "What do you know about pre-schools and job offers?"

"The job involves teaching young kids."

Andie chuckled.

"That's it, I'm afraid. But I mean it. If I can help, I'd like to."

She reached out and covered his hand with hers. "Thank you." He laced their fingers together, desperate for her to trust him with whatever help she needed.

The photo album of his youth laid open between the two of them with images from the middle school years. He really should have put that book in a locked cabinet.

"Hey, I've never seen you working on your projects."

He found the picture in question, him in the shop, sanding an oversized armoire with his grandfather. His bony arms poked out of his t-shirt as he used both hands to scrub.

"Yeah. I loved working with Grandpa. He taught me most of what I know."

"I can tell. Not many teenagers are that happy to do manual labor with family."

He caught her eye, not realizing she'd stopped looking at the photo. "I think I was eleven."

"And you're going to tell me an eleven-year-old doesn't aspire to teen instead of tween status?"

She smiled at him, wide and full. His dating life might have been sparse, but no one had looked at his love for antiques as anything other than a burden.

"I was roped into work."

Andie failed at swallowing a laugh. "I know kids, and the younger you in that picture was in his element. I bet you still look good when you work."

His mind scrambled more than cooked eggs. She saw his passion and seemed charmed by it. And somehow looked at his scrawny awkward preteen self and saw the hints of the man he became.

"Oh, woodworking, too?"

Andie flipped through the pages, the older he got, the more he worked with wood, old and new. It fulfilled him in ways nothing else had.

"Yeah."

"You are full of talent then, aren't you?"

As fulfilling as antiques and wood were, they didn't come close to this feeling right here, staring at Andie, having her see him, the real him, underneath all the layers. Like it was obvious. Like she'd support it and never tire of his sometimes obsession.

This woman right here got him, as simple and alarming as that. And she'd be moving soon. He'd finally found his perfect match only to lose her. A miracle for Chanukah that would only last for Chanukah.

From the kitchen, Gayle's voice called out, "David, are we making coffee or cocoa?"

"Cocoa, Daddy, cocoa!" Millie's voice joined her grandmother's.

Gayle stuck her head in the living room. "I need a vote, who wants what?"

"After having David's hot chocolate the other night, I have to go with that." Andie glanced at Leo. "And Leo's sweet tooth either means you have some fancy coffee maker or sweetener, or he'll be going for the same. I'm also guessing David often has to be persuaded to make his delicious treat."

"Of course Leo will have the hot chocolate. That man won't even touch my coffee," Gayle teased. She moved on to find the rest of his family.

"Has your doctor had a talk with you about your sweets intake yet?" A glimmer shined in Andie's eyes, a seductive underscore to a normal-sounding conversation.

He leaned in. "I'm young."

"For now."

"You know what I find the most sweet out of all the sweets?"

"David's hot chocolate?"

He shook his head. They were close enough his nose brushed hers. "You. You, Andie Williams, are the sweetest thing I've ever known. Or tasted."

Her cheeks flushed and he kissed her, keeping it short and sweet, trying not to lose track of his family being here. Her lips against his felt right, like she belonged here as much as the rest of them did. Now he needed to somehow show her the same and hope it would be enough to convince her to stay.

*   *   *

The kitchen bustled with everyone standing around. David manned the stove, Gayle at the coffee maker, though Andie noted only David and Dean had opted for the coffee. An array of mugs in different colors and sizes lined the island, each one with its own personality.

Voices crisscrossed over each other. The moment screamed family, loving family, with all the goodness Andie had seen in movies and shows. This family certainly wasn't perfect, but they loved and loved strongly and she started to believe their love conquered all.

Foolish thoughts. Each family had its strengths and weaknesses. Hers had a lot of weaknesses, but her father was the strength. Just because this family had what she wanted didn't mean it belonged to her.

"Hot chocolate's ready," David said. He filled a mug, added whipped cream and handed it to Millie. "One princess caticorn mug for my princess." The pink mug with a cat/unicorn drawing on it transferred hands and Millie beamed up at her father.

"Thank you, Daddy." Her feet took one careful step after the other, since her mug threatened to drip down the sides, before arriving at the kitchen table and settling in.

David prepped the next mug, holding it up to read the writing on it, though Andie suspected he knew it already. "Is there a . . . Jill of all Trades here?"

Jodie playfully slapped David's shoulder.

"Oh, that's you?" He grinned and gave his wife a kiss before handing over her cocoa.

"Jill of all trades?" Andie asked.

Jodie sat next to Millie. "I'm a stay-at-home mom who helps my father and brothers in business, my husband in business, am on way too many committees, and have an entire room with unfinished projects, varying from crafts to a set of drawers that need painting."

"I've told you, I can do that," Leo said.

"And I've told you, *you* are not the only talented member of this family. I just need to find the time."

"The mug I'm told would result in my death if I break it." David held a very old-looking mug with flowers on it.

Gayle collected it from him. "Right you are. This mug is older than you, and me."

Andie leaned into Leo. "Gift from your dad?"

"Yeah, back when he was sentimental."

This is absolutely charming. "I'm sensing a theme here. You all have mugs?"

"Mom has mugs for us all. She wanted to keep certain things special and give us kids a reason for coming home. I have to admit, now that I'm an adult out of the house, it is nice."

Dean stirred his mug of coffee. Andie squinted at the blue mug with white writing and made out, "I'm not spoiled, I'm the youngest."

"I think breaking mom's mug would be worse than the clock and plates."

Leo groaned. "I'm trying not to think about it."

Dean shrugged and sipped his drink.

"Here, you need sugar," David said, handing out a medieval-looking wooden mug to Leo. It had decorative grooves in the side, gold accents and, Andie had to admit, fit the man.

Leo collected it and placed it on the island near Andie.

"Medieval, of course you'd have a medieval mug."

Leo shrugged. "Anything old."

Gayle placed a mug with computer coding near David. "One coffee, no sugar. How are you in this family?"

David laughed, pouring cocoa into another mug. "I get my fill of sweetness with my wife and daughter."

A chorus of "aws" filled the room.

"More like buttering us up," Jodie said.

"Still sweet." David sent his wife an air kiss and placed a mug in front of Andie. Andie assumed she got a random one, but with the way Gayle studied her, she decided to investigate.

The white mug had childlike drawings on it. She read the text out loud, "I teach, what's your superpower?"

"I braved the mall, and it was worth it," Gayle said as though it was no big deal.

An avalanche of emotions hit her. Her heart swelled, and she had to blink back the sudden moisture in her eyes. Here, she'd been enamored with the love and care this simple routine held, and they'd opened their arms, and included her. She'd felt like an outsider when visiting her relatives, and yet here she had a spot made just for her.

The others chuckled and she forced a smile, because as shocked as she felt, she truly appreciated this. "Thank you."

Gayle patted her shoulder. "As I said, worth it. It's clear to me this mug fits its owner."

She moved over to the table and Andie let the underlying meaning slam into her. This mug wouldn't go home with her, it wasn't a parting gift. This mug welcomed her into the family, despite just meeting her, it said she belonged and would always have a place here. She'd never known a family to be like this.

Andie leaned into Leo and whispered, "Do they do this to all the random dates being brought home?"

Leo tapped his ear and leaned in closer. She repeated.

Leo rubbed his neck. "Not for Dean, he doesn't get serious. Jodie met David at a young age, so that was a given."

"And me?"

"I don't usually bring dates home, so it makes this, and you, special." He swallowed. "You are special, in case that wasn't clear."

"But what—"

Leo shook his head. "Don't even begin to worry about that. Mom has a lot of mugs, and even for one day, we will all enjoy."

Andie took a sip of her cocoa. Leo's family fit her dreams more than she thought could be possible. She finally found what she'd been looking for and she'd be moving far away.

The people around her chatted and smiled. A happy family. A family that supported each other. Did she really need to pass on this for a chance at extended education? With this type of support, she could do anything. Climb mountains, teach children, or simply gain a family.

While she didn't know who she'd meet in Ohio, she knew how rare a family like this could be. And as Leo laughed over something Millie said, she knew how rare a man like him would be to find.

Maybe staying would be worth the risk, since she now had a safe place to land. And a new mug that claimed those in this room believed in her.

CHAPTER TWENTY-TWO

"It's almost sunset, when's Grandpa coming back?" Millie leaned over the back of the chair by the window, gazing out at the sun beginning to disappear behind the trees.

They'd moved into the living room after drinks were finished and mugs rinsed out for later. Leo hadn't exactly missed his father's presence, but knew a child's focus would be on gifts, and those would wait for whenever Glen deemed appropriate to rejoin them.

"I called him earlier. No answer." Dean's scowl matched Leo's feelings on the matter.

Gayle stood, brushing at her pants. "I'll call him. That man knows better." She had on her mom face that made all three children cower and Leo felt a smidgen of enjoyment over that look being directed at his father.

"He better have a good excuse. It's not often we are all together like this," Jodie said.

Dean leaned over the couch where she sat. "What do you call the once-a-month dinner Mom insists we all attend?"

Jodie locked eyes with Leo and he knew he wouldn't like her answer. "Andie isn't there."

"Leave Andie out of this." Leo didn't want Andie to be put on the spot any more than she already had been. She reached over and squeezed his leg, giving him all the thanks he needed.

"Welp, that man is in the doghouse, but I'll let him figure that out tomorrow." Gayle returned to the group, putting her phone in her back pocket. "That said, he is on his way back, and apparently has big things to share, which I doubt means he's gathered more Chanukah gifts." She sent Millie a wink. "But it is getting late. Leo, come join me, I need a set of strong hands."

"I'm strong," Dean piped up, flexing a bicep.

Gayle patted the bicep. "I know you are, dear. This moment is for your brother."

Leo rose but before going anywhere he checked on Andie. She gave him a smile and a head nod in his mother's direction. Yeah, she'd be fine with his family.

He followed his mother downstairs to her work area/storage room. If someone needed something and Gayle had it, here is where it would be found. On her workbench were set up the special family menorahs she'd made for all the family members, a tradition she started when Jodie was born. The concept was simple, a row of nine wooden blocks, with a second layer in the middle for the raised shamash. Sometimes, the wood had two tones, or it was stained or painted. All of them had a woodworked etching of their names on it.

They still used traditional menorahs, old and filled with history and ritual over more years than any of them had been alive. These had been a special treat for the kids to participate, and that habit hadn't stopped when they grew up.

A cog clicked in Leo's brain and he did a quick inventory of the chanukiahs, counting eight when there should only be seven. He took a step closer, studying the one sitting on Gayle's work mat, shiny from recently dried varnish, with Andie's name in the center.

"Mom," Leo groaned. How would he ever explain to them that Andie had a job offer far away and he'd known about it all along? "Do you even sleep?"

"What? I'm supposed to bring out all of these and leave the poor girl out? Besides, you know it doesn't take that long to add a name and some varnish."

Because his mother, ever the overachiever, had extras made and waiting for a special name to claim them. "You already got her a mug."

"And it means nothing that she's here right now?"

"She's here right now because Millie plots more than you do."

Gayle laughed, pure joy on her face. "Oh yes, that child does."

"I don't want anyone making more out of this than they should, treat it the same as one of Dean's dates."

Gayle studied her middle child. "My dear son, if Dean had looked at any of his dates the way you look at Andie, I'd be down here including them, too."

He couldn't hold his mother's gaze. Somehow, he felt as though he'd been lying to them. This short interlude with Andie didn't call for big family gatherings, no matter what his feelings were. They were a Chanukah item and he needed more time to see if he could turn it into something bigger, something that matched what he felt and how easily she meshed in with his family.

Things had somehow turned complicated, so much so. He hadn't anticipated it. On the surface it all seemed so simple: bring Andie over for Chanukah. Give her a fun celebration, with some embarrassment for him, and continue their enjoyment of the holiday together. He hadn't truly fathomed what it would be like to bring a date home, hadn't anticipated the ongoing issues with his father boiling to the surface as he should have. It threw a wrench in his feelings. One area over-sanded and raw to the touch, another over-varnished and shining without the addition of light.

His mother's hand on his shoulder brought him back to reality. "She looks at you the same way. I know whatever you two have is new, and new can be fragile. But I've heard so much about her, from you and Jodie and Millie. I had a feeling before now, but if I had any concerns, I could have kept the mug and this menorah out of sight, my little secret. She matches you, fits in with you. And I hope you both take the time to figure it out."

He swallowed, but that sandpaper had traveled to his throat. He wanted to confide in his mother like he hadn't done since he'd been a kid. He wanted to lay it all out on this very table where things were created or fixed. He wanted his mother's advice.

"She's—" *moving, temporary, barely gave me this second chance* "—special."

Gayle picked up the new menorah and handed it to Leo. "Careful, this is still a bit sticky. And yes, yes she is."

* * *

"You teach little kids, right?" Millie plopped down on the couch next to Andie, making the cushions jump.

"Yes, I do. Three- and four-year-olds."

Millie stopped bouncing. "That's babies."

Amusement bubbled up. "Some see them that way."

Millie tilted her head to the side. "What do you see them as?"

"Young scholars eager to learn about their world."

"They don't even know their ABCs."

"How do you think they learn them?" Sure, they had bathroom issues and more germs than the older kids, but she loved the preschool age. Her job let her give children a foundation that would carry them through their lives. Or, at the very least, she hoped they left her class with a love of learning.

"Good point. Mom says I was born reading, but I think she just likes to say I'm smart." Millie sat up straight, clearly proud of her intelligence.

"I've known early readers like yourself, and late readers, and you know what's amazing?" Andie paused, waiting for Millie to lean in. "They both can end up at the same advanced reader state."

"Huh." Millie glanced around, tongue peeking out of the side of her mouth in thought. "I guess that's right. So when mom complains that Uncle Dean wasn't a very strong reader, that doesn't mean he can't read me books, he just doesn't want to."

"Hey, I heard that!" Dean walked over and squatted before them. "And I've read to you plenty."

"You won't read *Wings of Fire* to me."

"I told you, pick something that I like and then we'll talk."

Millie crossed her arms. "You can't read it." She faced Andie. "Andie, can you help him?"

Andie couldn't hold in the laughter, but at least she kept on a level of two out of ten. She'd never had a conversation quite like this, certainly not one that made her smile and laugh and feel warm about her career at a family gathering. "I think he's a bit too old for my specialties."

"Ha ha, she's calling you old."

"You, too."

Millie slumped.

The basement door opened and Millie popped out of her seat. "Are we lighting the candles? It's dark out there!"

Gayle placed two hands on her granddaughter's shoulders. "I'm told Grandpa will be here momentarily."

"He better be," Millie mumbled, stomping away.

Leo stood behind Gayle, an expression on his face she couldn't quite make out. He nodded toward the dining room and Andie got up, following him.

"We have a tradition here," he said softly, and Andie realized he held something behind his back. "We each have our own menorahs. Not to light, that would be a fire hazard, but as kids we would set candles in them with fake flames."

Tradition. Family. Love. It really was all here. "That's sweet. Don't worry about me, I'm not here to interfere, just being present means a lot."

"That's not why I wanted a word with you."

The dim lighting couldn't diminish the spark in his eyes, the squareness of his jaw. She wanted to kiss him, savor him, even with his family in the next room. "Oh?" She stepped forward, the heat in his eyes swelling. "It's not?" A lift onto her toes and her lips grazed the side of his jaw.

Leo groaned. "You make me forget my own name." He met her lips for a hot moment. "But that is not why I wanted you here either."

"Oh." She took a step back, allowing air to cycle between them.

Leo revealed the item in his hands. "Mom made each and every one of our menorahs. And now she's made you one."

Andie collected the wooden menorah. The blocks were shiny and smooth and expertly put together. On the front, a woodworked swirl of her name. She brushed her finger against the etching. "I guess you get your love of antiques from your father's side, but an additional love of woodworking from your mother."

"Yeah. I was doomed."

The item in her hands contained a heavy emotional weight. It came with history and tradition, more so than by simply being an item for an ancient holiday. Beyond the mug, this said she was welcomed here, and not for a day. It claimed she'd be back.

She pushed the menorah into Leo's arms. "This is too much." She searched his face, curious how he felt about all this. "I'm new and only here because Millie said something."

Leo took one of Andie's hands and pressed the menorah into it. "My mother has gone a bit overboard, sure, but I did talk about you, probably too much." A soft, gullible laugh escaped. He didn't hide his gaze, he kept it open and let her see that this wasn't a simple Chanukah affair for him. He wanted more. Like she did.

Andie took the menorah. "They stay here, right?"

He nodded. "Yes. And, should it be necessary, my mom could change that to a different name."

Laughter overtook her, breaking the tension. "Why didn't you lead with that?"

He brushed back a lock of her hair. "Because I like the thought that in a few minutes, a menorah with your name on it will be next to mine."

Belonging, she'd never experienced a belonging like this from more than her father. It brought on a world of complicated intensity, something she'd worry about later. "I'm glad Millie invited me here."

Now Leo laughed, letting the heavy mood dissipate. "Can always count on her to create trouble. Though she usually knows what the good kind of trouble is."

"So I'm the good kind of trouble?"

"The best."

He leaned in and she parted her lips in anticipation, when a door slammed off in the distance. "I'm back!"

Leo's shoulders lost their loose, relaxed state. "Speaking of trouble—that's not the good kind." He took her hand. "Come on." He tried to pull her but she dug in her heels.

"Wait." She cupped his face, staring into him. "I know things are uncomfortable. But it's still Chanukah and you have a wonderful and loving family. Don't let one bad egg ruin it."

Leo placed his forehead against Andie's. "You're right. I think I needed that reminder." He kissed her, sweet and sure, and Andie hoped she gave him some strength with her lips.

When they pulled apart, Leo's shoulders were relaxed again. "Now you're ready. Time to join your family."

CHAPTER TWENTY-THREE

Andie pulled Leo into the living room, where Glen had an arm around a very unamused Dean. "Ha ha, it's a good day, isn't it?" Glen said.

Dean shot a look to Leo that even Andie could interpret as "Help."

"And there's my other boy!" Glen raised a hand in Leo's direction, but his son did not move. If anything, Andie felt he shifted behind her ever so slightly.

The older man with his coat still on, but not zipped, did not resemble the grouchy grump who left earlier.

"Did you stop by the new cannabis place down the street from the store?" Dean asked.

"There's a cannabis store down the street?" Leo asked.

Dean snapped his fingers. "Keep up, apparently Dad knows. Me and you need a night out." Dean slapped a hand on Glen's shoulder. "What did you get? Gummies? Brownies? A drink? And good to know you need that for our family gatherings. I'm copying."

Glen pushed Dean away. "I know where the store is, but I have not been. Can't I enjoy spending time with my loved ones?"

Andie wanted to step out of the room where one could suddenly hear a pin drop. The only motion were faces looking at each other, carrying on silent conversations.

Gayle broke the silence and approached her husband. "Dear, are you sure you're okay?"

Glen leaned forward and kissed Gayle's cheek. "Splendid. This year is ending on a high note."

"Ha, high, see, he admits it!" Dean said.

"Get your head out of the gutter." Glen shook his head, but even that didn't hold the punch to any of his words or actions of earlier. Andie didn't know if Glen typically had mood swings or if something else had happened. The crowd around her suggested it wasn't expected behavior.

"Fine. Ghosts then, you were visited by three ghosts of Chanukah—past, present, and future."

"Uncle Dean, that's Christmas!" Millie crossed her arms.

He looked down at her. "A scrooge is a scrooge regardless of the holiday."

"Enough, I have a story to share." Glen grinned a bit too wide. The closest Andie could relate it to had to be a Cheshire cat. Or Scrooge at the end of the story.

"No, candles first! It's sunset!" Millie pulled on Glen's arm. "Come on, Grandpa. We waited for you!"

Glen smiled and laughed. "Of course, let us light." He scooped up a squealing Millie and carried her to the dining room.

Dean joined Andie and Leo. "He has to be smoking something."

Leo shook his head. "I have no idea. I wouldn't think Dad ever would, but his behavior makes no sense."

Millie popped up in the center of their little circle. "It's a Chanukah miracle, you made another wish, didn't you Uncle Leo? I know you did." Millie flung her arms around Leo. "This is the best one. After Andie, of course." Millie pulled back, a pink-cheeked sheepish expression on her face. "Oops."

Leo gazed over the top of Millie's head at Andie. "I didn't make a wish. I don't know what's gotten in your grandpa."

"Oh. Right. No wishes." Millie winked at Leo before skipping off.

Dean threw his head back, laughing. "Good thing you updated Andie on her theories, or this could become awkward," Dean sang the last word.

"Uncle Dean! We need colors!"

Dean saluted and followed after Millie. "The color master coordinator has arrived."

The conversations flowed into the dining room, leaving Andie and Leo on the outskirts.

"Hey, you okay?" Leo said softly.

Andie nodded. This affected her the least out of all of them, and yet he studied her intently with his brown eyes, as though he needed her answer to breathe. The other voices faded to the background, leaving them in their own bubble. "I'm okay."

"Sorry about Millie, and my father."

"Nothing to be sorry about." She wanted to kiss him again, hold him and touch him, but even in a bubble, she remembered the others around them. This was family through and through. The big family she'd always wanted.

A match striking pulled them to the crowd and they joined in on the prayers, voices rising in harmony, until eight candles glowed in the room.

Millie bounced. "Gifts!"

Glen held up his hands. "Not so fast. First I have a story to share, about how my sons pulled a fast one on me and saved the business."

* * *

Leo shared a look with Dean. His brother mimed smoking weed in their father's direction. Whatever Glen talked about, neither of them were in the loop. Which made any notion of a "fast one" make less and less sense.

Leo wracked his brain, trying to come up with something, anything that would have erased over a decade of bitterness. Nothing came to mind. Even the last few finds that Leo and Dean had obtained didn't equate to a bank-altering potential.

And yet, their father looked younger than ever. Face light and bright, and it dug deep that Leo hadn't seen him like that in far too long, apart from when he looked at Millie. Glen smiled at Leo, looking him directly in the eyes. The last time that had happened there were no smiles or crinkling eyes involved.

It stung; a sharp twinge harsh enough to break a back. Glen hadn't looked his middle child in the eyes since the incident. Not even his illness had changed it.

There were more wrinkles on his face now, the regular wear and tear of age and time, compounded by stress. A longing welled up in Leo, for the man he used to know, for the years they missed. Because while he had been a foolish teenager, Glen held grudges like no other.

Something had changed, and the only possible explanation Leo could scrounge up related to the Scrooge scenario. Maybe Glen had a near-death experience on the road and one of their dead relatives came to visit. Grandpa would certainly chide his son on letting go of the business he'd started.

"Saved the business?" Gayle approached Glen, as many questions in her eyes as the rest of them. "Your boys were there, ready to take over. What needed saving?"

Leo loved his mother; she always had their backs.

"History made me cautious."

Dean turned a choke into a cough. Glen didn't even flinch or glare.

"But I challenged my boys to prove to me they had what it takes. And they came through in a way I would have never imagined."

Leo thought over the transactions from the last month and came up empty on any that deserved this gratitude. "We've been here, doing the work, trying our best for years."

Glen crossed the room, placed a hand on Leo's shoulder. "I know. I let the past guide me. Let my fears over each of your weak spots overshadow the strengths. I'm done with that."

Weak spots, that meant Leo's hearing.

"Definitely cannabis," Dean whispered. At this point, Leo agreed.

"All this because McFadden needed a get-out-of-jail-free gift?" Leo asked.

Glen spread his hands wide, in larger-than-life story telling mode. "He needed a prize beyond other prizes. We scoured the store, and while we have some fine stuff there, it wasn't the right one. On a whim, I checked out back, searching for what we might have missed. And there in the back held the diamond we all needed."

Leo's blood turned very, very cold. The items were in the back for one reason: they weren't ready for sale. A fact his father knew and knew well. His head swam, the room narrowing to his father's glowing face, all other contents spinning. A dark and ugly rage built from the bottom of Leo, fueling so fast and so bright in one second he understood why his father had been pissed at him for so long.

In the next he knew things would never, ever be the same.

There were several items in the back, but only one worthy of this response. "You didn't," he said, his voice a harsh and quiet vortex. Some people got loud when angry, his father one of them. Leo got deadly silent.

"Of course I did. The perfect end to the perfect day." Glen laughed, clueless about the shallow grave he'd dug.

Dean glanced back and forth between them. "The only thing back there valuable enough . . ." Dean's voice trailed off, his eyes going anime wide, a swear crossing his lips.

"An amazing find. I'm proud—"

"It needed a final coat of wax, why would you even consider . . ."

Dean shot Leo a look, grimacing, and the words died on his now dry tongue.

"I waxed it for you. I wanted to help."

"Oh yes, the wax was still sticky, but that's okay, it'll still work wonders."

Leo couldn't take it anymore. He grabbed his father by the arm, dragged him through the living room, into the kitchen, and then had to keep going, had to get away from the rest of them before he exploded like he never had before. He all but pushed his father outside, onto the deck, where the cold air did nothing to quench the inferno inside him.

Dean followed, closing the door behind them.

"Tell me you are not so careless to think an item in the back, with a still drying coat of wax, that you know nothing about is for sale?" Leo said the words carefully, slowly, before he spat them out.

"Oh, the wax was fine, McFadden understood."

Leo's nails cut into the skin from the strength of his fists, and he welcomed the sting. "That. Was. Not. For. Sale."

"Everything is for sale my boy."

Leo saw red and couldn't be completely sure the violent blood bath in his head wasn't real. The lack of screams his only sure ground into reality. "I repeat. That was not for sale. Nothing in that area of the workroom is for sale. A fact you've drilled into us time and time again. A family heirloom doesn't have a price tag."

Andie's desk. Glen had sold Andie's desk. With the pictures and note inside that Andie didn't even know about. She'd trusted him to make it better, not to sell it.

"Heirloom? Oh, yes, that will make a wonderful heirloom, I like the way you think boy."

Leo took a step toward their father, unable to hold his out of control emotions in check.

Dean stepped between them. "Dad, you need to snap out of it before Leo snaps your neck. That desk belongs to Andie. It was her mother's. Her dead mother's. She didn't give it to Leo to sell. Leo offered to fix it for her."

Leo turned, hands tugging at his hair. He felt like he breathed fire. He stomped off the deck, into the yard. He wanted to ask for a chance at a future with Andie, maybe give her a reason to stay local. Especially with the temple job, perhaps there would be a potential.

The moment she found out about this, well, he'd just bought her plane ticket, for sure.

On the deck, he heard voices, but couldn't register what they said or the emotions behind them. He walked straight to a tree and punched the trunk, the bark scraping his knuckles. Better the tree and his hand than his father's neck.

He couldn't fix this. McFadden had bought the item fair and square. And being Christmas Eve, the damage would already be done. The blame belonged to Glen. And even that wouldn't fix this for Andie.

"Son?" Glen's voice grew close, Leo stared at the tree and slight spot where loose pieces of bark had splintered. "That was Andie's desk?" No gloating, no happy sounds came. It didn't soothe a thing in Leo.

"That's why it was in the back, not tagged and out on the floor." He turned, jaw tight as stone. "I promised her nothing would happen to it. I didn't realize we'd stopped communicating to each other, especially about important items like that. Or did you not see the personal items in the drawer, the items that I found for Andie and she has a right to?"

"Leo, I'm sorry. That find was—"

"You know what? Forget it. I should have known. Business first. Nothing sentimental allowed to get in the way. The minute I damaged one thing I became a nuisance, and then I became the damaged nuisance. And you will never forgive me, never see I was a teenager struggling to grow into my own. I needed to pay for my mistake, for sure, but I also needed kindness and forgiveness. And you refused to give it to me. Especially after that, when I got sick and needed my father to help me navigate a world that no longer sounded the same, but you held on to your disappointment. Only now, you'll take an important part of me, a growing potential, and destroy it with your greed."

Leo headed for the house, knowing he had to find a way to break the news to Andie. "You're a scrooge all right. But no ghosts have visited." The words sailed over his shoulder. To his father they came easy. To Andie, he didn't even know where to begin.

* * *

Andie stood in the kitchen with the rest of them, far enough away they weren't readily visible to those out back. Leo had grown scarily quiet, shoulders rigid. The kind, warm man had taken a flight far, far away.

"What on earth happened?" Jodie muttered.

None of them had any ideas, a mystery linking Glen's happy behavior, with Leo's grave one.

"All I know is that the tide has done a 180 in the business saga and Glen no longer has the upper hand. Or any hand at all," David said.

Andie clutched her leather cuff. The uncomfortable drama of earlier, before Glen had left for work, now held the weight of a teddy bear. This, right here, was the kind of earth-shattering conflict that divided families, a sea parted between, an earthquake, a destruction of a bond.

She wanted the good she'd missed out on, the peace her tiny world with her father had given her. The tension from the men outside should have her walking the other way, finding her own way home.

She stayed. Feet rooted in the spot. A yearning bloomed to go after Leo, to comfort him and fix things. Typically, the only scenarios she yearned to fix were the conflicts between her students, or even with their guardians. Perhaps the rest of the family soothed the level of theatrics unfolding. Andie feared the answer of why she wanted to stay would be simpler and scarier than that.

Leo made her stay. Him. The package he came with didn't matter, though she certainly reveled in the happy moments before Glen had returned. Leo was a puzzle piece, one that fit into the lock with hers.

Funny how quickly things could change. A week ago, she'd begun dreaming of a new life in Ohio. Now she wanted to stay, wanted to weather the storm with a man she'd grown too fond of.

Leo turned to the house and everyone scattered. Everyone but Andie. She stayed in her spot, watching him flex and clench his hand, red spots becoming visible as he entered the kitchen.

"What happened?" She asked, crossing to him, taking his scraped hand in her own. Red bubbles of blood had started to form and would spill if left unattended.

Leo shook his head, jaw clenched tight, as if it had been screwed shut.

"Come here." She tugged and he moved with her, allowing her to drag him into the downstairs bathroom.

Andie closed the door and ran the water, pulling Leo's hand under the spray. He winced but didn't otherwise retract. "What happened?" Andie asked again.

"Punched a tree," Leo's voice came out two octaves lower and softer than usual. "Better than my father."

Andie soaped up the scrapes and rinsed them off. She patted the banged-up knuckles dry with a towel. "Where does your mom keep the bandages, I think you're going to need one."

She moved to the door but Leo grabbed her arm with his dry hand, halting her action. "No. Andie." He swallowed, face pale and her heart sped, aching for him. "I need a word with you first."

He didn't seem to care about his hand, and those knuckles had to sting. It sent alarm bells ringing. Something was very wrong here.

She faced him, reached out but he pulled back. "Okay."

Leo scrubbed a hand down his face, paced in the small bathroom. "My father sold an item that he wasn't supposed to."

She nodded, heart racing, not knowing why this needed to be said in here.

Leo stood straight, looked her in the eyes. In his face, a cog twisted and Andie knew before he said anything what had happened. "We have a system in the shop, items in the back are being repaired or held for a customer, items in the front are for sale. Your desk was in the back."

Leo closed his eyes, pain on his face. A numbness took over her, freezing emotion, cracking all the new bonds and dreams that had formed.

"Dad ignored all of our protocols, all common sense. If I had even a small doubt this would happen, I would have never brought the desk there."

"He sold my desk? My mother's desk?" Andie didn't recognize the voice that came from her, she observed the conversation from a place far away.

Leo nodded.

"My one piece from the mother I never knew. From her family that she cherished and wanted me to have. It's now in the hands of someone cold-hearted enough to drag a person away from their family during the holidays?"

"Andie, I—"

She held up a hand. Stopping him. The numbness faded, the faraway view merged into reality. Pain sliced through her. Deep and rich. How had she ever thought this to be her family, Leo to be her home? No. He wasn't anything but a distraction she should have avoided. "And you didn't tell him that my desk was there?"

"It was in the back."

She shook her head. "That's not enough. It clearly isn't enough. If he's not respecting you and your worth, why would he respect your protocols?"

"His protocols."

"Really? Would he sell something he had there?"

"For the right price, he'd sell his son."

"A son that is still alive." She took in a shuddery breath. "I'm leaving."

She turned, grasped the knob. A hand on her arm stopped her. She remained trained on the wall, not wanting to face him.

"How was I supposed to know this would happen?"

Her anger bubbled to the surface. She turned and he stepped back in the cramped space. "Because you let life happen to you. You want your father to sell the business to you, so you can get that pat on the back you've been missing since you were sixteen. Or maybe you don't want to venture out on your own. It's not about the name-sake of your father's business it's about the safety net of taking over a wheel that works. So you don't have to make all the decisions and take all the blame, yet again."

His face blanched. "I'm in talks to branch out with Dean."

A dark laugh escaped Andie that she didn't recognize. "Branch out. With your brother. You would never even imagine moving far away from all your supports. You are so used to relying on your family. And you're only branching out because your father won't sell."

"You're only moving because your job is being cut."

"Correct. When the local searches were not giving me the options I needed, I expanded to maximize my chances. I took the risk. What risk are you taking?"

"Andie, it's more complicated than that."

She shrugged. "It always is. But the bottom line is still there, that nice little box you trapped yourself in."

"And you made your whole identity the poor little orphan one."

Shards of glass filled her. Leo's knuckles might have blood on them, but Andie had tears ripping through her. "Talk to me when you've lost a close family member and see if you still think that." She grasped the handle again, holding it all in, refusing to crack in front of him. "I guess that's one less item I have to move to Ohio. So, thank you for that."

She opened the door and stepped out. Voices rose in the house but it came through as muffled background noise. Andie grabbed her coat and her bag and left the house. The cold didn't register, only the pain.

No mother, no father, and one less item to remember them by. Maybe being alone really was the better place to be. Where families existed, so did conflict.

And pain.

CHAPTER TWENTY-FOUR

Leo hadn't meant to say those words, but Andie had riled him up on a day when he'd already punched a tree. How could she think he just let life happen? He didn't. He made his own destiny, his own mistakes.

Which is why he'd not only waited too long to ask her out, but also managed to mess it up in record time.

He ran a hand down his face, the motion causing his knuckles to sting. Didn't stop the desire to punch something else—or kick his own ass. He wanted Dentz Antiques. The field, the location, the name, all of it. That was why no other option existed for him. Approval from his father? Well, that was never coming anyway—no need to bother searching for it.

His thoughts fought each other, and he couldn't get the jumbled mess to settle. The seconds ticked past, each one sending Andie further and further away. Reminded him of the sight of her leaving, the pain and hurt on her face and knowing the part he'd played in putting it there, he couldn't hang back. He had to go after her, had to do what he could to fix it.

Not that he knew what he'd say.

He burst into the living room, aiming for the front door sliding shut. Andie stood just on the other side; he could reach her. He could grab her and . . . and he didn't know, but he'd find a way to make things right.

"Leo! I didn't know that was Andie's desk. I never would have sold it." His father's pleading voice halted his tracks.

Leo took in the older man standing there, no longer looking younger than his age but the opposite. The front door had just closed, Andie was in reach. His father wasn't.

Dean stepped into view and gave him a look, one hand on his coat hanging by the door. "I'll get her. She probably doesn't want to talk to you anyway."

Leo ground his back teeth together, hating the strong odds his brother was right. "You think you're immune, you're an accomplice."

Dean shrugged. "I'll take my chances." He slipped outside, leaving Leo to face Glen in a room filled with their family.

His breaths came fast, a struggle to get them in and out. Everything inside tightened, a live wire snapping and crackling. How could he have wanted a pat on the back from this man? "You didn't stop and consider the protocols that *you* set up and drilled into the rest of us for years? Didn't pause and wonder why the desk was out back with no information on it. Didn't think 'Hey, let me send Leo and Dean a quick text before I create an irreversible problem?'"

With each breath Leo moved closer to his father, until he stared at the man, nose to nose.

"I didn't think. I'm sorry."

Glen didn't back down. He stood his ground, owning his faults. If only this was one fault that could be owned.

"No. You didn't think. You haven't thought since you came to the shop and discovered the shards of broken plates and a clock destroyed. You watched me learn everything I could about restoration, ready to repair the one piece that I could fix. But no. You refused to think of me as anything other than a nuisance, to the point of giving up on your father's dream, even though you have two sons wanting to continue his legacy.

"So, of course, you wouldn't think that an item in the shop might not be for you. Because my skills don't register, my talents don't register. I'm an insignificant flea, and you'll be happy to sell the business to anyone, even let it fold, rather than to give your son an olive branch."

Leo backed up, fire blazing deep inside. A tiny voice whispered he'd just proven part of Andie's complaint, he'd deal with that later. "I've paid my dues. Made up for a mistake years and years ago. I was a kid. I needed support and guidance. I'm done trying. I'll start my own business. I don't need yours."

"Leo, I—"

Gayle touched Glen's arm, shook her head. "Give him time."

Leo pulled out his phone, heading for the door, then caught the text from Dean, *I've got her.* The rock-hard knot deep inside uncoiled a fraction. Andie was safe. And if Leo didn't want to talk to Glen, he doubted Andie wanted to talk to him.

A small hand grasped his. He glanced down at Millie's face. "Uncle Leo? I made you a special gift."

A part of the internal fire dissipated and a smile he wasn't sure he felt appeared for his niece. "A special gift, huh?"

She nodded and pulled him over to the couch. His parents had left the room, though raised voices could be heard. Leo found Jodie's gaze.

"I'm sorry," he mouthed.

She shook her head, brushing it off. "Not your fault," she mouthed back.

He focused on Millie. Somehow, everything became his fault. Maybe Glen took most of the blame for this one, but with Andie, Leo and Leo alone held the title.

* * *

Andie made it to the end of the driveway before pausing at the mail-box and realizing she had no transportation and no direction. The cold wind nipped at her, and she tugged her jacket closer, pulling out her phone.

A leaf blew across a neighboring yard as she debated her options. She could call Sarah, or a ride share, or simply walk and let off some steam. Her feet didn't want to stay still and either of the other options would require her to sit and wait.

Walking won.

She shoved her phone back in her pocket and let one foot flow in front of the other. The crisp ground crunched beneath her feet. She wanted to focus on nature, instead of the pain shattering her.

Why had she ever let Leo take her desk? Sure, it had seen better days, but she should have never trusted him, not with something so precious.

A car pulled up next to her, rumbling. The passenger window rolled down and Dean leaned over. "I know you're probably pissed at me as well, and rightfully so, but want a ride?"

"Why would I be pissed at you?"

Dean's eyebrows rose. "Beyond the fact that I helped Leo move your desk to the store? I waxed it for him last night. If I hadn't, it wouldn't have been ready to go. I'm equally responsible for what happened."

"You just helped your brother."

"Hey, I've done a lot of damage with my helping, let me have this one." He pouted and despite everything, she had to laugh.

"Okay. I hate you. Does that make you feel better?"

Dean shifted, crossing the seat, and the door swung open. "Definitely. Now get in."

Ahead of her a vacant street stretched out, houses on either side leading up to a more populated road. She'd have to walk past a lot of homes before reaching any sort of public establishment.

Andie got into the car.

"Thank you." Dean pulled out his phone and fired off a text. "To Leo, just so that he knows you are okay."

"Not his concern."

Dean put the car in drive and got on the road. "Perhaps. But my brother is still going to worry, and this prevents him from walking around, looking for you like one does a lost dog." Dean stopped the car, Andie lurched in her seat. "Unless you want him doing that? Might feel good to know he's out here wandering through the neighborhood yelling your name, right?"

Andie shook her head. "Can you take me home? And not tell him?"

Dean focused forward and resumed driving. "Whatever you want."

He let the silence take over, and she slumped in her seat, suddenly very tired.

"For the record, he really cares for you. And even if he didn't, he wouldn't want something to happen to any of his repair jobs."

Andie said nothing and thankfully Dean didn't press it further.

* * *

"The lobby has lights, that's got to be some small miracle."

Andie pulled her attention from the unfocused image of buildings and trees to the apartment complex in front of her, the one where lights shone in various places.

Small miracle indeed. It brought an ounce of comfort, knowing she had a warm, safe place to go to.

Dean parked and faced her. "And no, I won't tell Leo. It'll be our little secret."

Andie couldn't muster much more than, "Thanks."

Dean tapped his wheel. "Need anything? I feel bad about the crap that went down. You didn't even get dinner."

And the power had been out long enough that she doubted anything in her fridge survived. "It's fine." She wasn't hungry anyway. "Thanks for the ride."

"It's the least I could do."

Andie unbuckled, more than ready for this day to be over. Here, she'd thought Leo saved her from a depressing Chanukah. Instead, she doubted she'd be able to enjoy the holiday in the years to come.

"Hey, wait a second."

She faced Dean, hand on her door handle. He held out a card.

"At least take my card, it has my cell number on it. If you need anything, even kicking my brother in the pants, let me know."

Andie accepted the card and tucked it into her pocket. She'd already said thanks twice and didn't know what else to say. The day had turned into one of the worst she'd ever had, and considering she'd lost her father, that was a high pole to climb.

"Happy Chanukah, Dean." She tugged on the handle to open it.

"Happy Chanukah, Andie. Sorry this one repeated the destruction of the temple."

The early evening air swirled around her, welcoming her into the night. "Just my luck, no Maccabees around to save the day." She closed the door and headed to her building. The lobby held a warmth that guaranteed power restoration, and Andie breathed a little easier. At least she'd made it home.

Dean drove off as she opted for the stairs, climbing to her unit, desperately not thinking of taking these with Leo or of how they had later kept warm. No. Those memories would not give her any further comfort, since without them she'd still have her desk.

Her dark apartment greeted her and she flipped on the light, following how it pooled in the empty spot where her desk belonged. A sob wretched through her, but she shoved it down, used it to fill the new hole deep inside. She wouldn't cry over a desk, or the man who'd taken it from her.

In need of a distraction, she went to her fridge. The insides were nearly the right temp, but not quite. Made it easier in playing the game of toss or not, since toss had already won. She got rid of anything temperature perishable, filling an entire trash bag, leaving her with bread, soda, apples, and jam. It would make for an interesting dinner. In her freezer she kept only the ice, then sat down with her carton of half refrozen ice cream.

The tears wanted to come again, and she froze them with her treat. She needed action, needed to find a way to regain control over her situation. And one clear answer came to mind. She grabbed her phone, ready to fire off an email to accept the Ohio position, only to be derailed by her text folder.

A new message waited for her, and after biting her lip and claiming another spoonful of ice cream, unsure if she wanted a message from Leo or not, she clicked. Curiosity had always been her downfall. Only the message wasn't from Leo.

Sarah: How goes Chanukah with Leo's family?

The thought of having to share everything that had happened had a tear slipping free, sliding down her cheek. She didn't need Leo, not anymore, but she did need her friend.

Andie: I'm home. It's over.

The response came almost instantly.

Sarah: Over as in an early night and you're having fun solo time with Leo or over as in this should be read as an SOS friend message.

Andie wiped another tear, her vision starting to blur.

Andie: SOS.

CHAPTER TWENTY-FIVE

Millie placed a blue bag she'd decorated in menorahs and dreidels in Leo's hands. In the center big curvy letters spelled out Uncle Leo. The part of him not shattered by earlier events thawed.

"You made this for me, kiddo?" he asked.

"Duh." Millie rolled her eyes. "Open it!"

He pulled out the white tissue paper, finding a mug inside. Like the bag, this mug had been decorated by Millie. Hearts and candy wrappers covered the outside, surrounding text in the same curvy handwriting: To The Sweetest Uncle.

"I'm sweet?" He held up the mug, showing it to the others, begging them to answer the question.

Millie answered first. "Yup! You have a sweet tooth, so you're the sweetest uncle."

Sweet. Just what every man wanted to be called. "My love of sweets doesn't have anything to do with how I am as an uncle."

Millie wrapped her arms around him. "Nope. It does. You're sweet." She planted a kiss on his cheek and he expected her to skip off, instead she clung.

Leo glanced at David. "Help me out here?"

David shook his head. "Don't make me kiss your cheek as well."

Leo put the mug back in the bag. Millie hadn't let go, so he wrapped an arm around her. His father thought he was a screwup, Andie hated him, and Millie thought he was sweet. None of those matched or felt right.

Heated voices continued in the kitchen from his parents, and he strained, trying to send his hearing aids around the corner to get an inkling of what transpired. Not that he couldn't make a valid guess: his father would deny blame and his mother would encourage him to see the other side.

At this point, Leo wondered if *he* needed the faraway job offer.

David sat down next to him. "Hey, let them work through it."

Leo scoffed. "We still on for our New Year's plans? It's now my top option."

"On a scale of one to ten, how irreplaceable is Andie's desk?"

"Fifty."

David winced. "Yeah, we're still on."

"I'm sorry," came a barely audible voice from under Leo's arm.

He looked down at the kid still burrowed into his side. It knocked every other thought or emotion out of him and he turned his full attention to Millie. "Hey, what's wrong?"

She sniffed; he hadn't even realized she'd be close to tears. "I caused this."

"Sweetheart, you didn't do anything here," David said. He reached out, rubbing Millie's arm.

"I made Uncle Leo make a wish and he wished for Andie. Now that wish backfired, because a menorah shouldn't give wishes, and if I hadn't made him make that wish then Andie would still have her desk and Grandpa and Leo wouldn't be mad at each other."

Leo pulled Millie back into him. "None of that is your fault." He took a breath, debated his next words, if they would help or create more problems. Then he realized escaping problems had not been on the to do list of the day. "I actually didn't make a wish."

Millie's head shot up and Leo worried he'd chosen the wrong option. "You didn't?"

He scratched his neck, glanced at David, but his brother-in-law only leaned back, a clear "your funeral" vibe emitted. "I had already had dinner with Andie before you wanted me to make that wish. I only wanted to make you happy."

"Oh. So it's not magic?"

Through her eyes he watched her little heart break as if he'd just killed the tooth fairy. "I don't know. I haven't tried it."

Her eyes cleared and she stood up straight, the typical Millie headstrong stance coming back. "Oh. Okay. So this was just some rotten bad luck then."

Leo did his best not to wince at the low jab he doubted she meant.

"We'll still have to try it out. Those words are there for a reason."

"Maybe next year," David said, "we don't need any more trouble this year."

Millie nodded. "Yes. I see your point." She crossed her arms, faced Leo. "Next year, first night of Chanukah, we make wishes together."

Leo held out a fist to bump. "You've got it."

Millie bumped his fist, then skipped off to her mother. Leo slumped into his seat.

"How do you handle that?" he asked David.

"You either wing it and hope for the best or don't have kids."

"Well, good thing my romance track record supports the latter." This day needed a major do-over button. With his luck, the exact same mistakes would still happen.

Luck and Leo might start with the same letter, but that's where the similarities ended. He hadn't a chance to fully recover from Millie's little bombshell when his father entered the room and walked straight up to him.

"What now? Have another item that's not for sale to sell?" He could bite his tongue and the snark would still leak out.

"I'd like a word with you," Glen said.

"Been there, done that." He leaned forward. "It never works out in my favor."

"Son, let me—" Glen stopped talking when Leo held up a hand.

The room had gone eerily quiet, but Leo kept his gaze on his father, not on if they even had an audience. He rose, slowly getting to his full height. "No. A son is someone you support. Teach hard lessons to but show that you also have their back. You haven't had mine since I was sixteen and nothing I can ever do will change that."

He stepped to the side, away from where his father had blocked him into the couch. His heart ached, deep inside. Extra at the realization he had been waiting for that pat on the back that would never come. In such a short amount of time, Andie somehow managed to see into the very heart and soul of him. Something a lifetime of knowing him hadn't done so well with Glen.

"I'm not your son. You gave me up over a decade ago. Not even my sickness could change that." Leo grabbed his jacket. "I'm going for a walk." He let the words sail over his shoulder, not checking on who got the message or not. For all he knew, his father had already left the room.

* * *

The outside air did nothing to calm Leo or set his chaotic thoughts to a tranquil state. He shoved his hands into his pockets, walking along the grass border to the road. Neighbors had begun to turn their outside lights on, the artificial glow combating against the darkening sky. Several houses had multiple cars parked out front, with lights and movement happening inside.

Leo hoped their gatherings held more peace than his.

He had ambitions. He had dreams. And they all centered around Dentz Antiques. A day ago, heck, an hour ago he would have denied that it had anything to do with letting life happen to him. A passive man did that. Not one who had goals. Goals his own father blocked him on.

So what did he want? No, that wasn't the question. What was he going to do with what he wanted. Starting his own business with Dean and the support of David felt like a step in the right direction. He wasn't Andie; uprooting across the country felt too extreme. Because his home was here, along with his family. And the business he really did want.

The world spun a bit and he sat down on a stone fence. He could be an active player in his future and stay local, people did that all the time. Which meant the real problem went deeper and was more complex than that, rooted in his father's approval. He'd given up on it years ago, true, but secretly yearned for it.

No more. He only needed to prove himself to himself. And if he was honest, he didn't do that often. Helping Andie with her desk was one of those rare moments.

Andie's desk. It should still be in the shop, giving him a chance to check on Dean's wax job and charm Andie with a renovated family heirloom. Instead, everything had been messed up. He wanted to find an answer, a way to solve the problem. Short of knocking down McFadden's door and taking the possession back, he had no ideas. A dark, cruel twist of fate. He had found someone, a person he wanted to hold on to. The Ohio job already put a wrench into his plans, but there had been hope, and potential.

Not anymore. Now his future was as dark as the sky above his head, or as dark as the sky would soon be, with only a few natural spots of light.

An old mustang chugged down the street, dark clouds of exhaust trailing behind. A lot like his present life: what was once new and bright now existed with rust and dirty smoke. The fumes hit his nose, tickled his throat, forcing him to stand and get moving again.

He circled the block, then did it again, not ready to greet those inside and fake a smile for the rest of the family. The night had grown darker, and colder, and he finally zipped his jacket, the heat of his anger down to a low simmer.

Either the time, or the cold, or Andie's words finally settling, but his thoughts became clearer. He wanted Dentz Antiques. He wanted to take over the helm and help the business thrive. So help him, he wanted the chance to pass it down to his own children, or nieces and nephews. He could build a new legacy somewhere else, but this had always been his. He'd tried to win it, to earn it. A fruitless task. If he wanted it, and he did, he needed to make it clear. And now, with his father's epic mistake, was his chance.

The business would never be handed to him as it had been to his father. He had to take it. Like his father used his past mistakes to hold him back, he'd use his father's mistake to make things right.

His legs moved with vigor now, a new pep to his stride. Only when he made it to the house, a figure sat on the steps. Adult-sized, casual stance. He took a gamble, ambling closer, until Dean came into view. Leo's gloveless hands were ice cold in his pocket, and walking hadn't eradicated a new urge to shiver. He sat down on the steps next to Dean, blowing air on his hands.

"I came back and you weren't here, so I ended up talking to Dad," Dean began.

Leo had hunched over for warmth, only now he straightened. "And?"

"Point in his favor: he called McFadden."

An undeniable burst of hope struggled free.

"It went to voicemail. Dad left a message. I think you should hear him out."

Leo stared at his brother; eyes wide enough to catch the wind.

Dean raised his hands. "I know. I know. Believe me. I wanted to walk the other way when Dad approached me. But Mom was there, giving me her Mom look and I had no choice. So we talked. And I think some sense has gotten through the old man's thick skull."

Leo scoffed. "I doubt it. Maybe it's a brief moment of lucid thoughts." The type of moment he needed. "Actually, this could work in our favor."

Dean blinked. "Who are you, and what have you done with my brother?"

Leo wanted to ask what that meant, but he feared he knew exactly thanks to Andie. "I had a wonderful person get wrapped into our family drama say a few overdue words."

"Andie is something."

It hurt, how much he needed her and how much he'd hurt her. The least he could do was not to mess up this opportunity. "She is. You want the business?"

Dean straightened. "Of course."

"With me? Partners. Fifty-Fifty."

Dean smiled. "Wouldn't have it any other way."

Relief filled Leo, not the kind where he needed his brother's response, because he already knew what that would be. Relief that he'd finally gotten where he needed to be. No more inaction. "Then we use his mistakes like he's used ours and take it."

"Like a club to the head?"

A rough laugh choked out of Leo. "I'm still liable to hit him. Make sure that doesn't happen."

Dean gave him a salute. "You got it. Partner." He held out a hand and Leo grasped it. "Now, let's go talk to Dad, and then fix the wrong done to Andie."

"I want to. I'm not sure how."

"You'll think differently soon."

That got Leo's attention. He turned to his brother, trying to read the man's mind. "Seriously?"

"You won't know if I'm wrong or right until we talk to Dad."

Leo stood and dusted off his backside, an urgency to get inside that had nothing to do with the cold. "Let's do this."

*　*　*

Andie sat with her soupy ice cream, unable to move as she waited for Sarah to arrive. A tiredness wanted to claim her, one that wouldn't respond to sugar or an energy drink. She should have kept her distance, stuck to a lonely and boring Chanukah, braved lighting her candles on her own with the lingering hurt and memories of her father.

That hurt she could handle, this new vice around her heart was too much. She wanted to climb out of her skin, get away from the painful itch, but knew those to be foolish thoughts. She couldn't change what had happened any more than she could bring her father back. But life had options and even through all the emotional upheaval, Andie held control over her life and the outcome. The new pain would fade, and what she did next could help.

The email from Ohio shined up at her. While slurping ice cream she reviewed the offer, and the benefits package. And like the frozen state her ice cream should have been in, her heart no longer jumped with glee over the very appealing offer.

"It's just your mood. A million-dollar salary would look bland tonight."

A fresh start. She held it in her hands. A chance to leave all of this behind, continue her education, make new friends. The accept button glinted, winking into the harsh night. One click, and she could begin the process.

Her fingers wouldn't budge. Something didn't feel right, not anymore. Though that blame could be handed to Leo and her mood of the night. She wouldn't derail her thoughts because of one very bad night. Andie Williams was stronger than that.

The screen turned black before any action could be taken. Andie slumped into the cushion, placing the sloshing ice cream on the coffee table. On a whim, she clicked over to the temple preschool website. The job listing wasn't on the page, but for all she knew they didn't often advertise here. She clicked through, over pictures of happy students, paused when a pigtailed younger version of Millie smiled up from a group of kids. Her heart tugged at that, the ice thawing.

Andie shook it aside. She clicked over other details, landing on the mission statement. *Our mission is to provide a safe and loving learning environment, enriching and nurturing in values and ideals, where each child has the space and support to grow according to their unique learning styles. The success of the future starts here.* The words clicked a box deep inside, gave her the sense of focus on a night where she had no direction at all. Different opportunities existed here, beyond what the Ohio job had to offer. She read the statement again, and again, the ice nearly all gone from her heart.

No, foolish thoughts. Jumping without a safety net, making plans on a whim. She loaded the Ohio school, found their mission statement. While the job offer and benefits package had given her the good kind of chills, this statement didn't. It said generic preschool trying its best. Granted, that's where Andie wanted to step in and help, because trying is all one could ever ask of others. It left room for growth, and her position there could make a difference. Yet, Andie began to wonder if her vision truly did align with theirs.

"You're getting ahead of yourself." She tried to convince herself she was looking at the world through the lens of a broken heart. But her heart had always been strong and sure, even in the face of tragedy.

She clicked back to her email, closed the Ohio offer, and scrolled up. A new email winked up at her, one she hadn't seen before. It had arrived the previous evening, while Andie was occupied with lights and power outages. It was from the temple. Titled simply: preschool position.

"That was fast." Did that mean good things or not? Her finger shook as she clicked it open. She scanned over the email, seeing her second job offer had come through. Her emotions had already been on a rollercoaster, and now an additional corkscrew loop. Maybe two. And yet, a sense of calm spread as she read the details. Pay consistent to the area and the position, decent benefits package, time off for classes . . .

Andie paused and scrolled back up. Surely her eyes were playing tricks on her and the classes she saw were her own to teach, but no, the temple had a program to help maximize continued education. Not as big a benefit as her other offer, but still a benefit.

She leaned back, staring out into her room. In a day where everything had gone wrong, somehow the tide had turned. Two amazing job offers had landed on her lap. Two, when others had none. A smart person would take the time, draw up a list of pros and cons, and weigh all the options.

Her heart wanted the temple job. Maybe meeting Leo, spending this awful Chanukah with him wasn't about building a connection or joining a family. Maybe it brought her to the temple, and to the temple preschool. She could stay local, not leave her friends or the other memories of her life with her dad. She could go back to school, work toward her master's like she'd always wanted. Her desk would be lost, but the odds of safely moving it to Ohio had been slim.

"I'm staying." The words may have been soft, but they held a strong backbone she didn't currently feel. "I'm staying." She said it again, louder and surer, and some of the unrest deep inside settled.

"Well, what do you know—I really am staying." It felt right. Her neighbor had had a purpose in her life, one beyond a surefire trust issue she'd bring to her next relationship. He brought her to her next job.

CHAPTER TWENTY-SIX

Leo sat at the kitchen table, arms crossed, leaning back on his chair. Anything to give him extra space away from his father, who sat at the other end of the table. His leg bounced with the frequency of a fully charged drill. The plan might have formed in his mind, but anger continued to simmer, and one wrong move would bring it back at a roar. Dean sat at his side, elbows perched on his knees, ready to intervene as necessary. David had gone to pick up Chinese food for dinner—that Glen had clearly forgotten in all his misguided excitement—and taken the others with them, so there were no witnesses to any forthcoming bloodshed.

Glen leaned forward, hands clasped in front of him on the table, unclasping, clasping again, unclasping . . .

It was the opening Leo needed. "Give us the business." Unfortunately, any attempt at diplomacy had long since left him. "Or are you going to continue your attempt to hypnotize us with your hand trick there?"

Glen released his hands, placing his palms on the table. "I'm sorry."

The foreign words sailed across the table, landing in a puddle. "Right. Because that brings back Andie's desk."

Glen's jaw clenched and Leo prepared himself for a blowout, but no other signs of anger came. "I'm sorry for the way I've treated you both these past twelve years." The words might have come out strained, but they had full volume.

Leo's chair landed back on four legs.

Glen rubbed his jaw, ran a hand through his hair. "I may have been too harsh."

"May have?" Dean scoffed.

Glen addressed his youngest. "Okay. I have been."

Leo glanced back and forth between the two, revisiting the cannabis theory.

"And then Leo got sick and I didn't handle that well."

"You think? You told me I was lying when I told you I couldn't hear."

To his surprise, Glen nodded. "I was worried. I didn't know how your future would be affected, if you could still be successful."

Leo's back molars clanked together.

"I was wrong to worry." Glen continued. "You've both done a lot of good work atoning for your past mistakes and overcoming the obstacles life put in the way. I've ignored them all."

Understatement of the year. The words were long overdue, but instead of bringing comfort, it demanded more answers. Leo had needed this while he'd been recovering and adjusting to life with hearing loss, or at any point in the years that followed. "Why?"

The air in the dining room was thick with tension, but none of the participants cared much. This conversation was always going to require a high level of strain. "That's a tougher answer. My father was always tough on me. Your mistake was not a small one, and I foolishly kept the monetary bottom line of what you lost and cost me in the front of my mind. Along with the pressure to be perfect." He held Leo's gaze, a rare vulnerability on his face. "A dollar amount you made up for over and over again."

Leo tried to absorb the words, but after so long, it came with part shock, part disbelief. And yet, deep inside, the sixteen-year-old version of him took a much-needed deep breath.

Glen taped his fingers lightly on the table. "The image of those broken plates, I still see them. I had worked so hard to acquire them and they were gone, just like that, a good deal lost. You two absolutely deserved your punishment back then. You don't deserve it now. I should have done things differently, created a goal for you to rise up to, if for no other reason than to allow myself to let go."

"So do it now. Or are you still going to fight me on the business?"

Glen shifted in his seat, fidgeting, and if this conversation didn't come with a boatload of emotions, Leo would revel in his father's discomfort. "I think we can discuss logistics and create a plan."

"And what does that mean?"

Beside him, Dean leaned forward, arms on the table.

"It means that Dentz Antiques was meant to be a family business, and I'm not going to end that line."

It wasn't the business on a platter like Leo would have preferred, but he still got his win. Dentz Antiques would remain in the family. For once in his life he didn't wait for things to be handed to him, even if he could admit the situation created the avalanche. He'd finally get his chance to take his rightful spot as owner, the spot he'd worked hard for.

Relief wanted to take over but couldn't. The price paid for this transition was too high for this long-overdue moment to be what it should have been.

"I can't forgive you for what you did to Andie."

"I know. I plan to fix that." Glen reached into his pocket, pulled out his phone. "I'm calling McFadden again."

Leo scoffed. "Again? It's Christmas Eve."

"Again. I made a mistake. And I'll fix that mistake. Either McFadden will understand, or I'll lose a buyer. But I'm not continuing to lose my sons over this." He rose, then turned back to the table. "You said you found pictures in the drawer?"

Leo nodded. "Yeah, and a letter addressed to Andie."

The words seemed to wash over Glen, settle in somewhere deep. "I shouldn't have touched it. The French Polish you'd done had been just so exquisite. Well, Andie deserves the work and her desk back." Glen walked away, heading out to the porch to make his call.

Dean angled toward Leo. "What do you think, partner? Do we have our win?"

Leo studied his brother, and the confident way he held himself. Dean gave Leo a chance to back out and change his mind. And whatever Leo decided, Dean would be there. "Yeah, we have our win and our namesake."

"And Dad?"

Outside, Glen paced, free hand in his hair, voice muffled by being outside. No gloating smile, no lighthearted anything. Glen was there to do business.

"Dad's on probation."

"Only fair. He's had us there for twelve years."

Glen returned after awhile, a tentative smile on his face. "McFadden isn't happy, but he understands. They're having a family celebration now. We can pick it up in the morning. And Andie's items are still there."

Leo breathed out in relief. He had the urge to cross the room and hug his father. Not yet. Not after everything that happened.

"So tomorrow we will get it back and return it to Andie. She'll decide if she wants any further work done." He doubted it, after everything she'd want to be on the next flight out to Ohio.

"We will. After Jodie leaves, I'd like you two to meet me at the shop. But the decision is yours."

Glen tried to leave, but Leo called out.

"What for?"

"Fixing another one of my mistakes. I'm asking for a favor I don't deserve; you'll have to join me to find out."

* * *

"He did what?" Sarah's eyes bulged as she finished off Andie's other refrozen ice cream. "I'll kick him! How could he let your desk get sold?"

Andie had finished half her ice cream and it hadn't help freeze her heart or numb her pain like it was supposed to. "I don't know. He tried to blame his father, and Glen is the drama instigator over there. But how do you accidentally sell a desk that's not for sale?"

Sarah shook her head. "Should we leave bad reviews online? Something along the lines of 'don't use them for repairs, they'll sell your stuff instead.'"

Andie set the carton on the coffee table and curled up. "They don't officially do repairs. Not sure how much it will affect them."

"Then we'll say something else. There are a million and one ways to tank a business."

"None of this will bring my desk back." It still didn't seem real, and yet a piece had been carved out of her. "Besides, Glen isn't selling to his sons, so Leo will probably be working someplace new soon."

"Perfect, we'll save our review for then."

Andie clutched a pillow and gave her friend a half smile. She wanted to have the fire and anger that Sarah had, wanted to feel the need for vengeance. All she had was an aching heart in more ways than one.

Sarah put down her ice cream and curled up next to Andie. "You really liked him."

That aching heart constricted. She hated herself for it, but she couldn't deny how close she'd been to falling and how rough the rug being pulled from under felt. "Yeah, I did."

"Then we'll egg his car or change his locks or cover his door with yellow caution tape."

A small laugh climbed up in Andie but refused to be released. "Thank you for being here."

Sarah covered Andie's hand with her own. "Of course. Anytime. Though it might take a bit to get to you out in Ohio."

Andie turned her hand around to hold onto Sarah. "I'm not going to Ohio."

Sarah pulled back; eyes wide. "What? What else happened?"

Andie straightened, clutching the pillow to her. A real smile tugged at her lips. "The temple offered."

Sarah squealed and wrapped Andie up in a hug. "Congrats! I get to keep my bestie close by!"

Andie held tight to Sarah. "Thank you. Leo's niece went to that preschool, they had such good things to say. And then I saw the offer waiting for me, like it was meant to be."

"Of course it was. They'd be foolish not to want you. And that will give Leo a chance to win you back."

Andie groaned and pulled away. "Too late for that."

"It is really?"

Andie glanced to the empty corner, where her desk should still be. "Most definitely."

* * *

Leo stood in the dark workroom, breathing in the smells of wood and polish. The smell of home. He'd been coming here since he was a small kid, helping his grandfather sand down a repair job, testing legs. It had always been in his blood. Now it would continue to be his future.

They'd eaten dinner and exchanged gifts and stayed until Jodie's family had gone home. Then the three remaining men got into their respective cars and met at the workshop. Leo had arrived first, basking in the silence and solitude. It begged him to text the others, lock the doors, and keep this moment for himself. He didn't. The only reason he was there, and not at a bar or banging down Andie's door, was his father's request.

He pulled out his phone, waking it to the thread of texts with Andie he'd been staring at, trying to figure out what he could possibly say. *I'm sorry. I'm going to fix this.* He stared at the words, hesitating. Until he had the desk back in his hands, he wasn't confident in either his father or McFadden. He deleted the second statement and sent the sorry.

Dean's muffled voice alerted him to the end of his solitude, followed by the hum of the lights as they clicked on and flooded the space.

His father said something in response before coming into view; eyes trained straight ahead. He passed Leo, heading straight to the corner.

"No way," Dean breathed.

Leo could hardly believe it himself. If he wore glasses, he'd take them off and check the lenses. But there they stood as their father approached the busted clock and put his hand on it. He faced his sons and Leo couldn't deny the note of apprehension on his face, filling the room with an unsettled energy. As though all three men and each antique item held their breath. "Tonight, we fix this. Together."

Dean audibly sucked in air, his gaze burning the side of Leo's cheek.

Leo stared at Glen, his feet moving toward the clock before he fully realized he planned to. "Seriously?"

Glen's smile was tentative and cautious. "Seriously. It's long overdue. And I'm tired of having this busted up old thing in a corner."

Dean appeared beside Leo, rubbing his hands together. "Let's tear this baby apart!"

"We're missing a few pieces. I know we can get the exterior looking good, Leo has proven that time and time again. The working clock pieces are another story."

A switch clicked in Leo. "I might have an answer for that." He moved to the other end of the work area, the region his father rarely ventured, and dug out Rose's old clock. She'd given this relic to him for a chance at a new life, and now he'd be able to tell her he'd had that chance. The pieces would be nearly the same size, it might work.

"What's that?" Glen asked.

Leo held it up. "From our long-time customer Rose, to be fixed or to help another item be fixed, as long as it helped bring more good memories to life."

Dean chuckled and Leo found his lips curving, along with his father's. Leo expected Glen to take it from him, do the inspection, even though Glen rarely did more than light repair work.

"I think we can manage that. But what do you think? Will it work for this grandfather clock? Or is it worth repairing?" Glen said.

Leo nearly stumbled back. He'd never been given this level of input. It soothed old hurts, a stitch on an old wound, and he began to fear it had a lot to do with Andie's accusations. Still, Leo inspected the smaller clock and compared it to the bigger one. He took his time, going into repair mode, doing what he did best.

"This old clock might be worth a repair, but it's not going to yield much more than sentimental appreciation. The strongest pieces match what was damaged in the grandfather clock. I'd say there's a high chance it's going to work."

Glen patted Leo on the back. "Then let's do it."

"There's glass that needs replacing."

"I'm well aware. We'll get there later if we don't have options here."

The three of them got to work. They moved the grandfather clock to the workbench, removed the remaining broken pieces. In addition to what had been damaged, the years of neglect had taken its toll. It needed the full repair, from sanding down worn wood, to varnish, to finding the right spare parts for the splintered wood. They worked into the night, surprising Leo by being able to relax and joke as they worked. He still checked his phone, more than he should have, but his family wisely didn't comment. No new messages from Andie came through.

Glen took direction, allowed Leo to be in charge. It shifted things deep down, the praise he had so desperately wanted. Andie truly had been right all along, and he'd find a way to make it up to her, starting with ensuring her desk would be returned in the repaired state he promised her. He wanted to tell her, all of it, but forced himself to wait.

The time had clicked past 2 AM when they'd finished all they could. Glue from the repairs still needed to dry, and the whole thing would need a good sanding and fresh coat of varnish. They'd have to order replacement glass, which they expected. Thanks to Rose's item and their hard work, the clock ticked in the workspace once again.

Glen wrapped one arm around Leo, the other around Dean. "The three of us make a good team, I'm sorry it took me this long to appreciate it."

"Don't get soppy on me, or I'll break another plate."

Leo braced for his father to stiffen, instead Glen laughed and rustled Dean's hair. "You would do that, too, wouldn't you, if it would serve a purpose of helping others."

Leo took it in. The clock on its way to even better shape than it had been before. He'd fixed a mistake from his past. Now he needed to fix the current one.

"Can we get Andie's desk now?"

Glen patted Leo's back. "It's too early. This girl really means something to you, doesn't she?"

"He brought her home for Chanukah—of course she does," Dean said.

A twinkle in Glen's eyes made Leo's stomach twitch. No longer an estranged parent, and a hint that underneath it all he never had been. "He brought her because Millie initiated it."

Yeah, his parents had been on to him. Not that any of that mattered now. "Yes. Andie does mean something to me. She has for some time." He didn't know the real Andie before, had only been intrigued by her beauty and her kind demeanor. But he knew her now. Knew that her kindness came from the biggest heart he'd ever seen. How she somehow managed to see the positive side of things, even when life handed her a crappy share. She brought fun wherever she went. And he wanted that spark in his life for a long, long time to come.

"I see how you look at her. If we can fix this, I suspect we'll have a new addition to our family gatherings."

It should have been too much, but Leo couldn't deny it felt right. He wanted action, he needed it. "So let's get her desk back."

"Soon. Get some sleep. We'll reconvene in the morning."

"It's already morning," Dean said.

"Later morning. Normal hours morning." Glen turned to Leo. "I really am sorry. For everything."

Leo nodded. He wasn't about to jump into a fatherly hug. But he could accept the strength needed for everything that had transpired since the afternoon. He held out a hand. "Lucky for you, I've been taught how to hold a grudge."

Glen laughed ruefully and shook Leo's hand.

CHAPTER TWENTY-SEVEN

After a restless night, Andie woke up clutching the pillow Leo had used. Sleep had obscured her memories, and she breathed in the faint reminder of his woodsy scent, wrapping herself up in her sheets, imagining more happy times with a man she'd grown fond of . . .

The previous day's events slammed into her, an unwelcome tidal wave of emotion, and she tossed the pillow off the bed like a bug had landed on it. Ugh. She needed to do laundry and change her sheets. Her puffy eyes made focus a challenge and prompted the question of how she managed to wake with that sense of misguided peace?

Her dreams must have told her some happy lies, not that she remembered what they were. Pity, she'd love to go back to whatever reality had a smile on her face, rather than the broken heart she carried with her this morning.

Enough! She wiped her hands in front of her, clearing the air. She didn't do wallowing, didn't see the need to grieve a relationship, a short-term one at that, especially so soon after grieving a parent.

"Okay, Andie, you need a game plan."

She stared at her ceiling, ready to put on her well-used brave exterior and make the best of things. Life hadn't often been easy, but her father had shown her that sometimes the simple things, namely a positive outlook and a creative plan, made just about anything better.

"Focus on the facts. You've decided on the temple job."

The words soothed her in the morning light. Shadows danced across the walls from trees swaying nearby. Yes, here was her positive. She'd stay, accept the temple offer, and pass on the Ohio opportunity.

"What do you think, Dad, smart decision?"

The wind blew harder against her windowpanes, the most answer she'd get from a dead man. He'd tell her to look inside and do what felt right—and the temple job felt right.

"Okay then. I'm really staying."

She waited for the doubt, for the reality of her decision to cause a twinge. Nothing. The temple job had the pro column stacked well against moving to Ohio.

"One down. Job decided. The next fact is I no longer have Mom's desk."

The pain creeped back in, fresh and raw. Andie clutched the blanket closer to the hole in her heart. She'd do just about anything to get that desk back. If only the option existed.

"Okay, new plan, find all items that relate to Mom and create some other way to display that in the living room."

Not perfect, but she had some random items here and there. Not as good as the desk, but something to hold onto and bring the memories. She could even add items from her father, create a shelf somewhere to honor the parents who had created her. The image formed, a fancy shelf with scalloped trim, rustic coating. She'd put it in her living room, above where her desk used to live.

"That will work. I'll make it work."

Her heart still felt heavy, but she had her facts and she had her plans. She woke up her phone, ready to pass on the Ohio job.

Texts waited for her.

All from Leo.

She bit her lip, debating if she wanted to see what he had to say, but knew it would bother her until she checked.

Leo: I'm sorry.
Leo: Truly, I am. If I had thought there was any chance of something like this happening, I would have never let your desk out of my sight.
Leo: I'm going to stop by later today with something for you. Please let me in.

"The mug won't make up for the desk, Leo Dentz."

She nearly typed that but held on to restraint. Instead, she set her phone down, leaving him on read and headed to the bathroom. A nice warm shower in her own apartment was exactly what she needed.

* * *

Leo hadn't slept. How could he with Andie on the other side of his wall? He was tempted to knock, apologize through Morse code, not that either of them knew Morse code. Well, he didn't, but for all he knew, Andie did.

He got up. Paced the length of his apartment. Emptied out his fridge with no regard to anything that might still be good. He showered, took out the trash, and still managed to be the first one back at the shop.

He had one chance to fix things. On the last night of Chanukah. He didn't know if they would have a chance at a future, long distance or not. He had to right this wrong and give Andie what he'd set out to do: a good Chanukah.

The sun began peeking over the buildings and trees. He grabbed a chair, set it outside. Cold morning wind rushed up his pant legs and found any opening through his jacket. It rustled against his microphones in that mind-numbing sound. He didn't care. The sky turned purple, then reds and oranges crept up the horizon, warming the area, though not the wind.

Whether frozen to the chair in reality or figuratively or just plain exhaustion, his father found him there.

Glen looked down at his middle child but didn't say a word. He passed Leo and went into the shop. Had the previous night been a dream? Did Glen get some sleep and realize he'd made a big mistake? A sudden panic welled, fear that Glen had had a change of heart and a bigger bridge would need to be burned to get Andie's desk back.

The door opened and Glen returned, placing a chair next to Leo. He sat, staring out beyond the buildings and trees, at the light still holding some color from the transition to day. The silence lingered, enhanced only by wind or cars on the nearby street.

Glen said something and the wind drowned it out.

"What?" Leo turned to his father, expecting the typical snide remark.

"You sleep?" Glen showed no sign of frustration at repeating himself.

Leo shook his head.

Glen placed a hand on Leo's knee. "We're getting her desk back. I won't let McFadden back out."

It filled him with a hint of helium disguised as hope. Hope for Andie. Hope for his future, both professional and personal. A tide had turned in his life and he'd need to stay focused to ensure it shifted the way he wanted.

Another car pulled into the lot and Dean exited the vehicle, reaching back before reemerging with a tray of coffees. He walked over as though he expected everyone to be outside and handed each of them a hot cup.

Leo's fingers stung from the cold morning, and he cherished the hot beverage in his hands.

"Should we warm up lover boy over here before his fingers break off and drop the desk?"

"Ha. Ha." Leo couldn't muster anything more.

"No. We're going to sit here for a few more minutes and enjoy the scenery and each other's company." Glen sipped his coffee. "And then we'll force Leo to warm up before he does drop the desk."

Dean laughed and tipped back his cup.

Leo breathed in the morning air, with his father and brother by his side. The present and future of Dentz Antiques.

* * *

Andie had just finished putting away her replacement groceries when a knock at her door startled her. She reached for her phone, but no new messages awaited her. And she hadn't responded to Leo's text. Not ready to see him, no matter what he thought could soothe over the events of the previous day.

She gathered up her reusable bags and fit them back into their storage spot, ready to head to her bedroom. She very rarely had someone knock and wasn't worried about checking. The knock at the door came again, followed by, "Andie, it's Dean."

She paused. Did Leo send Dean with his sure-to-be-lackluster attempt at winning her back? It didn't make sense, not one bit.

"Hey, I know you don't want to see Leo, so I'm here. But I'm standing in your hall with a very heavy item, so let me in and then complain to Leo later."

Confusion rankled deep inside, but she made her way over to the door, and opened it wide. Dean stood outside her unit, smile on his face. Next to him stood Glen.

The older man rubbed a hand over his head. "You probably don't want to see me, either, but I did something that I never should have, and I needed to come here and own my mistake."

If Dean wasn't there, Andie would be convinced she'd hit her head or was still dreaming.

"He finished his Scrooge experience. Complete transformation, so far at least. No ghosts required," Dean said.

Andie didn't know what to say. What could they possibly do to fix the mess that was created? That's when she noticed Dean didn't stand as tall as usual, he had his hip leaning against—

"My desk!" She ran out into the hall, and the men parted like a beam of light shining down on her lost belonging. The stained wood was gone, it shined with refreshed life and vigor. A part of her stolen and returned and she couldn't help herself, she hugged it.

Dean chuckled. "Wanna let us bring this inside, or should I get my brother, who is pacing impatiently in his apartment, to help?"

Andie swallowed, eyes darting to her neighbor's unit. Some of her anger had dissipated, but she wasn't ready to extend any olive branches. "You can bring it in."

Dean straightened. "Works for me."

Dean and Glen each grabbed an end, lifting her desk carefully and gliding it into her apartment. Dean led, setting it back where it rightfully belonged. She took it in, marveled at how good and fresh it looked. No longer did it appear to be a yard-sale find; instead, it sparkled as the heirloom she'd cherished. It shined, more than the wax, bringing the quality of her room up several notches.

"Leo asked me to tell you he could take it apart and do a more thorough refurbish, but wanted to get it back to you and wasn't sure what you'd like. Your call. But the drawer works."

The drawer works. Andie stepped in, reached for the knob, and gently tugged. It slid out smoothly, revealing items inside.

"Did the buyer leave something in here?" she asked.

"Nope. Leo found that when he got it working again. He'd saved it for a surprise."

A surprise?

"I should have checked, nothing valuable should have left the shop," Glen said. He'd taken a step back, keeping a quiet composure. A more subdued version of the man she'd met.

"Yeah, part of his deal was this surprise, and he would never have forgiven Dad or himself if he lost it."

"I'd deserve that one," Glen muttered.

She reached inside and pulled out an envelope. It had her name on it and she placed it aside as the photograph underneath stared up at her. A picture of her mother, wild curly hair, big smile, holding a chubby-cheeked baby. Her. Three more pictures followed, pictures she had never seen, from the rare period of her life when she had had her mother.

Andie didn't know when the drawer had been busted, or how, but her mother must have left these here for her, somehow.

The handwriting on the envelope didn't immediately register, but she opened it. The paper inside felt old and fragile as she carefully unfolded it.

My dearest Andie,

I am so sorry my dear, that I will not be here for your future. I had planned to watch you grow, to dry your tears and celebrate your accomplishments. I had planned to be here for you and your children.

Life had different plans for me. So I write this now, and will find some way to lock it inside this desk. Your desk. Your father has very specific instructions. I want you to know that I love you, now and forever. I am leaving you in the best of hands, your father's, and I know he will give you the world.

Love always,
Mom

Tears pricked at the corner of Andie's eyes. She held the letter closer to her, a quasi hug from her mother. This desk never belonged outside of her family and a moment of terror at never knowing these special pieces existed threatened to consume her, but she pushed it aside. No use fretting over what had already been remedied. And the letter didn't appear to have been opened, so if lost she'd never have known.

"Was the letter important?" Glen asked.

She looked over, letter still clutched to her, and had to swallow a sudden wave of anger. "From my mother. She died when I was three." It came out harsh, but the situation called for it.

Glen's face sagged, aging him. "I really am sorry. I let myself get too caught up in the past and this should never have happened."

It occurred to Andie that her anger at Leo was misplaced if his father stood in her apartment apologizing. "So what should have happened?"

Dean crossed his arms, settled on the edge of her couch.

Glen gave a double head nod. "Items in the back are not for sale, but sometimes they might be checked for a potential match for a customer. In that case their tags need to be reviewed to see if it is for sale."

"And what did the tag at my desk say?"

Glen lost a bit of color. "It didn't have a tag."

Andie straightened, but so did Dean. "Because I had just finished waxing it and there was no place to put the tag. So it was on a nearby work bench, which any fool should have known to check."

Glen waved a hand at his youngest.

"And I didn't. I got carried away, and that is how this mistake happened. And, yes, if you are wondering, it's not Leo's fault." Glen swallowed, the words a bit strained.

She thought fresh anger would consume her, the admission at the carelessness he gave to her belonging. Hard to feel anything other than relief.

"So how did you get it back?"

"I called McFadden, took responsibility for my actions. McFadden wasn't happy, but he'll get another item to make up for it."

"You've got something else to check out." Dean nodded back to her desk.

Andie turned, finding one remaining item stared up at her from the drawer. Another letter, in different handwriting.

Andie,

I'm sorry. So very sorry. You were right. About everything. I needed to take charge of my life and I'm taking that to heart. I don't know if there is anything I can do to fix things. So I want you to know this: your desk is back, and I would have moved mountains to get it to you.

You showed me a lot about myself in our short week together and I will always be thankful for that.

I can do a deeper refurbish, if you want. And I'm here to fix us, if you'll allow me. I know you're moving and better things await you. Just know you will always hold a special place in my heart.

Leo

"So what should I tell him?"

Andie jumped, so lost in her own world she'd forgotten Dean and Glen were still there.

"For the record, he really does care about you. Unlike anything I've seen before."

Glen nodded at Dean's words.

Andie bit her lip. Leo's words touched her, smoothed over a crack in her heart. Perhaps she had been too harsh. After all, he hadn't been the one to sell her desk. And he managed to get it back.

"Oh, I'm a shmuck, I've got one more thing for you."

Dean headed out into the hall and came back with a wooden plaque. He set it up on the desk and it slid against the base as though it always belonged there. Etched into the wood were the words: Andie's Desk. Do Not Sell.

A smile grew on Andie's face and warmed her up from deep inside.

"Just in case there is ever any questions again," Dean said. "Leo thought about etching that onto the desk itself, but if you ever have children to pass it on to, he figured this was better."

Andie rubbed her cuff bands, staring at her desk. Her now-perfect desk, with the one addition she hadn't known she needed.

"He's home?" she asked.

Dean grinned. "Yeah, he is. Probably with his ear pressed against the wall, trying to hear us, even though he knows he can't, and waiting for me to return with an update."

That gave Andie an idea.

CHAPTER TWENTY-EIGHT

Leo paced his apartment. Back and forth. Back and forth. He fit his ear to his door, but no sounds came from the hall, not that he often heard much. He checked the peephole, but the narrow vision yielded much less. He tried his bedroom wall, but the odds of that giving him any clues were slim to none. He couldn't stand still—or sit still.

He needed to know how the drop-off went. Needed to see Andie's face and know she was okay.

The wait killed him, but he waited. Dean and Glen would stop by and update him soon. Time ticked past. Either his concept of it passing had gone completely off the rails, or Andie and Glen had more to talk about than he anticipated.

He couldn't blame her for that.

Exhaustion finally won out and he sat down, fatigue settling into his bones. Only one thing was certain: he'd never forget this Chanukah.

The knock at his door had him out of his seat so fast he nearly tripped over his own feet. He reached for the handle, wrenching it open.

"Took you two long enough, did you stall in order to torture me . . ."

His voice trailed off as he saw who had knocked on his door. He would have bet money, a lot of money, on it being Dean and Glen.

Andie stood there. Wide-eyed, pink-cheeked, and somehow more beautiful than she'd been the day before.

"I assure you any delay was not done to torture you."

Leo swallowed but the fist-sized lump in his throat remained. "Did you, uh." He cleared his throat—or tried to. "Did the desk meet your expectations?"

"It did. I hadn't known there were items in that drawer."

"I suspected as much. I was terrified that they might have been lost before they could be returned to you." He took a gamble, stepping closer to Andie, foot crossing the threshold of his apartment. "I really am sorry. I never intended for your desk to be in any harm's way. Though with the level of conflict at work with Dean and I and our father, I guess an issue like this was bound to happen."

"It seems like your father has made amends."

This was Andie. Heart so big she'd check in with him regardless of her own emotional state. He wanted to touch her, instead he put his hands in his pockets. "Yeah, he has. I almost can't believe it. Turns out mistakenly selling irreplaceable family heirlooms presents an opportunity to clear the air."

"Clear the air?"

"We're going to sit down and have a meeting, but the business will be passed down to his sons."

Andie's face lit up. "Leo, that's great!"

"Yeah. We even fixed the grandfather clock together."

"See, things do work out."

This amazing woman took care of others, even now, and she needed someone to be taking care of her. "Turns out I needed that kick in the rear that you gave me. But I'm more interested in you. Did you take the Ohio job?"

The wall that had been built between them had begun to crumble, replaced by a live wire. He wanted to reach out, touch her, pull her in. But he didn't have the okay to do so.

"I decided to pass on the Ohio job."

Hope bloomed so fast his heart nearly stopped. "Why?"

Her eyes flitted up, lost in thought. "When I checked my email I found an offer from the temple and I realized that everything I had learned about that job matched my wants and needs. Add the bonus of remaining close to my friends and memories with my father helped sway the decision."

"And your annoying neighbor who nearly lost your desk?"

She looked at him, her gaze colliding with his. "Turns out I may have been a bit too harsh on him." She held up her hand, her thumb and pointer finger close together. Her leather cuff came into view, so Andie, so charming.

"No. You were the exact dose of reality I needed."

They stood there, staring at each other. The wall had been removed, but they still had begun as a temporary Chanukah thing.

"Andie, would you like to light the candles with me tonight?" He swallowed. "And give me the chance at spending next Chanukah with you as well?"

Her smile grew large and wide. He'd take a picture but it would break the moment. "Are you asking me something, Leo Dentz?"

He stepped further into the hall, until their toes touched. "Date me, Andie Williams. I can't get enough of you."

She rose on her toes and he leaned down but a voice down the hall stopped them. "Kiss him already!"

They turned to Dean, standing by the elevator. Glen stood behind him.

"What? You expected me to leave and not witness this beautiful moment." He pretended to wipe a tear.

"Dad?" Leo called out.

Glen stood taller. "Yes?"

"Take the stairs."

Andie chuckled, resting her head on Leo's shoulder.

Glen nodded and grabbed Dean by the neck, the two exiting the hall.

"Do I need to remind you I come with them?"

Andie's soft chuckle hit his ears. "Then you haven't been paying attention."

He reached down, tipping Andie's chin up to him. "That they are part of my charm?"

Andie's face turned serious. "They are something I've been looking for, but I realized families are never perfect and I would have wanted a chance at this thing with you without them."

"I'm going to kiss you now." He needed to feel her against him.

Andie wrapped her arms around his neck. "I believe I was going to kiss you."

"Either way, as long as I can taste you." He pressed his lips to hers, absorbing her touch and warmth. Somehow, through everything, he'd gotten his ultimate wish for Chanukah: a chance with Andie.

EPILOGUE

One Year Later

Millie couldn't wait for sunset. The first night of Chanukah. It came earlier this year, which was fine by her. At eleven years old, gifts were very much her thing, and she had no intention of that ending.

This year, however, she'd been trusted with a super-secret task for her sweet Uncle Leo, not that he appreciated the moniker. And while she had been known to ruin a secret, or two, she knew when one needed to be carried out perfectly according to plan.

Which was why she currently messed with the family game of dreidels, in quiet stealth mode. She'd snuck away from the others and needed to act fast, before her whereabouts as the sole child was questioned.

"What are you doing here? Messing with the gelt?"

Millie swallowed a squeak. Andie stood in the doorway, arms crossed. Her pseudo aunt, the best aunt in her family by far, and not because the other aunts were her great-aunts. Andie had continued to date Leo and be a part of their family over the past year. She'd started working at the temple preschool, which Millie liked, because

291

if she got to temple early and Andie stayed late, she got a few minutes with her. Andie also had gone back to school, which Millie also liked because they sometimes got to do homework together.

And Uncle Leo had been happier since he started dating Andie, though some of that might have to do with taking over the business from Grandpa Glen. All Millie cared about were her favorite people being happy, and occasionally taking her out for ice cream.

She tossed her hair over her shoulder. "I'm making sure it's all here and no one had planted any unhappy surprises." Sure, there was a surprise in store, though only a happy one.

"Uh-huh." Andie checked behind her before making her way into the room. She bent and dropped her voice. "This wouldn't have anything to do with the surprise your uncle is planning?"

Millie did her best to swallow her reaction. "What surprise?" she blinked, working on the angelic expression she'd perfected years ago.

Somehow, Andie saw through her. "I think we can both agree that while your uncle is a very talented man, he doesn't have your knack for keeping surprises in check."

Millie relaxed. "Of course. He did not get that skill at all. Skipped right over him. He tries, though."

Andie nodded. "Exactly. Which is why I already found that small item you are about to put in my gelt bag."

Millie's hand closed around the ring in her pocket. She tried to read Andie's face, but didn't know the endgame here. "Do you need interference? Oh no, you don't plan to say yes do you?" A new urgency consumed her. This couldn't become a bad start to Chanukah, it just couldn't!

Andie placed her hands on Millie's shoulders. "Shh." She glanced behind her, but they were still alone. "I do plan to say yes."

Millie couldn't help it; she squealed and flung her arms around Andie. Her soon-to-be-real Aunt Andie.

Andie chuckled. "But, I think your uncle needs to work at it a bit first."

Millie let go. That she could handle. "What do you have in mind?"

"Don't put the ring in my bag."

Millie opened her mouth. Closed it. "But why? He'll be upset."

Andie moved to the table, picking up the bag of gelt that belonged to Leo. "Because I plan to beat him to it." She slipped in a piece of leather that looked like the cuff that Andie always wore.

"No way!" Millie placed both her hands on her mouth.

Andie gave her a look, that teacher look that said to behave. Millie knew it well. "Are you going to be okay?"

Millie nodded, still holding her mouth. Then, because she wanted to, she hugged Andie again. "I'm so glad you're joining our family."

Andie held Millie tight. "Me too. It's been so nice having a family again."

Millie knew that Andie didn't have much of any family, certainly not these big happy gatherings that Millie loved, and so did Andie. Her family was nearly complete.

And when the sun set, and her uncle was engaged, she'd use her opportunity to make a wish on his menorah that had to be magic. Because she had a second uncle, and that uncle deserved happiness, too. Last Chanukah Leo met Andie. This year Dean would find his partner, too.

Millie was sure of it.

ACKNOWLEDGMENTS

For years I have wanted to write a Chanukah romance, especially during the December holidays, when so few non-Christmas romance options were available. I'm thrilled to see more and more popping up featuring other holidays—because there are a lot of December-ish holidays—and equally thrilled to have my own Chanukah story added to the mix.

This story began as a novella, an idea simmering over more than one holiday season. And then I got the chance to flesh it out. The journey was not an easy one. Andie and Leo morphed along the way into the current characters I love so much!

Thank you to my agent, Lynnette, for believing in me and this story. You helped get this to the right place and helped me tweak and strengthen. So glad to have you in my court!

To my editor, Melissa, thank you! You fell in love with Andie and Leo and helped me shine them up. You believed in this story from the beginning and championed for it. You also championed for me adding back in Leo's hearing loss that I had removed, and I'm so happy to have that additional part of me in this novel.

Acknowledgments

To the entire Alcove team: You have been amazing to work with! I feel so honored and appreciate all of you for your hard work and support.

No book can be written without an author team, especially me, who has to run everything by someone! Rochelle, you are always willing to be my sounding board, in both writing and life, and I don't know what I'd do without you (probably pull out my hair). Jami, you also listen to my endless babbling and grammar questions! Heather and Kari, we may all be busy these days, but I know you will always be there for me. And Kari, thank you a million times over for helping me with the preschool side of Andie!

Thank you to the Schmoozers for simply being amazing! And helping me figure out what the Hebrew on the menorah needed to be. A special thanks to Jessica, Felicia, Hallie, Stacey, Elsie, and Francesca for reading early versions of *Eight Nights* and giving me feedback.

Rona, Sara, and Lisa, thank you for allowing me to join the Masterminds. I've learned so much from you and cherish your friendship!

Pepper and Marbles, thank you for occasionally letting me work without meowing at me and walking across the keyboard.

To my kiddo—Mom loves you!